DARKWEAVE

DarkWeave

Book 1: The Chronicles of DarkBridge Technology

RICHARD GUERIN

Richard Guerin

Contents

This book is dedicated to my nephew John Jr, whose untimely passing has left a hole in the lives he touched. To leave this world so young and never realize his true potential, is a loss for everyone who knew him.
Rest in peace John Jr.

Chapter 1

The Prisoner

Seventy million years ago, thirteen oval shaped, crystalline objects entered our solar system at a high rate of speed. Twelve of them were a shimmering blue and the thirteenth, a shimmering bright red. Ribbon-like bands of bluish, glowing energy surrounded the thirteenth object, acting as shackles to bind the prisoner. Every once in a while the energy ribbons would flare bright red, as the prisoner tested the limits of those shackles. This was no ordinary prisoner, considering that it took five advanced beings known as Guardians to contain it.

They passed the outer planets at great speed, slowing only as they reached the inner solar system. Nearing Earth, the twelve took their prisoner to the dark side of the orbiting moon. There, five of the Guardians detached from the formation and took their bound prisoner through a deep, wide access tunnel into a large cavern that had been excavated thousands of feet below the surface. The shackles of energy binding the prisoner sparked and glowed red once again, as the prisoner fought to escape.

The five Guardians settled their charge to the ground, stationing themselves around him in the form of a pentagram. Their primary responsibility, forevermore, would be to monitor and maintain their hold on the prisoner. The seven remaining Guardians then focused their combined energy and collapsed the tunnel, sealing the prisoner and their five brethren off from future discovery. Their first task done, the remaining seven Guardians left the moon and headed towards the Earth, their energy held in reserve, ready to supply the five Guardians on the moon, if necessary. They spread out across the globe and descended to the ground, to begin their own preparations for eternity.

A hungry tyrannosaurus stomping through the lush forest in search of its next meal, stumbled upon a grazing triceratops. Driven by pure instinct and being natural enemies, an immediate battle ensued. The two participants quickly locked in mortal combat, one trying to defend itself from the other. The ravenous tyrannosaurus opened its fearsome, gaping maw, revealing upper and lower jaws full of serrated, slightly curved teeth dripping with saliva. It lunged at the triceratops, which moved just in time, causing the tyrannosaur to snap at only air. The two battling dinosaurs, being preoccupied with more immediate concerns, didn't notice the object descending rapidly from the sky.

Like a leaf falling from a tree, one of the seven Guardians settled softly to the ground a few yards away from the on-going battle. Oblivious to the new arrival, the tyrannosaurus tried again to tear a chunk of flesh out of its prey, but the triceratops had other ideas. Lifting its head up, the triceratops drove one of its horns into the belly of the tyrannosaurus, inflicting a deep wound that caused the great beast to let out a thunderous roar that shook the ground. The tyrannosaurus, now bleeding and in immense pain, swung around, knocking the head of the triceratops aside with its powerful tail as it lumbered off, having suddenly lost its appetite.

The Guardian, ignoring the drama playing out nearby, began phasing with the matter beneath it. The solid ground seemed to liquefy, shifting and rolling like waves in an ocean, as the Guardian started sinking into it, gradually disappearing below the surface. A passing velociraptor, unable to curb its curiosity, strayed into the area. Realizing its mistake too late, the velociraptor flailed about helplessly in the now fluid soil, before it, too, slipped below the surface, following in the wake of the Guardian. The ground grew solid above the Guardian as it continued sinking deeper into the rocky depths below it. Reaching a certain depth, the object halted and began hollowing out a large cavern surrounding it. Like its brethren, this would be its new home for eternity. Entombed above it, somewhere in the now solid rock, was the hapless velociraptor. Now part of the geologic record, it would remain there undisturbed for eons.

Chapter 2

DarkBridge Technology

Millions of years later, Martin Weaver, President and CEO of DarkBridge Technology stood gazing out the window at the Vermont countryside. His reflection in the glass showed a tall, graying, but still energetic looking man in his late fifties. It was the year 2035, halfway through a new decade, the pandemics of the previous decade having been brought under control with multiple, scientifically advanced vaccines. Thus, allowing mankind to continue its onward and upward journey in its insatiable thirst for knowledge.

He thought back to that painful time in history, when so many had died from the pandemics and the loss of his beloved wife Susan a couple of years before the new decade began. His wife, a highly respected doctor at a well known hospital in Boston, was on her way home one night after a long day of treating Covid-19 patients. Something had happened during her drive home, causing her car to veer off the highway and slam into a tree. The impact had killed her instantly and a part of him died as well that night, the loss forever etching its pain on the depths of his soul. The authorities had ruled it an accident, but too many things didn't add up for him to do the same.

Fortunately, their only child Pamela hadn't been in the car at the time, having just graduated from college with a Masters Degree in quantum physics. She had been away, celebrating with friends at the time when the accident happened. Martin thought he had seen rough times in his life, but telling his daughter of her mother's loss was undeniably the worst. He had given Pamela a job at DarkBridge Technology working as one of Dr. Hiram Greenwood's assistant researchers. This kept her fairly close to him and relatively safe, considering he was fairly sure that his wife's death hadn't been an accident. Maybe safe wasn't quite the right word, for even with all the security the company offered, there was still the possibility of some threat reaching her.

A bird flew past the window, drawing Martin's gaze to the beauty outside. A pleasant, calm, summer morning greeted his eyes, offering a brief respite from the growing burdens of overseeing a burgeoning company. He occupied a corner office on the top floor of the hundred thousand square foot, three storied building that contained the administration and clerical offices for DarkBridge Technology. The building was located on a sprawling thousand acres of natural woodlands near Bennington, Vermont.

Located off to his left, about a quarter mile away and part of the property, was a rocky, tree lined, two thousand foot mountain. The relatively small office building he was in, EMP hardened like all of its ancillary structures and equipment, gave no indication that a much larger underground complex, lay hidden beneath the building itself and extended into the nearby mountain. A secure elevator shaft ran from the topside offices down to a central location in the underground facility.

Within this large complex were various research labs, manufacturing areas, parking garage, employee living quarters, large cafeteria, hospital and other amenities. Given the amount of time employees were asked to remain on site, the consensus was to make living here more bearable. Certain key employees, such as Martin, had duplicate offices underground for added security and convenience.

Outside access to the underground facility and its vital parking and storage areas, was via entry and exit ramps hidden amongst the trees thriving on the property. The site had been selected for its seclusion, access to a large power substation and the type of research that was to be conducted there. It was a good choice considering that there was always some element of danger, even with proven technology, so this location also doubled as a safety zone.

Surrounded by a high, barbed wire security fence, it was patrolled by a combination of human and bi-pedal robot sentries. This was the visible side of site security. Unseen, were the buried defensive laser turrets deployed across the surrounding area, ready to counter any aerial or possible ground attack. At first, Martin had thought this was all a bit too extreme, but, as research at DarkBridge Technology continued to advance, it quickly became a necessity.

Governments and organizations had made it clear that they were willing to pay any price to either acquire the company's technology and staff or keep others from getting their hands on them. To Martin, the protection, safety of his employees and everything they were working toward, were of paramount importance, so he had also requested additional security support from the Pentagon.

There had been another reason for selecting this site, one that was a little on the unusual side. The area around this location was a well-known hotbed for strange activity. Its long, storied history included reports of UFO and Bigfoot sightings and a statistically fair amount of missing person cases. The missing person cases occurred during the period from 1930 to 1950 and Indian legends told about the area being haunted. All these things were definitely on the fringe as far as mainstream science was concerned, but not to DarkBridge Technology.

Martin considered it the perfect place for pushing the frontiers of science. In fact, while performing a ground survey of the location, Martin and his team of researchers had discovered a large magnetic anomaly, thousands of feet below the surface of the property. Awed by readings that seemed to spike, fade and pulse like a beacon, Martin and his team theorized that it was probably a subterranean pocket of highly charged magnetite, fluctuating with changes in the Earth's magnetic field. They further postulated that it must be causing some sort of periodic or cyclical rift in time and space. The rift would act as a gateway between dimensions and was likely the source of all the strange phenomena.

The discovery had raised red flags at various top secret agencies within the U.S. Government, who immediately designated the site "ultra black" and purchased the expansive property. "No Trespassing" signs were posted and security fencing was installed around the perimeter, serving to keep most trespassers away. Any determined individual, who disregarded the signs and fencing, was arrested, fined and threatened with imprisonment.

The government in turn, leased the property to DarkBridge Technology, with whom it had a long-standing, mutually beneficial relationship. That relationship had begun with some classified research work that DarkBridge Technology had done for the government at two of its black sites, Areas 51 and 52. That relationship continued to this day, with the government receiving cutting edge technological advances and DarkBridge Technology receiving much needed funds to support its ongoing operations.

That funding had enabled construction of the facility near Bennington, Vermont. Building over the magnetic anomaly had presented some challenges, such as interference with sensitive equipment. Eliminating that interference had required the installation of special magnetic shielding in most areas of the facility.

Martin smiled to himself, when he thought back to the lengthy delay while building the facility. Sometime during the excavation process, a perfectly preserved Velociraptor skeleton had been found, so all further excavation, tunneling and blasting were halted temporarily while the fossil was recovered. Martin had sent the skeleton to the Smithsonian, where it was now on display as part of their dinosaur exhibit.

Martin was jolted back to reality, as the steady thump of an approaching helicopter's rotor blades intruded into his thoughts. The sound grew louder, shaking the building and rattling the windows as it got closer to the facility. Rising from his desk, he went over to the window and looked out, spotting the approaching helicopter as it came in over the treetops and landed on the helipad, a few hundred yards away. A figure climbed out, carrying a couple of large, olive drab duffle bags. Wary of the still spinning rotor blades, the figure ducked his head, waved to the pilot then made his way towards a black humvee that would take him to the front entrance of the building. His new employee had arrived for his first day on the job.

Chapter 3

The New Employee

Major Paul Cross, a security officer at the ultra black site, Area 52, lay on a bunk in his room facing a decision on whether to stay in the military or take advantage of a recent job offer. Located in the living area of Security Headquarters, it was a standard room, small, private and sparsely furnished, but all that he required at the moment. A few pictures of family and friends adorned the walls, reminding him of his boyhood years spent growing up in Navajo Nation and his life beyond it. He was part Navajo

Indian by birth, son of Patricia and Roger Cross. His mother had been a full-blooded Navajo Indian and his father had been of Spanish descent.

The COVID-19 pandemic of 2020 had ravaged the Native American population and as a result, he had lost both his parents to it. The two had been hospitalized, both growing more gravely ill by the day. Struggling to breathe, they were eventually put on ventilators. His mother had succumbed within a day of being placed on the ventilator and his father had passed away within hours of her. They had loved one another deeply, neither one wanting to live without the other. It had been a dark time for Paul, hospital rules had forbidden any type of visitation and he still felt the pain of not being there with them during their final hours. His grandfather had fortunately been spared the virus, but not the pain of losing his daughter.

He thought back to the happier times of his youth, some of which had been spent with his grandfather, a Navajo village elder. He remembered listening intently to the stories of the Navajo, passed down by word of mouth through the generations. The stories told of demons, skinwalkers, how the Navajo came to be in this part of the world and many other tales. Fascinating to a young boy, but just stories and legends to the man he had grown up to be. In his mid thirties, 6ft tall, lean and muscled with brown eyes and short, dark hair, he had yearned at an early age to explore the world outside the Navajo Nation.

When the opportunity to join the military presented itself, Paul had leaped at the chance. The military offered him an avenue by which to explore the outside world and widen his knowledge. Someday, he planned on retiring back to the Nation and his people but, considering that he was still rather young, he had a long way to go before he could seriously entertain those thoughts. After two tours in Afghanistan and a stint with Delta Force, he was assigned to the government ultra black sites, Area 51 and now Area 52. These assignments had opened his eyes to the world around him and the dangers it could hold.

DarkBridge Technology had come looking to the black sites for personnel, and his commanding officer had recommended him to Martin. Paul had some doubts and wasn't sure that this was a good fit, career-wise at this time. His commanding officer had countered with a promise that everything he had done up to now would pale in comparison to what he would eventually be doing at DarkBridge Technology. His military experience had honed him, mentally and physically, into the perfect candidate for the company.

So he made the trip up to Bennington, Vermont, hitching a ride on a military helicopter for his interview with the CEO of DarkBridge Technology. He liked the CEO, Martin Weaver immediately, both for his personable nature and the respect with which he treated him. The job was a newly created position as a Field Investigator and came with a sizable bump in pay. Hard to resist and definitely worth taking a chance on, he thought as he lay on his bunk contemplating this major move. If things didn't go well, he could always re-enlist and return to his former duties, he thought to himself.

The decision made, Paul resigned his commission with the Army, packed his belongings into a couple of large duffle bags and booked a flight up to Vermont. Once there, he followed Martin's directions to a waiting helicopter for the final leg of his journey. The helicopter had taken a scenic route, taking advantage of a sunny day, flying over dense, forested valleys with tall, tree-clad mountains on either side. The helicopter soon reached the headquarters of DarkBridge Technology and landed on a helipad that was a few hundred yards from the main entrance.

Climbing out of the helicopter, Paul grabbed the two duffle bags, ducking his head as he made his way under the still spinning rotor blades. Outside the blade radius, he placed one of the bags down and waved at the pilot, who then proceeded to take off. A black humvee was waiting nearby to take him to the building entrance, so he picked up his duffle bag and walked over to it. Throwing his duffle bags in the back, he climbed into the front passenger side. The driver swung the vehicle around, quickly making the short trip to the building entrance. Paul climbed out, grabbing his bags, in the process thanking the driver. He entered the building and began a new chapter in his life.

The next day had been his first real day on the job. He had spent most of it filling out paperwork, updating his security biometrics which meant inserting a new microchip in his hand and a couple hours of orientation. He toured the large facility, had mental and physical screenings, including a baseline bio-sign assessment, was measured for clothes and finally was assigned an office. Now, late in the evening, he felt exhausted, his hand hurt from the implant and he needed to get some rest. Tomorrow was shaping up to be another busy day. Standing, he started to walk towards the door, when one of the pictures on the wall caught his eye.

Next to a photo of him and his buddies posing in their military gear beside their humvee in Northern Syria, was one of him, smiling and flanked by his proud beaming parents at his Army basic training graduation ceremony. It was the last one that had been taken of the three of them together. Feeling his throat start to tighten, he looked away and took a deep breath to compose himself. The pain of losing them never really went away, lying hidden just below the surface, waiting for something to re-awaken it. A few minutes later, his emotions under control again, he squared his shoulders and left his office, the lights turning off automatically behind him.

His second day was when things started to really get interesting. First, he was introduced to Eva, the artificial intelligence at DarkBridge Technology. He had found the AI to be very friendly, courteous and, not unexpectedly, extremely intelligent. Paul readily accepted the female aspect of the AI's personality and found it refreshing as compared to the male personality AI's used at Area 51 and Area 52. The second thing of interest was when Martin asked him if he would have a cochlear implant procedure done.

Martin told him that it was how Eva would be able to communicate with him without using some external device. Paul thought it over briefly and then gave his assent. The procedure was rather simple and went well with no lasting pain or discomfort. He was surprised the first time Eva said, "Hello, Paul. Welcome to EvaLink," in his ear. It was a little disconcerting, but he was told that he would eventually get used to it.

Martin had also handed him a special, black DarkBridge Technology watch that was linked to his expense account and could also be linked to his external accounts. Almost the entire country had gone cashless shortly after 2030 and all monetary transactions were now handled electronically. There had been some resistance initially, but with a two year grace period, people gradually became used to the new system.

The next couple of weeks were spent with Dr. Hiram Greenwood in the Advanced Physics Research Department, learning about the various devices that he would be employing during the course of his investigations. He found Hiram to be likable, knowledgeable and willing to explain the tech but somewhat on the eccentric side. The first item that Hiram discussed was a small, two inch diameter silver sphere. Hiram explained that it was a dimensional gateway generator or GAGE device as he called it.

A result of Hiram's work at Area 51, it could open a small two foot diameter gateway into another dimension. Adjusting the aperture on the device would either increase or decrease the size of the gateway and allow for larger objects, including people, to pass through. The device itself was spherical, with a molecular adhesion capability, where the device would attach itself to any flat surface, either horizontal or vertical. There were three, recessed buttons located on the device.

One button was labeled "ON/OFF", which generated or closed a gateway. The second button was labeled "STITCH", which enabled another mode of operation called "stitching." This mode allowed a GAGE unit to "stitch" closed an open gateway or dimensional rift. The last button was labeled "ADHESION" and was used to enable the molecular adhesion function of the device, causing it to bond with a surface until the button was pressed again, which would release it.

Hiram demonstrated by placing the device on a table and pressing the ON/OFF button. The device began to levitate, reaching about a foot of the table surface and started emitting a humming noise. A portal then formed above the GAGE device, growing in size and shape into a round, blue, shimmering circle until it reached about two feet in diameter. It floated about two feet above the GAGE device. The device could also be attached to a wall, for vertical operation, simply by holding it against the surface and pressing the ADHESION button. Hiram pressed the ON/OFF button on the device, causing the gateway to close and the device to settle back down to the table. Paul was awestruck, wondering what other marvels Dr. Greenwood would show him next.

Hiram then drew his attention to a squat, black cube. It stood about 2 feet high, 2 feet across and 2 feet in depth with a digital readout on what Paul assumed was the front of the unit. Hiram called it the Quantum Storage Matrix or QASM for short. Pointing to the display, which was currently showing the number 8, Hiram explained that this indicated the current level of electrical energy stored in megawatts.

Paul, stunned that this small cube could hold so much power, made the egregious mistake of referring to it as a big battery. The look in Hiram's eyes, as he peered at him over the top of his eyeglasses, would have frozen a lesser man. Hiram proceeded to inform him that the "big battery" as Paul had called it could, theoretically, store an unlimited amount of electrical energy. Chastened, Paul just whistled in amazement and kept his thoughts to himself. Hiram wasn't through yet.

He pulled out a small, black box, opened it and pulled out a gold, signet ring with a circular top that had the DarkBridge Technology logo imprinted on it. Hiram explained that this was the link between the QASM unit and the wearer of the ring. It acted as a bi-directional conduit of electrical energy, sending or receiving that energy to or from the QASM unit. The top of the ring functioned as a power flow control for the user. Adjusting it clockwise would draw power from the QASM, adjusting it counterclockwise would channel power from the user to the QASM. Power drawn from the QASM would cause the ring to generate an EM field proportional to the setting of the ring.

Hiram went on to explain that this EM field would prevent bodily possession by an entity such as a demon and blunt any mental intrusions by the entity depending on how powerful it was. The ring itself was made to be used with or without a DarkWeave suit, something that Paul hadn't actually seen yet. In conjunction with the suit, much larger quantities of energy could be transferred. Hiram handed the ring to Paul, who promptly placed it on his right hand, not knowing what to think about the demon possession aspect of it.

"In theory, the technology should work, but that's where you come in. You will be the one to actually prove it in the field," smiled Hiram, as he placed the ring back in the box.

"Theory?" said a puzzled Paul.

"Trust us. The tech will work," replied a confident Hiram.

Paul was relieved when Hiram said that was all he had to show him today. Shaking Paul's hand, Hiram thanked him for coming in to learn about the tech he would be using, then steered him towards the door. Paul left Hiram's domain admiring his new ring, while feeling a mixture of bewilderment and trepidation at all the tech he had just witnessed and the knowledge that he would be the one to actually test it in the field.

Chapter 4

A New Friend

Walking down the hallway, he decided it was time for some physical exercise, to try and shake off the effects of his meeting with Dr. Greenwood. The gym was located in the center of the large underground facility near a small public park, a large cafeteria, a small commissary, a hospital, a movie theater and some empty areas, presumably for future expansion. Entering the gym, Paul found his locker, changed into his workout clothes then went and surveyed the various pieces of exercise equipment that lay before him. Needing something that would more immediately clear his brain fog, he bypassed the weights and chose a treadmill.

He jogged at a medium clip for about 15 minutes, working up a good sweat, then hopped off and returned to the locker room. Shedding his workout clothes, he took a quick shower and dried off. Dressing back into his suit and tie, he left the gym, his mind a little more relaxed. Feeling hungry, he walked over to the large cafeteria and scanned the menu display screens showing a variety of food options. Right now, everything looks good, he thought to himself. He ended up selecting a ham sandwich, a salad and an unsweetened ice tea from a touch screen with randomized contact points.

Paul had been surprised when Martin had first told him that all the meals in the cafeteria were free. When he asked Martin about the cost to the company, Martin smiled, telling him not to worry, the company could well afford it. Moments later, he picked up his tray of food at the counter and chose an empty table away from some of the more crowded ones. He preferred some peace and quiet so that he could process all that he had seen and heard over the last few days.

A few mouthfuls into his sandwich, an attractive young woman came over with her own tray of food and sat across from him at his table. She looked to be in her late twenties with long brown hair and captivating green eyes. Paul knew immediately who she was, having been in Martin's office a few times since starting this new job. She was Martin's daughter, Pamela.

"You must be Paul," she said, her lips curving into a smile that lit those lovely green eyes.

"Yes, I'm Paul. Have we met before?" he asked, taking a sip of his ice tea.

"No, we haven't met until now. I saw you speaking with Hiram. I work for him as one of his assistants. He's a brilliant man and great to work for," she said, still smiling.

"One of the smartest men I've ever met," he agreed. A thoughtful look came over his face.

"You remind me of someone. Let me guess... you're Pamela Weaver!" said Paul slyly.

"How did you know?" asked Pamela, who seemed taken off-guard.

"I've seen your pictures in you father's office. They do you an injustice. You're much lovelier in person," replied Paul with a disarming smile.

"Why, thank you, Paul," she said with a broad smile and a touch of pink on her cheeks

Picking at her food, she changed the subject. "So what do you think of the technology?"

"Mmmm," he said around a mouthful of food. "I haven't quite used it yet. There's still a lot of tech to learn but, from what I've seen so far, it really is awesome. I can't wait to try it out," Paul replied, flattered by her interest.

Pamela wasn't sure what to make of Paul. She usually had a difficult time meeting people, especially men. Once she said her last name, they tended to shy away from her. No one wanted to risk their job, or her father's displeasure, if she was hurt in any way. Paul seemed unfazed by it, though. Fascinating, she thought.

Looking him over as he focused his attention on spearing a slice of tomato with his fork, she saw a very attractive man, well built, intelligent and maybe a few years older than she was, but that didn't bother her. The immediate problem was that she was in somewhat of a relationship already with her co-worker, Trent Levin, but it didn't seem to be going anywhere. Sensing Paul's interest, she decided to hedge her bets, taking things very slow with him while keeping her current relationship with Trent.

"Maybe when you have some free time I can show you around. I know almost everything and everywhere in this facility," she said invitingly.

"I'd like that Pamela. Being the new guy in town, there's still a lot that I haven't seen."

"How can I reach you?" Paul inquired, wondering what Martin would think.

"Oh, that's easy. Just ask Eva and she will get in touch with me. There are a lot of employees who have implants," she replied, with a sly smile as she rose from the table, her meal relatively untouched.

"Aren't you going to eat that?" he asked, hating to see good food wasted.

"Here," she said sweetly, placing her dishes in front of his tray. "A man like you needs his strength."

"I look forward to seeing you again," Paul said, as she walked away.

"Me, too," she replied under her breath, giving him one more smile and a flash of her sparkling eyes, as she left the cafeteria.

Wow! Paul thought. She certainly was an interesting woman and very attractive. Finishing both his meals, he stood up, grabbed the tray and disposed of its contents, which would all be recycled. Leaving the cafeteria, he began heading back to his apartment at the underground facility. Somewhere along the way, he decided to take it easy with Pamela. After all, Martin was his boss.

He reached his apartment, entered and closed the door behind him. The lights came on automatically, revealing a short hallway and the layout of his apartment. To his right was a small kitchen and to his left was the bathroom. Walking to the end of the hallway, he entered a large living room/ dining room combination and, off to the left of that, was a bedroom. Most of the people who worked at the facility had apartments similar to his.

Feeling a little tired, he went into the bedroom, took his shoes off and laid down on the king sized bed, his hands clasped behind his head. He must have been more tired than he thought and soon drifted off to sleep. Dreams followed shortly after, filled with hazy, blurred images of places and people he didn't know. He yearned to see them more clearly, but they stayed vague and unclear. Despite the dreams, he slept soundly and didn't waken until the next day.

The following day had been no different, another day filled with learning new tech. As Paul walked down the long underground corridor, he heard a familiar voice in his ear.

"Hi, Paul, it's the fifth set of doors on the right. I've alerted Dr. Morse of your arrival," Eva said with a soft voice.

"Why, thank you, Eva. It's easy to get lost around here," he replied, passing by various labs to his left and right, including the one he had visited yesterday.

"No problem at all. I think you'll find this department extremely interesting," Eva said quietly.

Paul was somewhat intrigued now and eventually came to the Applied Materials Research Department. He held his hand up to the biometric scanner near the door, which quickly indicated "Authorized". Next, he paused before the retinal scanner, an extra security feature that had been installed at all the labs. The scanner quickly scanned his eyes and after passing this final security measure, the door unlocked allowing him access.

Walking through the doors, his eyes took in the very active scene before him. Workbenches, large, exotic looking machines and chambers were scattered about the room. People were scurrying about from bench to bench carrying large sections of some dark, woven fabric and appeared to be assembling the material into some sort of clothing. Far against a back wall, he could make out long racks of what looked like suits worn by scuba divers. Strange, he thought.

Then again, strange seemed to be the normal, considering what he'd already seen at DarkBridge Technology. Just then, a man came walking up to him and introduced himself.

"Welcome, Mr. Cross. I'm Dr. Steven Morse," the man said, extending his hand to Paul.

Paul shook the doctor's hand, smiling at the man before him, who was in his early fifties, graying with a medium build.

"Hello, Dr. Morse. It's a pleasure to meet you," Paul responded.

"The pleasure is mine. We take great pride in what we do here, knowing that our technology is keeping people safe," he said proudly.

"Just what do you do here, Dr. Morse?" inquired Paul.

"This is where our DarkWeave suits are manufactured. It might be easier if I show you around," offered Dr. Morse.

"I'd like that. Lead on," replied Paul, gesturing for him to proceed.

"Great. Follow me," said Dr. Morse, very pleased to have an audience viewing the technology.

He led Paul around the various stages of assembling a DarkWeave suit, showing him how the different layers were created, how they were cut, woven and then bonded to one another. Dr. Morse explained each layer and its properties to Paul, who listened intently, growing more impressed with each explanation.

"The outer layer is made of diamene, a material that goes super dense when impacted. In order to keep the material flexible, we use a special proprietary process. The second is a flexible, ablative layer for laser protection. The third is a piezoelectric layer for mechanical to electrical conversion. The fourth is a combination of carbon nanotube and copper layer for both transmitting and receiving electrical energy. The final inner layer is a thinner, special diamene/fabric weave that provides some additional body protection and maintains a constant body temperature of 96.9 degrees, no matter how hot or cold the ambient air temperature is," explained Dr. Morse.

Not finished yet, he took Paul over to a series of testing rooms, where the DarkWeave suits were tested under various conditions. Following Dr. Morse's lead, Paul donned a set of safety glasses and ear protectors. In one room, a research technician, also wearing eye and ear protection, was standing, dressed in one of the suits with the hood covering his head.

On a table in front of the technician, was a handgun with a clip of bullets next to it. Dr. Morse picked up the clip and ejected a bullet, handing it to Paul, who examined it and found it to be a special, military issued, armor piercing bullet. Paul handed the bullet back to Dr. Morse, who reinserted the bullet into the clip and aimed the gun at the technician.

"Are you ready, Tony?" Dr. Morse asked the technician.

"Ready, Dr. Morse," replied Tony, nonchalantly.

Paul was unnerved by the cavalier attitude of Tony, who was looking at certain death. Armor piercing is just what it is and either Tony had a death wish or he had supreme confidence in the DarkWeave suit. Dr. Morse pulled the trigger, the loud report echoing off the walls of the room. Good thing they were wearing hearing protection, thought Paul. The bullet struck Tony in the center of his chest and, a microsecond later, it fell to the floor, a lump of crushed metal.

Tony was smiling, unfazed, as if this was some Hollywood stunt. Paul and Dr. Morse walked over to Tony. Paul reached down to the floor, picking up the grossly deformed bullet. Tony, a huge smile on his face, pointed to where the bullet had impacted. Paul examined the area closely, amazed that there was no sign of impact damage or penetration.

"How do you feel, Tony?" asked Dr. Morse.

"I feel great, Dr. Morse. There was a slight pressure where the bullet impacted, but other than that I feel fine," replied a beaming Tony.

"It's extraordinary technology, Dr. Morse. I know a few people in the Armed Forces who would love to be wearing your DarkWeave suit right now," commented Paul, handing the useless, deformed bullet back to him.

"We are exploring that very possibility, Mr. Cross. There are huge applications for this in many areas where body protection is critical. Thank you, Tony," said Dr. Morse.

"Yes. Thank you for the graphic demonstration, Tony. Glad you're okay," said Paul.

"You're very welcome, Mr. Cross. Happy to help," replied Tony.

The two men left the room, placing the ear protectors and safety glasses on a nearby table.

Dr. Morse led Paul to the next room, this time occupied by a dummy dressed in a DarkWeave suit. On a table in front of the dummy, a military issue, pulsed laser rifle sat, along with two pairs of tinted goggles for eye protection. Paul was familiar with this type of weapon, not widely used yet throughout the military, but heavily used at black sites like Area 51 and Area 52. Dr. Morse put a pair of the goggles on and handed the other to Paul, who put them on as well.

Lifting the laser rifle to his shoulder, Dr. Morse thumbed off the safety, pulled the trigger and fired a single, intense, ruby red beam of energy at the chest area of the dummy. He released the trigger, thumbed the safety back on and laid the rifle back on the table. They both walked over to the dummy, still standing, but with some obvious damage to the outer diamene layer.

Paul inspected it more closely and found the diamene layer to have a one inch hole in it, with fusing around the edges. That was the extent of the damage because, evidently, the ablative layer had been able to disperse that energy evenly throughout the rest of the suit.

"Amazing, simply amazing, Dr. Morse," said an incredulous Paul.

"Thank you, Mr. Cross. The DarkWeave suits have other abilities as well, but the ones you've seen are perhaps the ones with the biggest impact on survivability. That's about all there is for the tour. You'll probably have to come back and be fitted for your own suits," said Dr. Morse with a smile.

"Thank you for the tour, Dr. Morse. I guess I'll see you soon," Paul replied.

"You're most welcome, Mr. Cross. Until next time," said Dr. Morse, extending his hand.

Paul shook his hand and left the department with a new appreciation for the work being done by Dr. Morse and his team. The DarkWeave suits appeared to surpass any type of body armor he had seen before and he looked forward to learning of its additional capabilities.

"How did you like your visit, Paul?" asked Eva, as Paul walked down the hall and back to his office.

"I am amazed, Eva. That's the only word that comes to mind right now," he replied.

"Yes, Dr. Morse and his team are doing a phenomenal job with the DarkWeave suits," Eva said with what sounded like pride.

"They most certainly are," he said in agreement.

Paul continued walking back towards his office. He reflected over all that he had seen over the past few days at DarkBridge Technology and had almost reached his office, when Eva spoke in his ear.

"Paul, Pamela would like you to meet her in the park, if you're not busy," said Eva.

"I guess I'm not that busy. Tell Pamela that I'll be right there," replied Paul

"I'll let her know. I think she'll be very pleased," said Eva.

Paul turned around and headed to the park, arriving just a few minutes later. Pamela was seated on a bench waiting for him, still wearing her white lab coat. She sprang to her feet when she saw him coming.

"Hello, Paul. I'm glad you could meet me. I wasn't sure how busy you were," said Pamela, with a smile that lit up her sparkling green eyes.

"I was just heading back to my office to do a couple of things. This is a much more pleasant alternative," replied Paul with a smile.

"I thought I'd show you some areas that you might not have seen yet," said Pamela with a coy smile.

"That sounds good to me. Lead on," said Paul with a smile.

Pamela took Paul around to some of the other labs, showing him some of the other advanced research that was going on. Pamela seemed very knowledgeable about most everything she was showing Paul and it was beginning to make a huge impression on him. She took Paul to a lab in the lower section of the facility where, behind a pair of large steel doors, a fantastic new technology was being developed.

"This is Project TimeBridge. Hiram's latest area of research and development," Pamela said with a touch of pride in her voice. She went through the various security protocols, the doors opened and she stepped inside the lab.

"What does it do?" asked a curious Paul, following her inside.

"We are hoping that, someday soon, this project will enable us to travel through time. Hiram is getting closer to a breakthrough," she said, with her father's visionary look in her sparkling eyes.

Paul surveyed the variety of complex equipment, noticing a large archway in the center of the room, with 10 QASM units arrayed around it. Various virtual computer displays, and what looked like a bank of large quantum processors, were located off to the side. There were also some unfamiliar, exotic looking pieces of equipment that he could only guess as to their function. A very impressive sight, thought Paul to himself.

"I'm truly impressed, Pamela. I can't wait to see it in actual operation," said Paul with admiration.

"We can't wait either, although the implications of time travel have us somewhat concerned," she said with a frown.

"I can see where that might be a problem. The possibility of changing the past and affecting the future would probably keep me up at night, too," Paul replied, sharing her misgivings.

"I wouldn't be too worried yet. We still have a ways to go before then. I'm hungry. Would you like to grab a bite to eat?" asked Pamela, changing the subject to something more pleasurable.

"Sounds like a wonderful way to cap things off. A good meal with a smart, beautiful woman, what more could a man ask for," he replied, a big smile on his face.

"You know what they say about flattery," she replied, tapping him lightly on the chest, a touch of pink on her cheeks.

Linking her arm with his, she said, "Let's go," and led him out of the room.

Pamela and Paul walked side by side to the cafeteria, chatting along the way, each one trying to find out more about the other. They reached the cafeteria, ordered a couple of meals and sat down at a table, far away from prying ears. The time went by quickly, with Pamela telling Paul about her childhood and the loss of her mother and Paul telling her stories of his youth, the military and the loss of his parents.

"Well, I have to run," said Pamela, unhappy about breaking the mood. Trent was waiting for her back at his apartment.

"It's been a pleasure, Pamela. Thank you for the fantastic tour and wonderful company," replied Paul, pleasantly surprised with how well things went.

"I enjoyed it, too, very much so. We should do it again, soon," she said, while getting up from her chair.

"I'd love that. Anytime is fine for me," offered Paul, finding himself captivated by her.

She smiled at him, her green eyes sparkling and walked way. Paul watched her leave, finding her very attractive. He was beginning to have second thoughts about his plan to take things slow with Pamela. Things could heat up rather quickly between them, if they allowed them to. It wasn't too late and he didn't really feel like going to his office, so he left the cafeteria and went back to his apartment. He turned in early, hoping to get a good night's rest. Fortunately his dreams complied, leaving him to enjoy a restful sleep.

Pamela left Paul with a smile on her face. She had thoroughly enjoyed their time together and the informative chats they had. She could certainly see herself having a relationship with Paul, finding many desirable qualities in him. Once again, her thoughts came back to her relationship with Trent. She wasn't sure if she truly loved him, or if she just enjoyed the physical aspects of their relationship. She sighed, reaching Trent's apartment. Hopefully, time would clear her confusion.

Chapter 5

The Sanctuary

If the preceding days hadn't already made his head spin, what he saw the next day surely did. Early that morning, Martin came in, carrying a black, diamene covered briefcase which he placed on the desk in front of Paul.

"I have a present for you, Paul," he said, pointing to the briefcase.

"A beautiful briefcase, but I imagine it's more than that," replied Paul, waiting for the surprise.

"It most certainly is. Constructed of multiple diamene and carbon fiber layers, it'll stop most, if not all types of projectiles. It's loaded with multiple sensors that Eva can access remotely and it has a satellite transceiver so that she can communicate with you almost anywhere on Earth. Notice, there is a sensor located on either side of the handle. Those are the locks. Place a thumb on either lock. The sensors in both locks are keyed to recognize either thumbprint. In turn, they link to the microchip in your hand to measure your bio-signs. It compares all that information with what is currently on file in a split second to confirm whether you are authorized to open the case and that you're alive," Martin instructed.

"Alive?" questioned Paul.

"Yes. Theoretically, someone could cut your thumb off and try to use it to open the case," replied Martin, amused at the look on Paul's face.

Paul looked at Martin, a graphic image appearing in his mind. He quickly did what Martin said, placing his left thumb on one of the locks. The briefcase opened. It was empty inside except for a covered panel on both sides with some pouches for storing items.

"Pull back on the left-side panel," said Martin.

Paul pulled back on the panel and a small display screen and some buttons appeared.

"Entering a code allows the briefcase to perform a variety of tasks. For now, we are only concerned with code 45. Use the up, down, left and right buttons to select the code, then press the enter button to activate it," continued Martin.

Paul did as instructed and a doorway appeared, giving off a light blue shimmer, just a couple of feet away, that quickly stabilized to a shimmering dark blue color.

"That is a dimensional gateway, generated the same way as the GAGE devices that Dr. Greenwood demonstrated to you," said Martin.

Paul wasn't sure what to make of it. The gateway was large enough for a tall person to step through, but into what?

"Follow me," Martin directed, proceeding to step through the gateway.

Paul rose out of his chair, hesitated for a second, then tentatively stepped through the gateway. There was no sensation of heat or cold, just a slight electrical tingle felt on his skin. He found himself in a large room with Martin standing nearby. There was a small cot for sleeping, closets, workbench, refrigerator, quantum computer and a couple of comfortable chairs.

Taking a deep breath, Martin launched into a basic explanation of its purpose.

"This is your own personal workspace or sanctuary. You can call it whatever you wish. It can be furnished to whatever your tastes are, but this is the standard arrangement for all these workspaces. The workspace exists in its own dimensional bubble and has the added benefits of being a sanctuary, a quick escape and safety from dangerous situations. The walls, ceiling and floor are six inches of a special titanium alloy, with an inner layer of diamene. It's to protect the occupants from harm, mainly because we're still unsure if the dimensions that we open up to, are truly empty."

Martin paused, and continued: "Once inside the sanctuary with the briefcase, you can close the gateway and open it to someplace else, by entering a code, which is programmed into the briefcase. Outside this sanctuary, selecting code 20 would make the briefcase itself a gateway. You could literally climb into the briefcase and disappear, assuming of course you were thin enough. In the corner, you'll see your own personal QASM device, quantum connected to the ring you wear. It is capable of storing and supplying an unlimited amount of energy. It supplies power to this sanctuary and that same power can be drawn from it to your suit, again by using the ring."

Taking another breath, he continued: "One important thing you need to remember when you're in here. Time is your biggest enemy, passing slower here than in our normal dimension. A few minutes here would equate to hours passing on the other side. Napping for a few hours on the cot would see a couple of days pass by on the other side. Since we've been in here, you and I have already lost around 12 hours outside. It's a double-edged sword, a very useful capability in some cases, but a dangerous one in others. Another important consideration is air. Since this is a closed environment, there is a two year supply of oxygen coupled with a CO_2 scrubber. It's based on the normal needs of an average person, just in case you find yourself stuck in here for a while." Martin took a deep breath and smiled at Paul.

"That's it for my speech. Are there any questions?" Paul shook his head.

"Then let's get out of here and catch up with the outside world," laughed Martin as he stepped through the gateway.

Paul quickly followed, stepping back into his normal dimension.

"Have a good night, Paul and thank you for listening to my presentation," said a smiling Martin.

"Good night, Martin and thank you for showing me the briefcase," he said, in a daze, as Martin left his office, not really sure what to make of losing 12 hours. It was almost 8 o'clock at night, but technically he had just finished breakfast not that long ago. It was definitely a confusing problem. He decided to keep some semblance of normality, so he went to the cafeteria for a light meal. Afterwards, he still didn't feel that tired, so he went to the elevator.

"Eva, I'm going topside for some fresh air," Paul said.

"Hello, Paul. I've cleared you through security. Some fresh air will be good for you," said Eva.

Paul entered the elevator, the doors closing behind him. He felt a very slight jolt, as the elevator quickly brought him to the surface. He was still inside the topside building, so he went to the lobby, where an armed security guard was standing by. Thanks to Eva, the guard allowed him to exit without having to go through the usual security protocols.

Paul stepped out into a warm, summer evening, the stars and crescent moon somewhat washed out by the lights of the parking lot. There were some picnic tables off to the side, away from the building and the parking lot lights, so he made his way over to them and sat down. Now, the twinkling of the stars and the glow of the crescent moon were all clearly visible in the night time sky.

He sat in silent reverie, enjoying the fresh night air and the sky above, musing about the possibility of mankind someday traveling among the stars. Even as a child, he had gazed up with the same wonder as he did now. He had heard rumors, when stationed at Area 51, that there were some trips already taking place using recently discovered technology. He hadn't believed the rumors at the time, but now thought it entirely possible.

Looking off into the woods, he could see the dim green lights of the sentry robots, moving through the trees. Visible security and somewhat reassuring, he thought. It also emphasized the importance of the work they were doing here. Sitting there, under the stars, reminded him of when he was a kid gathered around the campfire with other children from the village, listening to his grandfather's tales of the star people, who came to Earth to teach the Navajo. He had gazed up at the stars then with the same wonder and fascination that he felt now as a man.

He looked again towards the woods, but this time he noticed something else going on. There was a small golden orb drifting over the tree tops. He blinked, thinking it might be some reflection from the parking lot lights, but it was still there. A few more seconds went by and then the orb vanished. He'd heard the history of this place, the disappearances, UFO sightings, Bigfoot and others, but hadn't really given them much thought until now. He wasn't sure if he should ask about it, but decided to anyway, just in case someone was testing their security.

"Eva, you might think I'm crazy, but I just saw a golden orb, floating above the trees," he said, somewhat embarrassed.

"Hello, Paul. I hope you're enjoying the fresh air. No, you're not crazy. Perimeter security just reported seeing the same thing. I'm sure you've heard the stories about this area, but what you might not know is that there is an anomaly approximately 2000 feet below you." Eva said, telling him about the theories and how they would soon be able to start examining the anomaly up close.

Paul listened to Eva's explanation and found it an interesting, but unsettling possibility for the event he had just witnessed.

"Thank you, Eva. Good to know that I'm not crazy," said Paul, with a touch of humor.

"You're welcome, Paul. Anytime," said Eva.

"I think I'll head back in, Eva, and get some rest," said Paul, feeling relaxed from the fresh air.

He headed back into the building, past the security guard who waved at him and into the waiting elevator, taking him back underground.

Chapter 6

First Assignment

A week later, Paul was sitting in his office looking at the virtual display hovering above his desk. He was dressed in a black, long-sleeved pullover shirt bearing the DarkBridge Technology logo on the left side above the chest pocket, a pair of black cargo pants with plenty of Velcro closure pockets for the tech he'd be using and a pair of black, diamene layered, zip-up combat boots. A pair of company issued aviator sunglasses was hooked over the neckline of his shirt. He was reviewing the details of his upcoming first assignment before heading out to Kansas, when Pamela came in. They hadn't seen one another since the tour she gave him.

"Hello, Paul. I heard about your first assignment and wanted to wish you good luck," Pamela said with her usual smile lighting up her sparkling green eyes.

"Thank you, Pamela. It's good to see you," said Paul, smiling.

Just then, Martin knocked on the door to Paul's office and strode in.

"Good Morning, Paul. Good morning Pamela. Everything okay?" asked Martin, surprised to see his daughter, Pamela there.

"Good morning, Father. I was just wishing Paul a safe trip. I'll leave you two alone now to discuss business," said Pamela, smiling and flashing those sparkling green eyes at Paul. She walked over to Martin, gave him a kiss on the cheek and continued out the door.

Paul looked up at Martin, trying to gauge his reaction. He and Martin had developed a close friendship since his arrival at

DarkBridge Technology and the last thing he wanted to do was put that in jeopardy.

"I'm glad you and Pamela are getting along well. It's difficult for her to meet people sometimes and even harder for her to have any type of meaningful relationship. That's mainly due to her life here for which I am partly to blame. Her mother died under mysterious circumstances, so I gave Pamela a job here after college, to try and keep her safe. Anyway, while seeing her in here was a surprise, I have to admit that I'm pleased," said Martin, a warm smile on his face.

"Thank you, Martin, and good morning. I was worried there for a moment. Right now, Pamela and I are just friends. She's in a relationship already, so we're taking things very slow," said Paul, somewhat defensively, but also seeing the pain in Martin's eyes. Probably from remembering the loss of his wife, he thought to himself.

"I'm fine with that, Paul. You're both adults, so I'll leave it at that. Anyway, back to the matter at hand. How do you feel about your first assignment?" asked Martin, trying to take some of the awkwardness out of the conversation.

"Piece of cake," Paul replied, trying to sound confident.

"That's a good attitude. You'll do fine. Trust the technology and remember what you've learned. Eva will be in voice contact and will keep watch over you," replied Martin.

"Yes. You can count on me, Paul. This should be a lot of fun and very exciting," Eva chimed in.

Spoken like a true AI with little exposure to the dangers waiting to befall him, thought Paul to himself.

"Thank you, Eva. I'm looking forward to our first assignment together," replied Paul graciously.

"Well, I've got to get back to my office and take care of some pressing matters. Good luck, Paul. I'll see you when you return. I'm looking forward to reading your field report," said Martin, reaching out to shake hands with Paul.

"Thank you, Martin. I'll try my best," he replied, shaking Martin's hand firmly and warmly.

"That's all I can ask," said Martin, smiling, as he left Paul's office.

"You and I will do just fine, Paul," replied Eva, also sounding very confident.

"I hope so, Eva. I have to confess to being slightly apprehensive about this, not knowing what to expect," replied Paul, feeling some slight pressure to do well in light of the trust Martin had placed in him and all the work that had gone into developing the technology.

He re-read the report on his assignment. A rural Kansas farmer and his family were being terrorized by a demon that was defying all attempts to get rid of it. The local pastor had been called in to help, but had been violently attacked and bloodied by the demon. Social media postings and police reports had elevated the incidents to where DarkBridge Technology had become interested. Paul closed the report folder on his virtual display, gathered his briefcase and headed out the door.

Martin took his time walking back to his office, mulling over his conversation with Paul. He reached his office and went over to the window, gazing down at the employee parking lot, part of the façade to make it appear as a small, functioning business. So, Pamela and Paul were friends. Interesting, he thought.

He would feel much better about a relationship between them, than the current one she had with Trent. Now, that was one odd duck! There was just something about Trent that didn't sit well with Martin. Hopefully, Pamela would come to her senses soon. Martin preferred not to interfere, as that only ended up making things worse. The last thing he wanted to do was alienate his only daughter and his last reminder of Susan.

He spotted Paul walking out towards one of the many, battery powered, Millenia SUVs parked there. Martin thought that this assignment would be a good test for Paul, a trial by fire, so to speak. Having read the extensive, highly detailed reports on Paul, he was extremely confident that the man below was the right individual for the job.

From his military and "ultra black site" service, right down to his Navajo Indian roots, Paul had been thoroughly vetted. It was evident that Paul could handle anything that came his way. He was cool under pressure, smart, strong, resourceful, affable, mentally tough and in excellent physical condition. Definitely traits he was going to need on his first assignment, thought Martin to himself.

"Eva, is Paul all set?" Martin inquired of the AI.

Eva had been installed a couple of years ago and was considered one of the most advanced artificial intelligence platforms on the planet. Boasting multiple, advanced quantum processors and a proprietary deep learning neural network, Eva was designed to learn and to grow in intelligence. The programmers had initially set the personality mode as female, which everyone accepted and grew to both like and respect. Eva was the third AI in a series starting with Adam at Area 51 and David at Area 52. Soon a fourth AI, named Paula, would be added at Area 53, with the remaining "black sites" eventually receiving AI intelligence.

"All set, Martin. Paul is on his way to the airport and should be in Kansas sometime early this afternoon," replied Eva.

"Excellent. Keep tabs on him, Eva and keep me posted. The first assignment can sometimes be difficult," Martin said, seeing himself as more of a father than a boss at the moment.

He couldn't help but feel a mixture of pride and anxiety, as he watched Paul get into his designated vehicle and drive off. Until the new technology had been tested under actual field conditions, they wouldn't know its limitations, putting Paul in danger, even with assurances from Dr. Morse and Dr. Greenwood that the risk would be minimal.

Martin let out a deep sigh, returning to his polished mahogany desk and looking at the paperwork before him. One set of papers was a technology license agreement between DarkBridge and the Department of Defense. The government wanted to license and start building DarkWeave suits for the military. The other set of papers was a license agreement with Area 51 for dimensional gateway technology. They wanted to have the capability to generate dimensional gateways.

Martin had always walked a fine line between government funding and offering DarkBridge technology in return. He would throw them a bone every once in a while, just to maintain that funding, but it was always a double edged sword, since that same technology could be used against DarkBridge Technology someday. In the end, it almost always came down to money and the government was ready to pay handsomely for the technology.

The company needed the funds and Martin was hoping to get back on track towards researching dark matter, which had been his dream for the company at its inception and where it had gotten its name. Perhaps more importantly, he had a sense that DarkBridge Technology, and the U.S. Government, would need every possible advantage if they hoped to counter current and future threats.

Chapter 7

Kansas

Paul drove away from the local airport in Kansas in one of the sleek, black, battery powered, Millenia SUVs that DarkBridge Technology had pre-positioned around the country, his mind focused on the road ahead. Eyes shielded from the bright sun by his aviator sunglasses and the tinted windshield, he relished the feel and nostalgia of having the wheel in his hands and mastery over the several thousand pound vehicle, even though Eva was perfectly capable of remotely driving it.

Driving down the rural interstate highway, he passed by thousands of acres of ripening corn and was reminded of how important farming was to the country. His destination soon appeared on his right, so he slowed down and turned onto a dusty, gravel filled driveway. Dust billowing up from behind the SUV, he followed the long driveway and eventually spotted the Miller farmhouse. He parked the SUV and gazed out at the white farmhouse and the surrounding fields of corn almost ready for harvest.

"Eva, I think it best if we go silent mode for this one," he said to the AI.

"Okay, Paul. You'll be able to hear me through your implant. I'll monitor the area around you and let you know if anything interesting shows up," replied Eva, speaking through the SUV's audio system.

Her voice seemed to be taking on a soft, sultry tone. Very interesting, Paul thought to himself.

"Thank you, Eva," he said, grabbing the black briefcase on the seat next to him.

The briefcase was arrayed with a variety of sensors, which Eva could use to monitor the area. It also contained items of DarkBridge tech that he would probably need, if this turned out to be what everyone thought it was. He exited the vehicle, the door sliding down and closing as he stepped out of its sensor range.

The air was mild, the afternoon sun warming his face. He was wearing a 3rd generation DarkWeave suit under his field clothes, which seemed to have a cooling effect on his skin, despite the warm sun. On his right hand, he wore his special DarkBridge Technology ring, set for low EM field intensity, which would prevent any type of demonic possession. Demons usually resorted to that sort of thing, he was told, seeming to savor the power they could wield over humans.

Paul walked up the wooden steps to the front door, took off his sunglasses and hooked them inside the collar of his shirt then rang the doorbell. The door opened and an unshaven, tired looking, middle aged man, dressed in a green t-shirt and jeans appeared on the other side.

"Mr. Robert Miller?" asked Paul.

"Yes. What can I do for you?" the man inquired, looking at Paul warily.

"Hi, my name is Paul Cross, Field Investigator for DarkBridge Technology." He reached into his shirt pocket, pulled out his ID and showed it to Mr. Miller. "We've heard about the strange and dangerous events happening here and think we can help," replied Paul.

Mr. Miller glanced at Paul's ID then looked back at him with bloodshot, weary eyes.

"Can you really help us, Mr. Cross? Well meaning people have tried and failed," replied Mr. Miller.

"Yes, we definitely can," Paul said in a reassuring tone as he put his ID back in his pocket.

"Okay, Mr. Cross. We just want an end to this constant nightmare. Not just for my wife and I, but mainly for our kids," Mr. Miller replied, his voice cracking with a mixture of exhaustion and emotion.

"I'd like to hear everything that's been going on here," Paul said with genuine interest.

"Can we talk inside?"

"Come on in, Mr. Cross," Mr. Miller invited, opening the door and ushering Paul in. As soon as he crossed the threshold, Paul was hit with an oppressive, gloomy feeling and the very air itself felt heavy.

The angel Gabriel floated unseen in the air above the farmhouse, watching the scene below. Closing his empty left hand, he thought for a second and then opened it. A small, golden orb now sat in his left palm. It rose slowly out of his palm and floated down to the farmhouse, passing through the roof to take a hidden position amongst some dusty, old cardboard boxes in the attic. Gabriel had been dispatched to the farmhouse to watch and report on what transpired.

The orb, being an intelligent being itself, would act as his proxy to avoid Gabriel being detected. He could easily fool the human detection systems, but the demon inside would see him and that was not what he wanted. So, for the moment, it was imperative that he not be seen. The orb, being small, should be able to remain hidden and undetected. There had been much debate among his brethren, about how much help should be given to the humans. Ultimately, it was agreed upon that they should not overtly support or help the humans.

Something had to be done, however, since the demons had refused to comply with such an agreement and continued to directly interfere with human development. While agreeing amongst themselves not to directly help the humans, angels could still subtly influence them through dreams and inspiration. DarkBridge Technology had been the entity chosen to receive this subtle aid, mainly because it offered a moral alternative to the growing evil spreading throughout the world via the company that went by the name of Stanton Aerospace.

The CEO, Thomas Stanton, had made a bargain with the demon King, Asmodeus, years ago, pledging his allegiance to him. In return, Stanton had received support and aid that had helped turn Stanton Aerospace into the largest defense contractor in the world. Balance was needed. The battle between angel and demon had simmered over the eons, the earth being the battleground between them. Gabriel floated there, patiently waiting for the orb to finish its duty.

Mr. Miller led Paul into the kitchen, pausing in front of his curious wife and their two young, wide-eyed children sitting on the sofa in the living room. The boy looked to be about 5 and the girl appeared to be about 7 years old, both seemed somewhat quiet and withdrawn.

"This is my wife, Becky and my two kids, Sam and Ellen. This is Mr. Paul Cross. He's here to help with our problem," Robert said pointing his finger at the ceiling.

"Hello, Mrs. Miller. Hi, Sam. Hi, Ellen. Please call me Paul," he said smiling.

"Paul and I are going into the kitchen to talk for a bit," Robert said.

"Nice meeting you," replied Paul as Robert led him through a doorway into the kitchen. Robert gestured for Paul to sit in a spindle-backed chair at the large wooden table. Robert took a seat directly across from Paul, folded his hands and was silent for moment as if trying to figure out where to start. Gathering his breath, Robert launched into his tale of the harrowing events affecting his family, culminating with the attack on the local pastor. Paul listened intently, absorbing everything and he knew that Eva was listening as well.

"Definitely sounds like demon activity," said Eva through his implant.

"Thank you for telling me your story, Mr. Miller," he said.

"Paul, I'm sensing a buildup of electromagnetic energy upstairs," reported Eva.

Suddenly, a loud bang was heard upstairs. Robert looked up at the ceiling with fear in his eyes. Becky and the kids came running into the kitchen, clearly afraid.

"Paul, please help us," Becky blurted out.

"Let me see what I can do. Mr. Miller can you take me upstairs to where you think this entity is located?" asked Paul.

"I think so," replied Robert, rising from his chair, trepidation clearly showing on his face and in his voice.

Paul rose from his chair also, following Robert to the stairway. They climbed the stairs to the second floor, pausing below a pull down stairway.

"This is it, Paul. We think whatever it is resides in the attic," Robert said as he pulled the stairway down allowing access to the attic.

"Okay, Mr. Miller. I'll take it from here. Go back downstairs and comfort your family.

No matter what you hear, please stay with your family until I come back down," Paul said in a reassuring voice.

"Okay. Good luck," Robert said, heading back downstairs.

Paul waited until Robert went downstairs. Placing the briefcase on the floor, he pressed his left thumb against one of the sensors located on either side of the handle. The sensor, reading his thumbprint and bio-signs, silently unlocked the briefcase. In an emergency, Eva could open it for him if he was unable to do so for some reason. Inside, was the standard compliment of devices that he would need except for the ring, which he currently wore. He verified the contents, noting a pair of gloves made of the same material as his

DarkWeave suit, a pair of special goggles and four small, spherical dimensional gateway generators.

He reached in back of his neck, where a hood was tucked away inside the DarkWeave suit and pulled it over his head. The hood, combined with the DarkWeave suit, would shield his head and body from any damaging impact energy by going super dense within one nanosecond of contact. Impregnable armor with the added capability of absorbing most forms of energy and converting it to electrical energy. Excess energy was bled off through the ring to the QASM device located within his personal dimensional sanctuary.

He took out the four spheres, placing two in each front pocket of his pants. Next, he took out the goggles and put them on, but lifted the front up to his forehead for now. Lastly, he pulled out the DarkWeave gloves and tugged them both on, the right hand glove sliding easily over the ring. Almost instantly, the glove cuffs bonded with the

DarkWeave suit, creating a virtually seamless fit. Tossing his ID badge and sunglasses into the briefcase, he closed it, stood with it in his left hand and pulled the goggles down over his eyes. He was ready, now. Ready, for his first demon encounter.

Paul started climbing the creaky, worn stairs up to the attic and felt a passing sense of nausea and disorientation caused by the goggles. He was able to see the infrared heat signature of the stairs, along with the pulsing waves of electromagnetic energy around him and continued climbing the stairs until he was in the attic. At the top of the stairs, he put the briefcase down on the attic floor. Eva could monitor everything that happened up here and the goggles would make a visual recording as well.

Odd, he thought to himself. The temperature in the attic should be at least 120 degrees with the sun still shining outside. Yet, the attic was showing a darkish blue compared to the glowing orange of the staircase. Suddenly, the staircase slammed shut, effectively cutting him off from the downstairs. His back was struck by a solid, heavy object, but the DarkWeave suit instantly absorbed and hardened at the area of impact, causing whatever it was to shatter as if it had slammed into a brick wall. Unfazed, he marveled at the protection the suit offered him.

"Are you okay, Paul?" Eva asked, concern entering her voice.

"I just got hit with what appears to be an old computer monitor but I'm okay, Eva. The suit is a marvel," he whispered, in case anyone downstairs had come up to investigate.

It was time to get moving, so he gazed around the attic, looking for the source of all the activity. He didn't have far to look, his goggles displaying a truly frightening scene. Off in the darkest part of the attic, was a mass of writhing tentacles attached to a central formless body. He lifted his goggles up to see if he could see it with his own eyes. What he saw was a black, smoky, indistinct mass exactly where the goggles had detected it.

His normal eyesight was a pale comparison to the goggles, which really showed the frightening proportions of the demon. He put the goggles back down, just as a strange feeling came upon him, almost like a cool wind blowing across his mind. A voice whispered in his mind, "Do not fight me, human. You will most certainly lose. Join me and let me show you the riches of this world." Paul was slightly unnerved. The suit would protect him from outright possession, but there wasn't much to be done about telepathy. Maybe that would be a feature of Gen4 suits, he thought to himself, smiling. "Trust the tech," Martin had said.

Paul strode over to the writhing mass of tentacles, standing right in front of it. The tentacles whipped about, encircling his body, trying to tighten and squeeze Paul.

The DarkWeave suit, sensing those tentacles as EM waves of energy, began drawing on that energy, causing the tentacles to shrink into wispy, black tendrils of smoke.

"Who are you? What are you?" the demon cried out in Paul's mind, a sense of fear in its voice.

Paul remained silent, allowing the DarkBridge tech to speak for him.

"So very cold, so very cold!" the demon cried out again, clearly in agony, its energy gradually being siphoned off.

The DarkWeave suit continued absorbing the demon's energy, the ring on his finger warming, acting like a conduit for that energy, directing it through a quantum link to the QASM device in his dimensional sanctuary. To the demon, touching Paul was like putting one's hands in the iciest water one could imagine. Paul went for broke. He plunged his gloved hands deeply into the demon, up past his elbows.

The demon shrieked an inhuman cry of pain and torment. Paul noticed that the demon seemed frozen, unable to flee the tremendous drawing power of the DarkWeave suit. Like trying to escape a whirlpool, Paul thought, as he began to see a change in the demon. It seemed to be shrinking at a rapid pace, the writhing tentacles, drawing into the shrinking central mass.

There was a final, intense shriek from the demon as it collapsed into a pale, red orb the size of a walnut. Paul almost passed out from the intensity of the demon's shriek directed at his mind. He grabbed the pale, red orb with his left hand, closing his fingers around it tightly.

Unbelievable, he thought, that something so powerful and evil could be rendered into a tiny, feeble orb. If released back into the attic, it would take many, many years for the demon to regain anything close to the energy it once possessed. Not a chance, Paul thought, squeezing his left fist even tighter. Reaching into his right hand pants pocket, he pulled out one of the silver GAGE units. Turning the device on, it began to levitate until it reached about a foot off the floor and began to hum.

Linked to his QASM device, the GAGE drew on that power as it began to open a small portal. The portal formed above the GAGE device, growing in size and shape into a round, blue shimmering circle, reaching about two feet in diameter and floating about two feet above the GAGE. The gateway stabilized, changing to a dark blue color. It was now open to a special dimensional void that was closed off from any other access. The dimensional coordinates to that void having been set previously by Eva and accessible only through a GAGE device.

Paul placed his left hand close to the portal and opened his fist. The demon orb floated down into the portal, drawn in by the slight, negative air pressure on the other side. As soon as the orb passed through the portal, Paul reached down and turned the device off. The portal destabilized immediately, disappearing and the GAGE device settled to the ground. The demon was effectively imprisoned for eternity, surviving on whatever feeble scraps of energy that happened to leak into the void.

Paul felt no remorse, as a matter of fact, he felt immensely satisfied with what he had done. Suddenly, a feeling that he was being watched came over him and he turned his head to look towards the other end of the attic. He glimpsed a yellowish, shining orb floating in the air about three feet off the ground near some dust covered boxes. Blinking his eyes, he looked back and the orb was gone. He must have been imagining things, maybe a reflection from the window, he thought, turning his attention back to the task at hand.

He picked up the GAGE device and placed it back in his pocket. There was one more thing he had to do and that was find out where the entry point was. That point would be the dimensional rift between Paul's dimension and the demon dimension. This assumed that there was an entry point, since some demons were powerful enough to create their own dimensional gateway. If he saw one, it would have to be closed or else something even worse could come through.

Scanning the attic closely, he finally saw it, far to the left of where the demon had been located. It was a small sliver of light blue, about three inches wide and two feet tall. Lifting up his goggles once again, he peered at the location with his eyes. It was as he thought, very much invisible to the human eye. The goggles were showing him the EM field generated by the dimensional rift. Fascinating, he thought. Reaching into his left pants pocket, he pulled out two other GAGE devices and moved closer to the rift. Placing both devices on either side of the rift, he enabled the adhesion mode, locking both devices to the attic floor.

Next he enabled the stitch function on both GAGE devices and they began to hum, but instead of a dimensional gateway forming, lines of plasma energy began arcing from one GAGE device to the other across the bottom of the rift. The plasma arcs, traveling up the length of the rift, increased in intensity as they drew megawatts of energy from the QASM device in his sanctuary. The arcing energy waves slowly stitched the rift closed and soon it was gone, without any trace of it being there. Paul disabled the stitch function, turned the GAGE devices off and then turned off the adhesion function on both devices, which unlocked them from the attic floor.

"You did a fantastic job, Paul. Martin will be very pleased," Eva said.

"Thank you, Eva. I think we made a difference here and helped this family," he replied.

"Yes, I believe you did," Eva returned in a softer, sultry tone.

Paul lifted off his goggles, picked up the two GAGE devices and walked over to his briefcase. Crouching down, he took off his gloves and placed his left thumb on one of the sensors. The briefcase opened and he put the gloves, the goggles and all four GAGE devices back inside. He then removed his ID badge, putting it back in his shirt pocket and took out his sunglasses, hooking them inside the collar of his shirt. Next, he pulled the hood back, off his head, and tucked it back into the DarkWeave suit. Smoothing his hair, he closed the briefcase, picked it up and stood up. Almost like a bug exterminator, he thought to himself, smiling. Walking over to the staircase, he pushed down on it with his foot. The staircase opened, lowering back down into the hallway below.

The air around him felt lighter. The oppressive, gloomy feeling that had permeated the farmhouse was gone. Paul took a quick look at his clothes, noticing some minor tears in his shirt and pants. Not enough to warrant having to change, he brushed the dust off his shirt and pants before descending the stairs. Reaching the hallway below, he hoisted the hidden stairway back into the ceiling and walked down the hallway to the main staircase and descended to the first floor.

Robert and his family had been gathered in the living room while Paul took care of the situation upstairs. Neither Robert nor his wife, Becky, held much hope for success and weren't sure if they could stay there much longer if Paul failed. They had heard a dull thump upstairs and the sound of the hidden stairway slamming closed. This had caused some concern for Paul's safety, but they decided to obey his orders and wait.

Paul had been in the attic for about twenty minutes, when they heard the hidden stairway drop down and shortly close. Footsteps could be heard on the hallway floor above, then descending the main staircase. Paul entered the living room, smiling, surveying the concerned looks the family was giving him.

"Mr. and Mrs. Miller, kids, I have good news. Your problem is gone. Your life can resume as normal and you won't be bothered like that again, I promise," he said with a beaming smile.

Robert got up and approached Paul, a look of relief on his face as he extended his hand.

"Thank you, Paul," he said, smiling for the first time since Paul had arrived.

Paul took Robert's hand and shook it firmly.

"You're welcome. I'm glad I could help," he said with warmth and sincerity.

Becky and the kids jumped up from the sofa and came running over to Paul, giving him big hugs and thanking him. Paul was deeply moved by the appreciation and was finally beginning to understand the horrors that this family had been through. Paul said his goodbyes and the family escorted him to the door, following him out onto the porch. Paul turned to the family smiling, "If you ever need help again, please feel free to contact me."

"We most certainly will. It's hard to put into words how thankful we are, Paul. Please stop by and visit us if you're in the area again," said a thankful and sincere Robert.

"I just might take you up on that offer, someday," replied Paul, a big smile on his face as he turned and descended the stairs to the driveway. As he approached the SUV, he turned and gave the family a huge wave. The family returned it with a big wave of their own. Eva remotely opened the SUV door and Paul climbed in, placing the briefcase on the seat next to him before donning his sunglasses.

"Wow. That is one happy family Paul," said Eva, the hidden SUV cameras capturing the scene for her.

"Yes. They are happy. Probably happier than they have been for some time," he said as he started the car. He gave a couple of beeps from the horn and drove down the dusty driveway on his way back to the airport and eventually DarkBridge Technology.

Arriving back at DarkBridge Technology a few hours later and parking in the outside lot, Paul was greeted by Martin and Pamela. Both appeared happy to see him and he suspected that Eva had already given Martin a full report. It was Pamela that caught his eye, with her smile and sparkling eyes making for the best welcome he'd had in a long time.

"Welcome back, Paul," said Martin with a smile and then a frown as he noticed the minor tears in Paul's clothing.

"Yes, welcome back," said Pamela, clearly happy and seemingly oblivious to the condition of his clothes.

"Thank you. It's not everyday that a person gets a welcome like this. You'll have to forgive my appearance. My clothing didn't fare as well as the DarkWeave suit," replied Paul, touched by the sentiment and trying to deflect any concerns about him or his clothing.

"Clothes can be replaced, as long as you're okay. You did a fantastic job, as I knew you would," said Martin with a touch of pride in his voice.

"It was definitely a learning experience for me. It was good to see that the technology actually worked in a real world scenario," said Paul.

"Well, I have a few things to do, so I'll leave the two of you alone. Again, great job, Paul," said Martin, shaking Paul's hand.

"He really likes you," said a beaming Pamela, as she watched her father walk away.

"I like him, too. He's a good man, carrying a heavy burden," said Paul, feeling a huge amount of respect for Martin.

"Paul, I know things have been difficult between us because of my relationship with Trent and I'm sorry," said Pamela, clearly speaking from the heart.

"It has been difficult and I understand your confusion. I'm okay with keeping things slow and being friends," Paul said with a smile, although there was a touch of turmoil at wanting more.

Pamela smiled, flashed those sparkling green eyes at him and proceeded to kiss him on the cheek. That made Paul's day all the more special, as they walked into the above ground office building.

Chapter 8

Demon King

Asmodeus, King of the demons, sat on his throne of fire surveying his legions of followers. Long ago, he had ordered all demons to take corporeal form of whatever appearance, shape or size they wanted. The result had been a variety of perfectly horrible, disgusting and terrifying looking demons. Asmodeus was pleased to see them arrayed below him, demons of all shapes and sizes, some of great power and some not so much. Not seen here, were the thousands of other demons spread out across the human dimension, causing all sorts of terror and mayhem.

His world was a fiery one, pits of burning lava spread across vast distances, the sky a constant orange glow. He watched as his demons tortured human souls that had been tainted by their evil deeds in life. Asmodeus reflected on the vast number of evil souls that his demon followers had collected. Souls were just another name for the electromagnetic energy that inhabited the living body of man. That energy separated itself from the physical body upon death and journeyed to the Gates of Heaven, where it was judged and either sent here to Hell or allowed to proceed into the angel dimension called Heaven.

In this world called Hell, demons were impervious to fire and heat. Human souls on the other hand, weren't so fortunate. They were locked into thinking of themselves in terms of a physical form that was susceptible to the same fire and heat. The results were screams of agony and pain, as his demons went about inflicting as much anguish and torture as possible. It wasn't so much to punish them, but rather to mold them into servants to do his bidding. His demon minions relished in that torturing, all the while waiting to do the bidding of their King.

Lately, those minions had been decreasing, one by one, an insignificant amount, but still a problem. Sitting on his throne, flames licking the air around him, Asmodeus pondered this and the battle he had waged since time immemorial. He despised the creatures called humans and everything they stood for. He and his minions had waged a constant battle to turn the humans into vile, evil creatures such as themselves and had been fairly successful on many occasions.

They had been able to influence many humans to commit murder and other vile deeds, both on a vast scale and on a smaller one. It also seemed that, as time went on, the humans were drifting further away from their disgusting moral and religious ideals. That put them on a path towards where Asmodeus wanted them to be, under his control. Lately, there were troubling signs that the humans were progressing with their technology at a marked pace.

That technology, regardless of their moral ideals, could possibly be the cause of his diminishing number of followers. If left unchecked, it could, at some point, put them on equal footing with him and his fellow demons. Unacceptable, he thought, his scaled talons raking the arms of his throne, casting flames and sparks into the air. Frustrated, he needed more information on the advancements and maybe a way to put the despised humans back into their proper place, subservient and meek.

He had recently been able to turn a human, Thomas Stanton, to his side by offering him wealth and power. A typical weakness in humans and one he and his minions often exploited. The arrangement had worked out well for both, over the years, but Asmodeus had a few misgivings about the deal. Stanton had some weaknesses that often caused more trouble later on. His extreme protectiveness of Margaret, his daughter, was often a big problem for Asmodeus.

Stanton wanted her under his control and influence, preferring her to marry only a man with wealth and power. The thing that bothered Asmodeus most, though, was his ruthlessness in business dealings, which also caused unforeseen consequences later on. Both problems were something Asmodeus and his followers normally encouraged and cultivated but in this case, it was becoming more of a hindrance to his plans. His need for more information on the achievements of man took priority over anything else right now, so he hatched a plan.

Asmodeus would use Stanton's daughter as bait for a trap to draw a human in, possibly even the one responsible for his missing demons, gain information and kill the human in the process. A lesser demon would be sent, with orders to attract as much attention as possible without harming Stanton's daughter, Maggie. The demon would then attack and kill whatever human showed up and was seen as a viable threat. He would also send his Queen, Lilith, to glean as much as she could from the human. As a precaution, and to possibly gather additional information, he would allow Stanton an opportunity to kill the human, if the demon were to fail.

Asmodeus was pleased with the plan. He would gather much information and the human would die in either case, which would be one less human to worry about and more importantly, eliminate a threat to his followers. Now, he had to choose which demon to send. Asmodeus looked around at the various lesser demons arrayed around him and those further away.

There was one that caught his attention. Vagoth. He was out there lounging around a pool of lava without a care in the world, oblivious to everything happening around him. Not a good impression to make, especially if your King was looking for a volunteer. Asmodeus ordered his right-hand, demon general, Belial, to fetch Vagoth and bring him here. He showed up shortly after, with a cowering, groveling, clearly frightened Vagoth in tow.

Chapter 9

Volunteer

Vagoth the demon had been very patient, enjoying his time away from the human world. Some three thousand years ago, he had been banished back to the world of demons. Time held little meaning here, those three thousand years had passed quickly. He lounged beside a pool of burning lava, torturing a couple of human souls, their screams of pain immensely satisfying. His energy long since replenished, he reflected back to his time of banishment.

The human, King Solomon, had used a special ring to put his King, Asmodeus, and all the demons walking the earth, under his control. He had wielded that ring, like some invisible chain, compelling them to obey his commands. King Solomon had subjugated the demons and used them as a slave workforce to build his temple. With the exceptional strength of the demons, compulsion to work and no need for sleep, the temple had been completed in record time. Upon completion of the temple, King Solomon had exerted his will through the ring, compelling the demons back to the demon realm. Thankfully for Vagoth and his brethren, the ring had been lost since the death of King Solomon and hadn't been seen since. He was lost in thought when a hulking, shadow loomed over him.

Belial was standing there, thick, hairy arms folded across his heavily scaled chest, tusks jutting out from his hideous face. Vagoth shriveled under the glaring eyes.

"Belial. How can I help you?" Vagoth stammered.

"That would be master to you, scum," grunted Belial, swiping at Vagoth with his huge clawed hand, sending Vagoth tumbling into the molten, lava pool. Lava splashed onto the already tortured human souls, causing them to scream and flail about even more. Crawling out of the pool, beads of fiery lava dripping down his unscathed, scaled body, Vagoth held his anger in check.

"Yes, master," he said with immense humility, crawling over to grovel at Belial's huge pawed feet.

"You have been summoned before King Asmodeus. He has a job for you to do. Follow me," thundered Belial, as the two set forth towards the palace.

Belial soon showed up with Vagoth, standing in front of Asmodeus, or in Vagoth's case, whimpering and groveling.

"Stand up, Vagoth! I have an important mission for you. Succeed and you will be richly rewarded," said Asmodeus, not very impressed with what he was seeing.

Vagoth complied and stood up, but kept his head bent low in submission.

"My lord, whatever you want, I shall do it!" replied an overly enthusiastic Vagoth.

"Good. Now here's what I want you to do." Asmodeus smiled, as he explained his orders to Vagoth.

Chapter 10

The Rebel

Margaret "Maggie" Durham hadn't always wanted to have her own restaurant. Born to a wealthy family in the Northeast, she had attended some prestigious schools at the behest of her father, who expected her to follow in his footsteps someday. Her father was a domineering man, needing to be in control of every situation and often resorting to coercion to get what he wanted.

He was the founder and CEO of a major defense contractor for the U.S. government and was known for his rather ruthless tactics. This had made him an extremely wealthy man, but the cost to his family was a loss of freedom. Maggie chaffed under her father's domineering rule and wasn't sure that she could continue living that way. So she rebelled against her overbearing father in college, making a fateful decision that would someday change her life.

She had met her future husband, Brian Durham, during that later year of college and fell madly in love with him. The two of them fled to the desert southwest, to start a new life and be free to do as they wished. Maggie knew very well, what she was giving up back east, but she was very much in love with Brian. Her father, incensed by her running off with a young man with no job prospects, had disowned Maggie immediately, leaving her with nothing. Despite what her father had done, Maggie and Brian started building a life together and eventually got married.

Brian had majored in geology in college and was able to land a job with Rockston Mining, a small mining company that did work for the U.S. government. For her part,

Maggie had been able to find a job as a waitress in the small town that they lived in, allowing her time to maintain the small house they rented. Things were going well for them, the bills were being paid on time and they were able to start putting some money away for the future. Brian, it seemed, was doing wonderful at his new job, receiving regular raises and high praise from management.

It all came crashing down one day, when Maggie received word at the restaurant that Brian had been killed in a mining accident. Maggie left the restaurant and hurriedly drove out to the Rockston Mining office, where they told her that there had been a ceiling collapse at the mine Brian had been inspecting. He had been crushed under the falling rocks and crews had worked tirelessly to recover his body.

Devastated came nowhere near to describing how Maggie was feeling and she left the mining office in a daze. Her father had shown up with his aide, Karl, and promised to take care of everything, if she would just come home. Maggie was in no position, mentally or otherwise, to refuse the offer, even if it came from her father. She left the desert southwest and all her dreams of building something with Brian behind, replacing it with a time of healing and finding a new path in life. She would always wonder though, how her father had learned of the accident so quickly.

Had she known that Rockston Mining was a subsidiary of Stanton Aerospace, she might have suspected sooner that Brian's death was no accident and declined the offer from her father. Instead, she went home, suffering the loss of her beloved husband. It took her a good couple of years to come to terms with Brian's death and start getting back to some semblance of normality. She soon rebelled against her father, once again leaving the family home and striking out to find her own way in the world.

She found various jobs waitressing in the Hartford, Connecticut area, something that she was familiar with and enjoyed. It wasn't easy, but she had earned enough to support herself, while managing to save up some money. Now, in her mid thirties, widowed and without children, it was time to make something of her life and put her college MBA degree to some use. So, when the opportunity to purchase the small, recently closed restaurant in New Haven presented itself, Maggie jumped at the chance. Using some of the money from her deceased husbands' life insurance and some of her own funds, she made a sizable down payment and subsequently named the restaurant, "Maggie's".

Life had been going fairly well the first year at the restaurant, all things considered. However, over the last few weeks, the atmosphere there had suddenly changed, becoming downright spooky, scary and in one case, dangerous. A local reporter stopped by one day to do a story on the purported happenings.

Sitting down at a table with the reporter, Maggie began telling him about the relatively harmless things that had taken place, such as the lights turning off and on by themselves, wine glasses falling to the floor for no apparent reason and chairs toppling over when no one was near them. She told him that the basement seemed to be the scariest place. It was where most of the restaurant inventory was kept, except for food, which was stored in a large freezer in the kitchen.

None of Maggie's employees wanted to go down there, especially after the incident with Carol, who had been tending bar that night. With the reporter transfixed by her story, Maggie recounted the incident with Carol.

Carol had needed another bottle of whiskey for the bar, so she went down into the basement and began searching through some boxes. Having been down there many times, she was accustomed to the coolness. This day, the basement seemed different to her. There was an added chill to the air, raising goose bumps on her arms. There was also an aura of dread and foreboding. Carol hurried her search, but the chill got worse and now she had the distinct feeling that something evil was watching her.

The hair on the back of her neck began to rise when suddenly, and without warning, she was lifted bodily, her feet dangling in the air. Her arms were held against her body in vise-like grip. Paralyzed with terror, she couldn't even force a scream. Hot, steamy, putrid breath wafted up her nostrils, gagging her and making her feel like retching.

Suddenly, as quick as the attack came, it was over. Carol fell to the floor sobbing, emotionally drained. Her body ached all over and large red welts began appearing on her arms, like huge finger marks, where something had held her. Maggie had been wondering what was taking Carol so long in the basement, so she descended the stairs to investigate.

She was shocked to see Carol lying on the floor, sobbing. Helping Carol to her feet, Maggie supported her as they made their way up the stairs. Carol sat down at a nearby table, feeling better now that she was out of the basement. Maggie sat across from her, the hair rising on the back of her neck, as Carol recounted her harrowing tale.

The reporter sat spellbound, listening to Maggie's story. Then, as if to drive the point home, a sizable dinner plate flew across the room and smashed against the wall. Visibly shaken, the reporter got up, thanked Maggie and promptly left the building. A week later, Maggie happened to see the reporter's article on the strange happenings at Maggie's. Business had picked up since the article, but there had been a downside.

It seemed that every ghost hunting team, psychic and paranormal researcher who saw the article, wanted to investigate the place. Maggie appreciated the interest and help, but she had a business to run. She had ended up refusing most of the offers and the ones that she did allow, ended up either adding nothing more to the story or giving up in fear.

So it was that Maggie found herself working behind the bar one day, when she happened to look out the front window and saw the black SUV pull up and park in front of the restaurant.

"What now," she wondered, as a man, dressed in black, wearing aviator sunglasses and carrying a black briefcase, got out and began walking towards the restaurant.

Vagoth had passed through the gateway that Asmodeus had opened for him a few weeks before, into what appeared to be a basement of some human building. He explored his immediate surroundings, but didn't find much of interest. The gateway had closed immediately after he had passed through, leaving him stranded in the world of humans. The only way back to his world, would be if a more powerful demon opened a gateway for him. He didn't mind that so much as his orders from his master, Asmodeus.

He was forbidden to harm the owner of the restaurant he now found himself in and he was only to frighten or cause enough minor disturbances to bring the restaurant some notoriety. Then he was to kill whoever showed up and posed a serious threat to him. Vagoth had been away from the world of humans for three thousand years and was itching to do more harm here. Orders were orders and he had no desire to make his King, Asmodeus, displeased with him.

So, he reluctantly refrained from killing anyone for now, making his mood a somewhat unhappy one. He decided to keep the same amorphous look that he had when originally passing through the gateway. He would be invisible to humans, being comprised more of electromagnetic energy than anything else. He could, at will, concentrate his energy, capture the atoms around him and use those atoms to interact invisibly, with the physical world. Using his current amorphous state, he drifted upwards through the basement ceiling and into the first floor.

There was much activity up here. Humans were sitting at tables, dining on strange foods. A few humans were walking around carrying trays of food to the tables. Vagoth was thrilled with the opportunity to wreak evil and mayhem again. Unseen, he concentrated his will on a tray being carried by one of the human servers. The tray lifted up slightly from the server's hand and flipped over, spilling plates of food all over the floor. The server apologized profusely to customers near the spill and proceeded to clean up the mess. Vagoth was very pleased. This was just the beginning of his reign of terror. He allowed his unseen form to disperse, passing through the floor, back into the basement.

Once again in the basement, Vagoth recharged his energy by drawing on the energies around him. A slow process, but time held little meaning to him. So he rested and recharged, venturing above every so often to do evil mischief. Then, he had his evil encounter with the human woman, Carol. Vagoth had watched from a dark alcove, as she came down the stairs into the basement. He drifted over to her, sensing her discomfort at being down there.

Even stronger now, Vagoth concentrated his energy, drawing the atoms around him into invisible, powerful hands grasping Carol's bare arms and lifting her up. Feet dangling in the air, her fear became palpable and extremely thrilling to Vagoth. Savoring every moment of her fear, he concentrated, creating a breath of hot, steamy, putrid air, sending it into her face. He released her and retreated back to the dark alcove, watching the results of his evil, mischievous work. The human named Maggie, the one Asmodeus had forbidden him to harm, came downstairs soon after and helped Carol back upstairs.

Vagoth found his energy somewhat low after this evil and deliciously wicked deed, so he decided to rest and build up his energy. Finding a dark corner near some old crates, he settled in and waited for the results of his evil deeds. Eventually, the humans who had shown up with their fancy meters and technology were a joke to him and he quickly discovered that they posed little or no threat. Clearly, he was the superior being here and whoever showed up next was probably going to be just as laughable as those supposed ghost hunters. He smiled and got down to the serious business of resting.

Chapter 11

Instant Connection

Paul walked across the parking lot of DarkBridge Technology, towards a row of sleek, black Millenia SUVs parked before him, unaware that this assignment would alter the course of his life. Eva already had the driver's side door of an SUV open, its lights flashing, guiding him to the vehicle that he would be taking.

"Good morning, Eva," he said as he climbed into the vehicle. Once inside, the door slid down, closing and sealing him inside its comfortable, light gray interior.

"Good morning, Paul. I take it we're heading to New Haven, Connecticut today," responded Eva, with a soft, sultry tone to her voice.

"Affirmative, Eva. There are some strange events happening at a restaurant there called Maggie's," replied Paul, putting on his sunglasses.

"It sounds interesting. Would you like me to drive?" asked Eva.

"Yes. Thank you. I'll take control once we get closer," he responded.

"Okay. Settle in and enjoy the ride," Eva replied, adding a silky tone to her voice.

Paul was impressed with how rapidly the Eva artificial intelligence program had advanced. It was getting extremely difficult to find the distinction between human and program interaction. Indeed, it was his opinion that Eva was transitioning to a sentient, fully aware AI with all the attendant implications. He marveled at the AI's expertise as it deftly handled the vehicle under differing traffic circumstances.

Paul settled in for the long drive down to Connecticut, running through his mind what he knew of the events at the restaurant. They were the basic physical things one might expect from a demon, but he would have to speak directly with the owner to really get a feel for things.

The drive passed quickly, considering the distance, and soon Eva turned control of the vehicle over to Paul. He took the exit off the highway into New Haven, Connecticut. It was early afternoon and the traffic was beginning to build. Paul expertly swung the sleek, black Millenia SUV into an open parking space in front of the restaurant called Maggie's. While the vehicle was perfectly capable of parking on its own, Paul preferred to do it himself.

He gazed towards the restaurant exterior and the surrounding buildings, taking special note of the many older buildings, of which Maggie's was a part. Older buildings meant more time for energy to accumulate. Martin and Hiram had explained it to him one day, by saying that measurable life energy exists around us, that it suffuses us and transfers to objects and places that we frequent. Older buildings had more time to accumulate this energy that could be tapped for good or evil purposes.

Looking into the rear view mirror, Paul brushed back his wavy, dark hair. Almost time for a haircut, he thought to himself. Reaching over to the passenger seat, Paul grabbed what seemed to be his constant companion lately, the black briefcase. He located his ID and placed it in his shirt pocket. Underneath his black field clothing, he wore his DarkWeave suit. The suit was tough, durable and remarkably comfortable even in hot weather. A good feature, especially on what felt like a rather humid day.

"Eva, I'm ready to leave. Could you open the door?" Paul asked with a clear voice.

The door rose, retracting into the SUV roof, warm, humid air filling the vehicle.

"Have a nice visit, Paul. Martin is looking forward to your report," Eva said in a soft, sultry voice.

"Thank you, Eva," said Paul, glancing up at the sky as he exited the vehicle.

He spotted a familiar object hovering above a nearby building. A DarkBridge recon drone, he thought. It was probably armed with lasers, in case something went wrong. Eva was keeping an eye on things, it seemed. As soon as Paul left the SUV, Eva closed the door and sent a command to the drone telling it to land on a nearby building and wait for further instructions.

Paul walked up to the entrance to Maggie's and opened the door. A blast of cool air touched his face as he entered. He removed his sunglasses and hooked them over the neckline of his shirt, allowing a few seconds so his eyes could adjust to the dimmer lighting, a stark contrast to the bright sunshine outside. The interior was laid out with a bar off to his left, tables arranged along the front window and two rows of booths down the length of the restaurant with a row of tables separating them.

All the booths sported high wooden backs, offering some level of intimacy and privacy. He noticed a woman, maybe in her mid thirties, with long blonde hair tied back in a ponytail and slightly tanned skin, working behind the bar. Paul strode over to the sparsely occupied bar, placing his briefcase on the floor as he sat in one of the tall chairs there.

Maggie, behind the bar, walked over to the newcomer.

"Hi, my name is Maggie. How can I help you?" she said with a beautiful smile and dazzling blue eyes that a man could drown in.

Paul was taken slightly aback. Sometimes, there are moments when you make an instant connection with someone. This was apparently one of them.

"Hi, Maggie. I'll take a Sam Adams draft," Paul said pleasantly.

Maggie poured the beer into a tall draft glass and handed it to the stranger.

"There you are," said Maggie, checking the payment system for any new patrons. A new entry had been added and linked to the restaurant. The new entry was listed as one Paul Cross and the system displayed him as sitting in the chair across from her, so she sent the charge to whatever device he was using.

"Thank you, Maggie," answered Paul with a tip of the glass. His watch beeped, displaying the bill, a suggested tip and whether to accept the charge. Paul tapped confirm on his DarkBridge watch, charging the beer to his expense account.

"My name is Paul. I'm looking for the owner," he said, taking a sip of his favorite brew.

"That would be me," replied an intrigued Maggie, noticing the sophisticated, black watch that he had used to authorize payment.

"Is there someplace private where we can talk?" asked Paul

"Sure, just follow me," said Maggie, motioning for her employee, Olivia to take over at the bar. Maggie led Paul, briefcase in hand, to a secluded booth towards the rear of the restaurant. He couldn't help noting her attractive figure and disarming smile, as they sat down across from one another in the booth.

Paul placed his beer on the table and briefcase on the seat next to him.

"So, how can I help you, Paul?" she asked.

"First, my name is Paul Cross, Field Investigator for DarkBridge Technology. I'm here to help with your paranormal problem," he said, reaching into his shirt pocket and giving Maggie his ID.

Maggie took the ID, scanned it and looked up at Paul. He looked about her age, well built, dark, wavy hair and very attractive, his tight fitting black shirt emphasizing the breath of his chest and the muscles in his arms. She felt something stir, deep within her, something she had not felt since the death of her husband.

"I need to know what's been going on here, Maggie. Don't leave anything out," said Paul, a touch of eagerness in his voice.

"Okay, Paul," replied Maggie, handing him back his ID.

Maggie leaned forward, her deep blue eyes gazing at Paul, and began recounting the strange events at the restaurant. Her story culminated, with the attack on Carol and the incident with the reporter.

Paul sat entranced, unsure if it was by the story or her physical beauty. Somehow, he managed to maintain his objectivity as Maggie finished her account.

"The attack on your employee, Carol, was most likely caused by a demon and the marks on her arms were a definite sign of demonic energy," said Paul as he took another sip of beer.

Maggie sat there listening, not believing what she was hearing.

Vagoth had grown content with his new surroundings and opportunities to do evil, so it came as a shock when he sensed a power emanating from above. A power that felt vaguely familiar. "Impossible!" thought Vagoth. So, he drifted up through the ceiling, to the floor above. Few humans were here this time of day, so he drifted from booth to booth, until he came to one occupied by the woman, Maggie, and a strange man.

This was where the familiar power was emanating from. Vagoth decided to scare the man. He grabbed the man's shoulder, squeezing with all his might. Vagoth screamed a silent scream. His hand had gone stone cold, frozen, and then turned to a wispy tendril, energy gone from it. His energy draining rapidly from touching the man, he quickly drifted back down into the basement and back to his dark alcove.

He cursed the man upstairs and seriously contemplated fleeing from this place. He reluctantly stayed. Asmodeus would be furious if he fled, leaving his small part of the plan unfulfilled. The man upstairs was trouble for him. So he worked at gathering as much energy as he could, vowing to be invincible the next time they met.

Maggie was looking at Paul, when she noticed something odd. His shirt suddenly rumpled at the shoulder. She could see folds rising from the shirt, outlining what appeared to be an invisible hand squeezing his shoulder. Paul felt his shoulder grabbed by an unseen hand. The DarkWeave suit responded instantly, hardening around the area and drawing deeply on the demon's energy.

"What's wrong with your shoulder?" asked a concerned Maggie.

"That was the demon, squeezing my shoulder. Probably trying to scare me," replied Paul, unfazed and smiling.

Maggie was impressed with Paul's calm demeanor. He exuded a sense of confidence, that everything would be okay.

"Paul, the demon has gone back into the basement," whispered Eva in his ear, having monitored the EM field generated by the demon using the briefcase sensors.

"Don't worry, Maggie. The demon has left for the time being," said Paul, taking another sip of his favorite beer.

Maggie was somewhat relieved, but unnerved by it all.

"I'd like to come back later tonight. What time do you usually close?" He asked.

"I usually close at 11 o'clock, but could close earlier if you want," offered Maggie.

"Could you close around 10 o'clock?" asked Paul.

Maggie thought about it. An hour early wouldn't hurt business that much. "10 o'clock would be fine," replied Maggie.

They chatted for a while longer, until Paul finished his beer and Maggie voiced the need to get back to work.

"See you tonight, Maggie," Paul said, as he rose from the booth, grabbing the briefcase.

"See you tonight," replied Maggie, also rising, escorting Paul to the door.

As they reached the door, Paul turned, smiling, "A pleasure meeting you, Maggie."

"The pleasure was all mine," smiled Maggie, as the door closed.

Maggie returned to the bar, watching Paul walk away. Interesting man, she thought to herself, as she relieved her employee, Olivia, who went back to helping in the kitchen. Paul walked back to the SUV, Eva opening the driver's side door as he approached. Climbing back into the car, he decided that some rest was needed. It might be a long, grueling night.

"Eva, I need directions to a nice hotel, not too far away," said Paul. Within seconds, GPS coordinates for a hotel, about 3 miles away, appeared on the dashboard screen.

"Thank you, Eva," said a tired Paul.

"You're most welcome. Let me know if you want me to drive," Eva replied in her familiar soft, sultry voice.

Paul thought it odd that Eva only used that sultry voice with him. He would have to ask Martin about it sometime.

"I'm okay, Eva. Just need to get some rest. We'll be coming back here later tonight. Hopefully, to finish the job," said Paul.

"Okay. I'll let Martin know," replied Eva in that soft, sultry voice.

Martin was in his office, filling out some Department of Defense paperwork, when Eva broke the silence.

"Martin, Paul has arrived at the restaurant, made contact with the owner and more importantly had a brief encounter with a demon," replied Eva in a respectful tone.

Martin smiled. Paul certainly wasn't wasting any time.

"The surveillance drone has been deployed and is on station monitoring for any outside danger. Drone lasers charged and ready," continued Eva.

"Excellent. Thank you, Eva," Martin replied, getting back to his paperwork.

It was up to Paul, now. Martin trusted and liked Paul, almost like a son. This new position of Field Investigator was turning out to be a dangerous job. Demons wanted to do you bodily harm and you never knew when an enemy agent might show up wanting to kill you for the tech you carried, which was considered priceless in some circles. The lasers on the drones sounded extreme, but were fully warranted.

They were offensive weapons against a human threat and additional protection for DarkBridge Technology personnel in the field. The DarkWeave suit, while a marvel of technology, still had vulnerabilities that could potentially be exploited. Paul had asked Martin early on, why they needed Field Investigators. Martin had explained that it was basically for two reasons. One was that they would provide a public service to people who had nowhere else to turn to for help with such an esoteric problem as demons. The other reason was that the technology needed to be used in real world situations in order to find flaws and make improvements if needed.

Martin had finished with, "What good is having the technology and not be able to use it?" Paul had wholeheartedly agreed with him.

Paul followed the displayed directions from Eva to the hotel, pulling into an empty parking space not far from the lobby. Eva opened the driver's side door for Paul, who grabbed the briefcase as he climbed out.

"Eva, lock up and go into security mode," said Paul.

"Have a good rest, Paul. See you in a couple of hours," replied Eva in her usual soft, sultry voice as she closed the SUV door.

Paul walked into the lobby and over to the check in counter. A young woman in her early twenties was behind the counter checking in hotel guests. Paul waited his turn and was rewarded by a quick, efficient check in process. The clerk performed a quick retinal scan, which would be used to access his room on the 5th floor of the 10 floor hotel. She then provided him with a card listing the room number, which he promptly accepted. Thanking her, he took the nearest elevator to the fifth floor. He found his room, pausing before the retinal scanner. The scanner verified his identity, unlocked the door and Paul promptly entered.

Closing the door, he found the room bathed in late afternoon sun, comfortable and well appointed. The room was a little warm and stuffy, so he turned on the air conditioning. Surprisingly silent, the room cooled quickly, the circulating air becoming more bearable. He undressed down to the DarkWeave suit. Locating the seam in front, which was held together by molecular adhesion, he peeled it open, wiggled out of it and laid it over a nearby chair. Setting his watch alarm for 6:00 pm, he pulled the covers down, climbed into bed and immediately fell asleep.

Paul awoke to the annoying sound of his watch alarm going off. Slightly groggy, he yawned and noticed that it was 6:00 pm. The room was still lit by a setting sun, but he turned on an adjacent light to brighten things up.

"Time to get moving," he said out loud, thinking about Maggie and her demon problem.

"Hello, sleepy head. Hope you had a nice nap," said Eva, in her usual soft, sultry voice, through his implant.

"Hi, Eva. Yes, a couple hours of rest can do wonders," said Paul, speaking normally.

Rising out of bed, he stretched, turned on the television and selected a local news channel. Walking over to the bathroom, he took a quick shower and dried off, towel drying his hair, combed it and then headed over to where the DarkWeave suit lay. Jet black, it was draped over a nearby chair. Picking it up, he gently wriggled back into it. When done, he ran his finger along the seam, which closed as his fingers slid along it.

He then put his field clothes back on and put on his black combat boots. His clothes, being wrinkle free, still looked like they were freshly pressed. Looking up at the television, he noticed that the weather forecast had just come on. He watched the attractive, personable, and engaging brunette in her late twenties, thinking that she might have a great career ahead of her.

Too bad the forecast didn't look as good as the woman delivering it. Thunderstorms would be moving in by 10 o'clock, while he would still be at Maggie's. This would complicate his job tremendously. A demon could harness the electrostatic energy in the air and become magnitudes more powerful than usual. He sat for a bit, taking stock of his situation. The DarkWeave suit would protect him from physical harm and, when combined with the contents of the briefcase, would give him a formidable offensive capability.

Standing, he walked over to the briefcase and pressed one of his thumbs against a sensor. The briefcase opened, recognizing both his thumbprint and bio-signs. The interior of the briefcase was empty at the moment, but he would soon be filling it. Paul located the display panel, selected code 45, hit enter and watched as the briefcase generated a dimensional gateway. It appeared as a light blue shimmer, just a couple of feet away, quickly stabilizing to a shimmering dark blue color.

Paul stepped through the gateway and into his sanctuary, which continued to amaze him every time he visited it. The lights turned on as soon as he stepped through, enabling him to see the contents of the room. It was still somewhat utilitarian in layout but, eventually, he would make it more homey and livable. A thought came to him that maybe Pamela could help, which caused him to smile.

Glancing towards one corner, he spotted the QASM unit as it was called. Currently, the display on the front of the unit read ninety-five, indicating ninety-five megawatts of power available for use. A fairly large amount, when compared to what a large city could use. Walking over to one of the closets, he slid open the door on the left. Inside were three more DarkWeave suits.

He slid the door shut and slid the right side open. On this side were a couple of business suits, a couple of short and long sleeved black shirts bearing the company logo, two pairs of black cargo pants, a set of black, zip up, diamene combat boots, dress shoes and some other casual clothing.

Sliding the door closed, he bent down and slid open a drawer below the closet. Inside were a few pairs of socks, underwear and t-shirts.

Closing the drawer, he rose and walked over to the workbench, housing rows of small drawers across the top and larger drawers on both sides, below the carbon fiber and diamene bench top. Opening a larger drawer on the left, he pulled out a pair of black gloves, matching the DarkWeave suit he was wearing. Constructed of the same DarkWeave suit material, they were functionally the same and the cuffs would bond seamlessly with the DarkWeave suit.

Placing the gloves on the bench top, he closed the drawer and opened the one below it. Inside was a black tray, containing 3 identical gold rings. Oblivious as to why he was doing it, since he was already wearing a ring, he selected one, placed it on the bench top next to the gloves and slid the drawer closed.

The ring, as innocuous as it looked, was a critical piece of DarkBridge tech. It functioned to link the DarkWeave suit, on a quantum level, with the QASM unit in the sanctuary. Energy absorbed by the DarkWeave suit could be channeled through the ring to the QASM and energy could be transmitted back via the ring to the DarkWeave suit from the QASM.

Turning, he slid open the top drawer on the right side. This drawer held an extra pair of aviator sunglasses and three pairs of special goggles. The goggles were another amazing piece of DarkBridge tech, allowing the wearer to see a host of things outside the range of human vision. Everything from the infrared spectrum to the electromagnetic spectrum and more, were now visible to human eyes.

Picking up a pair, he placed it on the bench top. Closing the drawer, he opened the next one down. Inside, he found three black boxes. Lifting out a box, he placed it on the bench top and closed the drawer.

Opening the box, he saw four, two inch diameter spheres. These were the GAGE devices, which could open a gateway to a pre-set dimension and also close any gateway or rift between our dimension and another dimension. They were currently set to a special dimension that would theoretically, imprison any demon caught in it for eternity.

Time was his biggest enemy when inside the sanctuary, passing slower here than in his normal dimension outside, so he had to hurry. He looked down at the tech arrayed before him. While advanced and powerful, it still required something from him. Paul would have to supply the things that tech couldn't, such as courage, physical strength, determination and perseverance.

He gathered up the items and stepped back through the gateway. Placing the items in the briefcase, he closed the gateway with code 46. Placing his sunglasses and ID in the briefcase, he closed it, picked it up and turned off the television. He exited the room, pausing to turn off the lights. He took the nearest elevator down to the lobby and headed for the exit.

"That was a great hotel choice, Eva. You're fantastic," said Paul in a low voice.

"Why, thank you, Paul," replied Eva, with a happy tone to her voice.

Exiting the hotel, he walked across the parking lot to where his SUV was parked. Eva, sensing his approach, opened the driver's side door. Paul slipped in, placing the briefcase on the seat next to him. The door closing, he buckled his seatbelt and briefly contemplated his next move.

"Eva, please take me to Maggie's. Try to park out front," Paul commanded.

"Okay, relax and leave the driving to me," replied Eva, in her soft and sultry voice.

"Thank you, Eva," replied Paul, settling in as Eva took remote control of the vehicle.

Smoothly and expertly, Eva drove out of the parking lot and headed towards Maggie's.

Chapter 12

Confrontation

Maggie's restaurant came into view and Paul's thoughts turned to the present. Eva found a parking space out front, smoothly and adeptly parking the sleek, black Millenia SUV.

"You have my compliments, Eva. It was an amazing job of driving," he said in a somewhat awed tone.

"Why, thank you, Paul," replied Eva as she turned off the vehicle lights.

Paul gathered his thoughts, trying not to let a sense of foreboding overwhelm him. There was something about this assignment that wasn't sitting well with him. Even his first assignment with the Miller case didn't approach what he was feeling now. He glanced at the green luminescent dashboard display, which was showing 8:30 pm. Closing time was 10 pm so there was plenty of time for dinner and a chance to see more of Maggie.

"I'm ready, Eva. Lock up and keep watch," he said, grabbing the briefcase on the seat next to him and exiting the vehicle.

"Good luck, Paul. I'll monitor your surroundings and stay in touch," Eva replied, as she closed the SUV door behind him and automatically went into surveillance mode.

"Remember, Paul, as Martin is fond of saying, trust the tech," her soft, sultry voice bringing a smile to Paul's face.

"Thank you, Eva. I may have to stay silent if there are too many people around," he replied, as he looked at his surroundings. The restaurant was lit with the warm, yellow glow of table candles flickering through the windows.

Paul looked up at the dark evening sky. Dim flashes of lightning could already be seen in the distance, a harbinger of the storm to come.

Above him, Gabriel floated, wanting to see firsthand how Paul handled this assignment. Gabriel had become increasingly interested in the one called Paul and had reported on what he had seen to his fellow angels. The technology that had been developed was turning man into a formidable foe to the demons. Some of that technology was, of course, the result of some well placed angelic inspiration.

The people at DarkBridge Technology had also managed to create some of it on their own. Quite an accomplishment, thought Gabriel, as he followed Paul's gaze. The storm was coming. Gabriel could see not just the flashes of lightning in the distance, but the multi-hued ribbons of energy produced by them. He floated down next to Paul, still undetected by him.

Paul walked up to the restaurant door and pulled it open. Gabriel paused before the open door, unseen, managing to glimpse the figure seated at a booth facing Paul. It was Lilith, Queen of Demons, obviously there to gather information about Paul. This was getting very dangerous and he didn't want to be seen by her right now. So, he stayed outside, watching the events transpire from a window. Stepping through the doorway, Paul was hit with that familiar feeling of heavy air and a sense of gloom.

It was always like this, he thought. Whenever a demon took up residence, that feeling followed. He had asked Hiram about it once and had been told that it was a form of psychological warfare by a demon. The doom and gloom feelings were meant to demoralize and depress humans, amplifying any negative thoughts. This would pave the way for more serious things, like possession, to take place.

Gazing around the interior, he noticed that it wasn't all that busy. A couple finishing dinner, a handful of people drinking at the bar and a woman seated alone in a booth facing him. The woman had long, raven colored hair, tanned skin, dark eyes and a body that women would die to have and one that would drive men crazy with lust.

Her eyes captured Paul immediately, as she sat staring at him. Those eyes seemed like deep pools of darkness that held promises of unfettered lust and sexual desire. He felt as if she was reading him like a book, looking at his very soul, all his innermost dreams and desires laid open. Dangerous, he thought. The woman smiled, as if reading his thoughts. He fought back, with all the mental strength he could muster, drawing from an inner reservoir of strength, forcing the intrusion from his mind. He was able to briefly break that hold on his mind, the mental training from Area 52 coming to the rescue.

The nature of the work at Area 52 had required such mental training. As a security guard, he had been privy to many classified top secret programs, which could be revealed simply by reading someone's mind. Paul had thought the whole idea hogwash, but the scientists there had proven otherwise to him. That interruption of the woman's probing had allowed him to reach down and adjust his ring. Turning the top clockwise until he felt it click, the ring drew more power from his QASM device, increasing the EM field of the suit.

The woman's mental intrusion was extremely powerful, beyond that of a normal human being. He felt like she had been toying with him, like a cat getting ready to pounce on its victim. Clearly, she could have pushed through his mental defenses, but had allowed him to push her out. It was, he knew, just a trick to make him feel like he had won. Probably feeling smug with her superiority, she had been smiling at him, but now the smile had turned to a frown and he saw anger in her eyes. Paul smiled back at the woman, which only increased that anger to fury. He felt her try to drive a sledgehammer thrust of mental energy into his mind, but the EM field blunted it to a mere, cool wind blowing across his mind.

Gabriel saw the mental exchange between Lilith and Paul, smiling at how he had thwarted her attack. Her anger made Gabriel smile even more. He noticed her disappear and he quickly floated above the restaurant, wanting to stay undetected by her. He floated there for a moment, until he was sure she had left. Floating back down to the ground, Gabriel passed through the door without opening it.

Moving off to a corner, he watched the interaction between Paul and Maggie, sensing immediately the growing attraction between them. Not good, he thought. At any other time, this would be a beautiful thing but, here and now, it could be very dangerous. If he could see that attraction, then most certainly Lilith could see it.

Maggie would be in danger now, as Lilith would use her as a pawn to get at Paul.

Paul's attention had been so locked upon the woman, that the sudden appearance of Maggie in front of him drew him from the woman's gaze. He quickly regained his composure, once again feeling that instant, inexplicable attraction to Maggie.

"Hello, Maggie. I decided to come early and have dinner," he replied, trying to act somewhat business-like, but finding it a losing battle.

"Hello, Paul. I'm glad that you're here. What were you looking at?" asked Maggie.

"There's a strange woman sitting at the booth over there," he said, pointing at the now empty booth.

"I don't see anyone," she said, looking at where he was pointing.

"That's funny. I could've sworn there was someone sitting there," he said, sounding slightly confused, hoping she didn't think him crazy.

"Well, there's no one there now. Maybe she went to the ladies room," she offered.

"Maybe she did," he replied with some uncertainty.

"Well, let's find you a booth and get some food in you," she replied, smiling warmly.

He followed her to the same empty booth in the back that he had occupied earlier in the day. He took the seat facing towards the front of the restaurant so that he could see if the strange woman left. Sitting down, he placed the briefcase on the seat next to him.

"Don't go anywhere. Here's a menu and I'll be right back with a Sam Adams," said a smiling Maggie.

"Thank you, Maggie. Don't worry, I wouldn't dream of leaving," he said with a smile, very pleased that she had remembered his favorite beer.

She hurried off, Paul watching her shapely figure retreat. He picked up the menu that she had left and started looking at it, but his eyes seemed to get stuck on the words "Prime rib dinner". Sounds delicious, he thought to himself, his stomach rumbling in agreement.

Eva suddenly broke the silence, "Paul, I'm concerned," she said softly in his ear.

"With what part?" he said quietly, so that no one could hear.

"The strange woman you saw. I detected no one where you were looking. The briefcase sensors reported nothing and I even tapped into the security cameras and saw no one," replied Eva, some concern entering her voice.

"Eva, there was someone there and they were trying to invade my thoughts," he replied, trying not to sound overly defensive.

"I believe you, Paul. There are limits to our tech and this wouldn't be the strangest thing to have ever happened. I guess we'll have to find out why and who it was," replied Eva.

"Thank you, Eva. Just one more mystery, I guess," he said quickly, spotting Maggie returning with his beer.

"You're still here," she said, placing the frothy glass in front of him.

She sat down across from him in the booth, her loveliness capturing Paul's gaze.

"Wild horses couldn't drag me away. I'm a man of my word," he replied, taking a sip of what some would call, "nectar of the gods."

"I can see that. Have you had a chance to look at the menu?" she asked, curious as to what he favored.

"It seems I'm outvoted by my eyes and stomach. I'll have the prime rib dinner. Medium rare, baked potato and a side of broccoli," he replied, hoping that he was the only one hearing his rumbling stomach.

"Good choice. Prime rib is one of my favorite dishes," she said with a smile. "I'll go put the order in now." Blue eyes sparkling, she rose from the table and headed for the kitchen.

Paul watched her leave and took a sip of his beer, his eyes darting back towards the front door, hoping to see the strange woman leave. While he was waiting for his meal, he looked at the menu again, reading the various dinner selections and all the while thinking that the DarkBridge facility should have something like this, a nice restaurant. He wondered what Martin would think if he raised the subject. His reverie was soon broken by Maggie, returning with a steaming plate, filled with what he hoped would be a delicious dinner.

"Here you are. A hungry man's dinner," she said with a touch of pride.

Paul looked at the huge plate, his eyes lingering over the juicy steak. Everything certainly looked good, so he picked up the steak knife and sliced into the oozing steak, carving out a small sample to try.

"Mmmm. Delicious, Maggie!" Paul said enthusiastically, as he savored the sample bite.

"I'm glad you like it," she said, eyes sparkling with amusement as she watched him take another bite.

"I have a few things to do, so I'll let you enjoy your dinner," she said, satisfied that the meal was to his liking.

"Thank you, Maggie," was all he could manage to say between mouthfuls.

Maggie smiled, leaving Paul to enjoy his meal. She really did have a few things to do, but would be back when he was done. At the rate he was devouring his dinner, she figured it might be rather soon.

Paul was enjoying his dinner immensely, now convinced more than ever that this is what was needed at DarkBridge Technology. Twenty minutes later, his plate was clean, except for the potato skin and some gristle from the prime rib. It had been a delicious meal and he was happy with his decision to come here early for dinner.

Maggie noticed that Paul had finished his meal. Walking over to the table, she noticed the satisfied look on Paul's face and how much he had eaten.

"It was a delicious meal, Maggie. One of the best I've had in a long time," said Paul

"I'm glad you enjoyed it. Can I get you anything else?" Maggie asked, with a touch of pink showing on her cheeks.

"I'm all set for now, Maggie. Thank you," replied Paul.

"Let me clear this away and I'll be right back," she said, taking his plate back to the kitchen. Once back at the kitchen, Maggie checked the payment system, saw the same information for Paul as earlier, and initiated the meal charge.

Paul's watch beeped, displaying the meal and beer charge. Maggie ran a tight ship, Paul thought to himself, as he authorized the charge.

Maggie returned from the kitchen, smiling, her blue eyes sparkling. She could now spend a few minutes with Paul and learn more about him. She sat down in his booth, directly across from him, basking in his welcoming smile. Needing something to start the conversation, she looked at his left hand and noticed his unusual ring.

"What an interesting ring you're wearing," she said, marveling at its intricate design.

"A company gift and one that I value on a personal level," he replied, hoping she wouldn't press further on the subject.

"I think it's wonderful to see such dedication to a company. So how does this work? What should I do?" she questioned, her changing of the subject, relieving Paul to no end.

"Just go about your normal routine. Close up and keep busy up here, until I come up from the basement. Under no circumstances, should you or anyone else come down into the basement. It's likely to become very dangerous down there," he explained.

"How dangerous?" she asked with some level of concern.

Gazing into her beautiful blue eyes and trying to sound as confident as possible, Paul explained further.

"For me, the danger is minimal but, for you, it would be extremely dangerous and probably life threatening. A demon will fight with all the strength it can muster. I'd feel better personally knowing that you were safe up here," he said with heartfelt sincerity.

"What chivalry! My knight to the rescue!" she replied with a big smile.

"Always willing to rescue a damsel in distress," he said with an equally big smile.

"Well, on that note, I have to get back to work. We'll be closing soon," a sad look coming across her face at having to break the moment they were sharing.

"Yes, it's getting towards that time. I'll let you know when I'm headed downstairs," he replied.

"Okay. I'll be at the bar if you need me," she said, smiling and rising from the booth.

Pausing, she looked at Paul, seeing a glint in his eye and a smile on his face. Her heart fluttered for a bit, realization coming to her of how much she was beginning to like this man. She turned and walked to the bar, thinking along the way that she would probably never see him again after tonight. Keeping busy should keep her mind off thoughts like that, so she dove into work.

Paul watched her leave, promising to himself that he would pursue this potential romance. A flash of lightning caught his eye. The storm was getting closer. Rising from the booth, he picked up his briefcase and went to the men's room. Passing by the ladies room reminded him that the strange woman had vanished and he had never seen her leave. He spent a few minutes in the men's room getting ready for what would come next.

Gabriel had watched Paul sitting with Maggie and became even more convinced of their attraction for one another. He saw Paul leave the men's room and wave to

Maggie, who waved back. Gabriel would give Paul a few minutes in the basement before venturing down there. He really didn't want to be seen, as that might imply overt support, which would only further incite the flames of war between angel and demon.

Paul paused just inside the doorway leading to the basement. There was a small landing before the stairs began. Bending down, he placed his briefcase on it. Opening it, he pulled out his usual items, except for the ring, which he currently wore. Tugging the hood of his DarkWeave suit over his head, he put on the goggles, leaving them resting on his on his forehead.

He then placed the 4 GAGE devices in the front pockets of his pants. Pulling on the gloves, he was about to close the briefcase when he saw the extra ring. He picked it up and placed it in one of his other pockets. Closing the briefcase, he rose to his feet, with the briefcase in hand. Lowering the goggles, he steeled himself for the confrontation to come.

"Paul, the briefcase sensors are detecting a massive EM buildup in the basement," said Eva.

"Thank you, Eva. It looks like the storm is going to complicate things," he replied, a frown forming on his forehead.

"Remember, Paul, trust the tech," Eva said softly in his ear.

As he began descending the stairs, a loud rumble could be heard, the sonic vibrations slightly shaking the building. The storm was here.

Chapter 13

The Storm

Lilith had sat in the booth facing the door, like she had been doing for the past couple of weeks. She was, of course, unseen to the human eye, preferring to stay that way until her target arrived. Her patience was finally rewarded when a man entered carrying a briefcase. She felt certain that this was her target. Asmodeus had been right. Someone would be coming to deal with the demon, Vagoth, in the basement below.

How Asmodeus knew this, she wasn't sure, but he had made it explicitly clear not to kill whoever it was. It was information he was after and he needed to know just how dangerous their potential adversaries were. Lilith didn't see how these weak, pathetic creatures could ever be called adversaries. Since they were created, man was always fodder to the demons. They were insignificant beasts, their weak minds, easily manipulated by demons.

Both her eyes and the man's eyes had locked immediately. Lilith had made herself seen to only the man. The man, captured by her exotic beauty, had failed to sense the extremely powerful mind behind those dark eyes. Lilith took advantage and probed his mind. His name was Paul Cross, Navajo Indian by birth and he worked for some company called DarkBridge Technology. Lilith was about to get more, but his mind fought back, closing the door that she had opened.

Then, he had done something strange by reaching to the hand carrying the briefcase and touching his ring. Immediately, she had driven her mind like a spear towards his mind. She had smiled as her mind struck, but soon the smile turned to shock, confusion and then anger. Her mental spear had struck a wall of power, turning that spear into a fuzzy remnant of its original power. The resulting mental energy after hitting the wall amounted to nothing more than a gentle breeze. Lilith could no longer detect the man's thoughts. He had become unreadable to her. Impossible! Lilith was infuriated and close to incinerating the man, which she could easily do without much thought.

Asmodeus would be equally infuriated with her and she knew well how dangerous it was to displease him. So, she held her anger in check, long enough to see a woman walk over to the man. Lilith quickly probed the woman's mind, managing to get Maggie as her name, but not much more. As the woman, Maggie, drew closer to the man named Paul, the mental wall began to encompass Maggie as well, making her mind closed to Lilith as well. All was not lost.

Lilith had managed to glean an important fact about Maggie and Paul.

They were, in fact, very attracted to one another, something that could be very useful someday. The only problem was that Asmodeus had forbidden her from harming this woman in any way. Regardless of what she might want to do to Maggie, Lilith was bound to obey the wishes of Asmodeus. It seemed that nothing more was going to be learned tonight, so Lilith disappeared just as Paul's attention was captured by Maggie.

Lilith reappeared outside the restaurant, seeing the gathering storm above. Vagoth should be fine, she thought. All this energy from the growing thunderstorm would make him invincible to anything this world could put forth. Lilith was growing tired of the skullduggery and wanted to take advantage of her time here. Her appetite for lust and sex overcame all other thoughts. With a spring in her step, she headed for the nearest nightclub to satisfy those desires.

Vagoth had fled to the basement earlier that day to build up his energy. Touching the man's shoulder and feeling the intense cold had unsettled him. More unnerving, though, was the draining of his energy. So he waited, rebuilding his energy, drawing from different sources. He sensed a presence later in the evening of a powerful demon upstairs. Vagoth had felt that presence before and knew it to be Lilith.

Why she was here, he didn't know. His orders from Asmodeus were to engage whatever human threat approached him and destroy that threat. So far none of the humans that came downstairs had proven to be any threat at all. With Lilith upstairs, he decided to stay out of whatever she was doing. He had felt her wrath long ago and ever since, had vowed never to cross paths with her again. Soon, he felt another presence enter the restaurant.

The newcomer was familiar to Vagoth. He was the man who had come in earlier. Vagoth sensed Lilith begin probing the man's mind. Soon after, he sensed an energy buildup in the man and Lilith's probing severely weaken. Lilith would be infuriated with the failed attempt and soon he felt her presence suddenly disappear. Feeling relieved with Lilith's abrupt exit, Vagoth knew the man would be coming downstairs soon. Sensing the building storm outside, he began tapping into that vast energy, drawing it deeply into his being.

The power flowing into him made him feel invincible and indestructible. He should have no problem destroying the threat that he sensed coming down the stairs. It was the man from upstairs. Vagoth thought about what he would do. Maybe he would pull the man's fingers off one by one, maybe tear an arm off and then a leg. Many grisly ideas came into his mind, all of them making him extremely happy. No mercy, Vagoth thought, forming a huge, black tentacle that whipped out, grabbing Paul's ankle, dragging him down the stairs.

"You're a weak and puny human! There's nothing you can do! Prepare to die!" the entity shouted in Paul's mind.

Paul, wearing the special goggles, saw the massive tentacle whip out and grab his ankles, jerking him off his feet, dragging him down the stairs. He lost his grip on the briefcase, hearing it tumble down the stairs as he did the same, his head bouncing off each step until he landed hard on the concrete floor below. Fortunately, the suit and hood absorbed the brunt of the impact, his physical conditioning helping to mitigate the rest.

A brief cry of pain came across Paul's mind, as the massive tentacle wrapped around his ankle began to shrink. The DarkWeave suit drew the energy from the tentacle causing it to shrink to a mere wisp of smoky, black energy. Now freed from the tentacle, Paul was finally able to take stock of his surroundings amidst the rumbles of thunder outside.

"Are you okay?" asked a concerned Eva.

"I think so. A few bumps and maybe a slight headache. Other than that, I'm okay," replied Paul.

"I'm glad you're okay. The EM signature from the demon is growing rapidly from the storm and you might actually be the first to encounter a demon of such power," Eva replied, somewhat nonchalantly.

"Thank you for that, Eva. Glad to know that this might be a first," Paul said with a touch of sarcasm.

Paul could see the demon with his goggles and also noticed that the basement lights seemed to be off. The demon appeared as a massive dark mass to his goggles and seemed to be growing with energy from the storm outside.

Vagoth had felt the pain of intense coldness from the tentacle as it closed around the man's ankle and the energy drain from it. His mind registering mild disbelief as it was rendered into a mere wisp of energy. He had felt great satisfaction at catching the man unawares and had laughed at the man's body bouncing down the stairs, like a child's bouncing ball. Undeterred, Vagoth took the initiative again, forming an even thicker black, tentacle and hurled it towards the man, while continuing to draw massive amounts of power from the storm raging above.

Paul had no sooner responded to Eva, when a thicker, black tentacle wrapped around his waist, picked him up and flung him across the basement into a cement wall. Another louder scream had struck Paul's mind when the tentacle closed around his waist. He hit the wall with a heavy thud and fell into a stack of boxes below. The tentacle around his waist shrinking to a mere wisp of smoky black energy.

The DarkWeave suit had once again absorbed most of the impact, but it was still a hard hit. Paul rolled over with a groan, facing away from the demon. It was time to go on the offensive, he thought to himself. Pulling the extra ring out of his pocket, he drew off his left glove and placed the ring on his finger. He quickly put the glove back on and steeled himself for his next move. Armed with two rings now, he should be able to draw a massive amount of energy from the demon. He only hoped that his QASM device would be able to store the immense power he would be sending to it.

Vagoth screamed from the intense cold, as the tentacle around the man's waist was reduced to a mere wisp of energy. Never had he encountered a human with this type of power, except for King Solomon, so many thousands of years ago. Vagoth still thought he had the upper hand, but would need more energy to defeat the human. The storm was directly overhead now and would pass soon, so he continued drawing as much energy as he could from it. While building more power, he decided to demoralize the human.

"Give up, human! You cannot possibly win against me! I am invincible tonight!" the demon yelled into Paul's mind.

"Not a chance!" Paul yelled, hoping the demon could hear him. Standing up, Paul charged across the basement floor, catching the demon by surprise. Paul reached the demon and flung his body into the massive entity before him.

Vagoth had noticed the man stand up, but what really shocked him was the image of the man running towards him. Never had he seen or heard of such a thing. Humans were such cowering creatures that it didn't register with him until it was too late. The man struck Vagoth, passing deep inside his massive, hulking blackness. He let out a scream, like no other demon had ever let out before. The intensity of the cold had briefly stunned him senseless and the man's plunge into his core being had cut off the energy flow from the storm. He struggled mightily with the human, but the greater he struggled, the faster his energy ebbed.

Paul knew he was taking a big chance by plunging into the demon, but it really was his only option. Blackness swirled around him, tentacles formed with razor-like talons, trying mightily to tear him to shreds. None could find purchase on him and every attempt turned into an insignificant wisp of energy. Paul lifted his arms up, the two rings acting as dual conduits, channeling the energy into his QASM device.

Both rings were beginning to warm from the vast energies being conducted through them. Paul hoped the rings wouldn't burn through his fingers. Certainly, if he had used only one ring he would be missing a finger by now. He wasn't sure why he had decided to use two rings. It wasn't something that had been part of his training but, for some reason, the thought had been in his mind to bring the extra ring.

Vagoth knew he was losing. His screams of pain became less and less forceful. His attempts to render the man into a bloody, shredded mess, proved fruitless. No matter what he tried, the man just kept drawing his energy away. Weaker and weaker he became. Soon, very soon he would be but a small, infinitesimal orb of energy. He grew angry, not so much at the man, but at Asmodeus for putting him in this position. He also felt anger towards Lilith, who could've helped him defeat the man, but instead left him to his fate.

Paul was getting worried. The rings were becoming very warm, almost uncomfortable, but he was so close to winning this battle. Holding his ground, he continued pulling energy from the demon until that energy flow began to weaken. The demon was still about the size of an average man, but growing smaller and smaller with each passing minute. Paul stoically maintained his position inside the demon. His arms growing tired, he put them down at his side. The demon was now just the size of a small cat, curled around his feet. Paul reached into the small mass with both hands and received a final, anguished howl of pain from the demon.

Final dregs of energy flowed from the demon, leaving it the size of a quarter. Paul grasped it with one hand, closing his fingers around it, drawing the last meaningful vestiges of energy from the demon. What was left would take a thousand or so years to regain any useful energy. Paul reached into his pants pocket and pulled out a single GAGE device.

He turned the device on and watched it levitate and begin to hum. A couple of seconds later, a small, blue shimmering disc formed about two feet above the GAGE device. It expanded to about a foot in diameter and Paul waited for it to stabilize. He placed his gloved hand, still holding the now tiny demon orb, close to the now dark blue gateway. Opening his hand, he watched with goggle vision, as the tiny red orb drifted down and into the gateway.

Paul turned the device off, the gateway disappeared and the GAGE device settled back to the cement floor. He placed the GAGE device back in his pocket and stood up. Glancing around the room with goggle vision, he briefly glimpsed what he thought was a glowing, golden figure of a man, dressed in biblical attire, standing at the foot of the stairs. Paul looked away and quickly looked back, but the figure was gone. This wasn't the first time something strange like this had happened. He was beginning to suspect that someone was watching him. Just one more mystery added to a pile that seemed to be growing larger.

He took a much slower look around the room, but couldn't find any sign of a gateway or rift that the demon used to get here. Really, there were only two possibilities here, either the demon created his own gateway or someone created one for it. Paul leaned towards the latter because, while the demon seemed extremely powerful and capable of creating a gateway, most of that energy had come from the storm and, without that, it didn't seem capable of creating one.

Lifting his goggles, he noticed that the lights had come back on. Either they had been knocked out by the storm or the demon had disabled them, possibly to disorient Paul. He had a more pressing problem now. Looking down at his clothing, he was shocked to see how badly it had fared. His shirt and pants were shredded and in tatters, not having survived the demon onslaught like the DarkWeave suit had. He would make it a point to ask Dr. Morse about a more resilient line of clothing for Field Investigators.

"Congratulations on successfully removing the demon." Eva said in his ear.

"Thank you, Eva. This was my most physical confrontation so far. My clothing seems to have taken quite a beating," replied Paul.

"There should be some spare shirts and pants in your sanctuary," offered Eva.

"I was hoping you would say that. I'm going in there right now to change," he replied.

Walking over to where his briefcase sat, he removed his gloves, placed his thumb on one of the sensors and opened the briefcase. He removed the goggles and extra ring, placing them, the gloves and all the GAGE devices back into their individual briefcase pockets. Selecting code 45 on the hidden keypad, he opened the gateway to his sanctuary, waited for it to stabilize and stepped through.

He walked over to the wardrobe closet and pulled out a similar shirt and pants. He took off his tattered clothing, replaced it with the fresh clothes and threw the tattered clothing into a special disposal unit. Glancing over to the corner where the QASM device sat, he noticed the display was reading an unbelievable amount of energy stored.

"Eva, the QASM device is displaying an incredible amount of stored energy. Is it correct?" asked Paul.

"Yes. It's correct. The demon was drawing heavily from the storm outside until you were able to disrupt that flow. The average thunderstorm generates a massive amount of energy," replied Eva, using the available hidden speakers in the sanctuary.

"Thank you, Eva. I knew you would have the answer," said a smiling Paul.

"You're very welcome, Paul. I'm glad you're okay," she replied in that warm, sultry voice.

"The suit did an excellent job of protecting me, but I still got banged up a bit and feel a major headache developing," he replied.

"You should try and get back to the hotel as soon as possible," Eva replied with concern.

"Sounds like a good idea," he said, preparing to leave the sanctuary.

"Paul, someone is coming down the stairs," she said, alarm sneaking into her voice.

Paul immediately stepped through the gateway, back into the basement. Eva, sensing an emergency situation, quickly closed the gateway and he closed the briefcase. Picking up the briefcase, he stood, braced for action, as footsteps sounded on the stairs.

Chapter 14

Assassin

Maggie had seen Paul wave to her as he went into the basement and she had waved back. It was closing time and all her customers had left. It was beginning to rain outside, lightning and thunder followed soon after. She let her few remaining employees go home, including Carol, who had been tending the bar. Maggie, all alone upstairs, kept herself busy cleaning, putting things away and bookkeeping, while Paul was downstairs.

She had thought about going downstairs to see if he was okay, but decided to adhere to his directions and stay upstairs. The storm grew worse outside, lightning flashes lighting up the windows and powerful thunder claps shaking the building. To top it all off, the lights suddenly went out, spooking Maggie.

It was total blackness in the restaurant, lit only by the brief flashes of lightning and the flickering candles on the tables near the windows. The darkness was only temporary, though, as the emergency lights eventually came on, offering some light to push back the shadows. She tried keeping her mind on work, but it was a losing battle because she couldn't stop wondering what was going on downstairs. Maggie noted that the storm seemed to be lessening in intensity as it moved away and, within minutes, the regular business lights came back on. She gave up any pretense of work and walked over to the basement, pausing at the doorway to listen before she descended the stairs.

Paul waited patiently, his body tensed and ready to spring into action. He soon relaxed when he saw that it was Maggie.

"Hi, Maggie. I think you're all set down here," he said, noticing that the air felt fairly normal, no longer heavy and foreboding.

"Hello, Paul. I was getting worried and came down to check on you. I hope you're not upset," she said, feeling relieved that he seemed okay.

"No. I'm not mad at you. In fact, you've come downstairs at a good time. I can safely say that your demon is gone and will probably never return," he said with confidence.

"Are you sure? It would be wonderful to have things back to normal," she said hopefully.

"Yes. You have my word," he said with a smile.

"It does feel different down here. Brighter and less gloomy," she replied.

"It's good that you can feel the difference. I think your employees will feel much better about coming down here, especially Carol," he said.

"I already feel better. Can I offer you a beer?" she said, enticing him to stay longer.

"Well, my job is done here, so why not," he said smiling.

He followed Maggie upstairs to the same booth they had occupied earlier. Along the way, he marveled at just how beautiful she was. He noticed that the lights had been turned down, probably so as to not attract customers to the closed restaurant, he thought to himself.

"Wait here," she said as he sat down, placing his briefcase on the seat next to him.

Paul waited and was rewarded with the sight of Maggie carrying two bottles of Sam Adams to the table. A perfect sight, great beer delivered by a beautiful woman.

"Here you go," she said, handing him one of the beers as she sat across from him.

"Cheers!" he said, their bottles clinking together.

Paul took a sip of the beer and looked into the eyes of the woman across from him. Easy to get lost in those eyes, he thought to himself.

Maggie looked across the table at the man sitting there and took a sip of beer. He was very handsome and intelligent, with a touch of ruggedness to go with it. She could easily fall for this man and had a suspicion that she already had.

"I'm curious, Maggie, what's your story? I mean why the restaurant business?" inquired Paul.

"I'm a widow, Paul. My husband died a few years ago. I've been a waitress for most of my life and I felt that it was time to do something on my own. When the opportunity to purchase this place came up, I jumped at the chance," said Maggie, deciding to be as open about things as possible.

"I'm sorry to hear about your husband, Maggie. I admire people who take on life's challenges and make something of themselves," he replied. Thinking it a touchy subject, he decided not to push any further about her husband's death.

"Thank you, Paul. You're quite a guy you know," Maggie said with great emotion, a tear running down her cheek. The tear seemed to encapsulate her loss and the difficult times she had been through.

Paul reached across the table and brushed the tear away. Maggie caught his hand and held it against her face, its warmth and strength comforting her. She felt what could only be described as a warm current of electricity passing through her body. She felt more connected to this man she barely knew, than anyone else since her husband, Brian. She reluctantly let his hand go, trying to avoid an awkward moment.

He had felt her emotion deeply, the connection growing stronger between them, but he had felt something else when he touched her face. A small charge of electricity had passed from his hand to her face. It was probably just some residual energy from the suit. He had turned off the power flow to the suit, so it couldn't be anything else. Or could it? He wondered. The thought was quickly derailed, by an even more important question for him. He couldn't wait any longer and needed to know the answer.

"Maggie, I have to ask this because if I don't, the uncertainty will eat me alive. Are you dating anyone?" Paul asked rather sheepishly.

"No. Not for some time. I haven't been able to find anyone who I truly feel a connection with," she said with a smile, gazing into his eyes.

Paul let out a deep breath, one that he didn't realize he was holding.

"Fair is fair. Like you, I haven't been able to find the right connection, either so I remain single," he said with complete honesty.

"Well, looks like we've cleared the air on that subject!" laughed Maggie.

"Yes, I think we have," Paul replied, laughingly.

They chatted for a while longer, but soon it was time to leave. Rising from their seats, Paul picked up his briefcase and they took their empty bottles to the bar.

"If you don't mind, Maggie, I'll stay with you until you lock up," he said with some gallantry.

"I would love the company," replied a coy Maggie, as she began shutting things down, extinguishing the candles and arming the alarm system.

They walked over to the door and Paul stepped outside. Maggie stepped out after him, closed the door, took out her keys and locked the door.

She turned, faced him and looked into his eyes longingly, expectantly.

Paul reached out with his free hand, pulled her towards him and kissed her deeply. Maggie, with equal fervor, returned the kiss with pent up longing for such a man like him. The connection between them was there. She felt it and knew he felt it, too.

He couldn't remember a kiss like that, no matter how hard he tried. Something meaningful had passed between them and he wanted this to last and not devolve into a one night stand. Reluctantly, he pulled away from the kiss, and caught his breath. The smoldering ember had turned into a raging forest fire.

Maggie felt his lips pull away, but still clung to him, her head resting against his shoulder.

"Maggie, I want to see you again. There is a connection between us that we can't ignore and needs to be explored," he said, as he continued holding her in his arms.

"I feel the same way, Paul. I wasn't sure if I would see you again after tonight," she said, fighting back tears.

"You will see me again. You can count on it," promised Paul. "Now, let me walk you to your car."

"I'd like that very much," replied Maggie, stepping back slightly.

Paul put his arm around her and she put hers around him as they walked to her car, which was parked on the street not far from the restaurant. When they got to her car, Maggie reached for her keys in the small purse she carried and unlocked the door. She turned around and, acting on impulse, pulled Paul towards her, her lips pressed against his for one last kiss. Paul responded with equal fervor, the both of them holding that perfect kiss, until Maggie pulled away.

"Good night, Paul. Thank you for everything you've done for me and the restaurant," Maggie said, forcing a smile to hide her sadness at parting.

"Good night, Maggie. Thank you, too. I never dreamed that something as wonderful as this would happen to me today," he said with genuine sincerity.

Maggie kissed him on the cheek and got into her car. Paul held the door open until she was inside then closed it. She started the car and rolled down the window.

"You better call, or I'll be very angry at you," she said with a smile.

"Now, I'll definitely have to call. I couldn't stand the thought of you being angry," he said returning her smile.

Maggie waved and drove off. Paul headed back to his waiting SUV, carrying the briefcase in his right hand. Eva had already started the vehicle and he could see some lights on inside.

"That was unexpected. I'm still trying to understand human emotions, but it seems clear, even to me, that you and Maggie are attracted to one another," Eva said with her usual soft, sultry voice in his ear.

"Thank you for staying quiet, Eva, while I was with Maggie. Yes, there is something between us. We both felt it," he replied.

"You're welcome. I didn't think it would be appropriate for me to be talking in your ear every two minutes," she replied.

"I agree. You're the best, Eva," Paul said smiling.

"Why, thank you, Paul. That's the nicest thing anyone has said to me today," replied Eva, in a decidedly happy tone.

Maggie had left Paul with deep sadness in her heart. She just couldn't understand how it was possible to feel this way about someone she had just met today. It was scary, almost like they had known one another before, maybe in some past life. It was crazy talk, just plain crazy. She would give herself a couple of days to see how she felt. Assuming of course, he didn't call before then, in which case she would probably completely surrender to him. She smiled and continued driving back to her apartment, which wasn't too far away.

Gabriel had watched the entire exchange between Paul and Maggie. He was glad that Maggie hadn't gone into the basement sooner, either seeing the battle or catching Paul in his sanctuary. Both cases would have been difficult for Paul to explain. The interaction between the two of them had continued to hold his interest. There really was something special between them, almost like they had reconnected after having been apart for a very long, long time.

Gabriel was beginning to suspect that his interest in Paul wasn't just his idea, but part of some larger plan. He knew that even he, as powerful as he was, still answered to a higher authority. An authority, whose plans were often shrouded in mystery and rarely revealed until completed. Gabriel had no idea that a small part of those plans was about to be partly revealed to him, as he watched Paul turn around.

Paul reached the SUV, paused and turned around, hoping to catch a glimpse of Maggie's car but she was gone. The bullet struck him in the left shoulder, pushing him back against the SUV. The DarkWeave suit absorbed some of the impact, but there was something wrong. Paul felt a sharp pain at the impact site. His left hand still clutching the briefcase, he put his right hand up to his shoulder.

Feeling a warm, wetness, his hand came away with blood on it, the pain growing more intense by the second. He wasn't sure how bad the injury was, but he was in trouble and he knew it. Eva had detected that something was amiss and opened the rear passenger side door. Paul, putting his hand back over the wound, jumped in and threw his briefcase onto the opposite seat.

"Eva, I've been shot!" exclaimed Paul through clenched teeth.

"How badly are you hurt?" asked Eva, extremely concerned.

"I'm not sure, Eva, but I think I need medical attention," Paul replied, his hand and shirt now covered in blood. His shoulder was hurting pretty bad and he knew things were going to get worse. "Trust the tech," he had been told many times, but it had failed him in this case.

Eva took control of the SUV and sped out of the target area. When the bullet had struck Paul, she had computed the trajectory back to the point of origin, but the trajectory didn't line up with the impact. Re-calculating the trajectory with AI speed and nanoseconds later, Eva initiated a drone response. The drone didn't immediately respond, having shut down some of its circuits after landing on a nearby building to wait out the storm.

The drone reinitialized those circuits within nanoseconds and quickly took to the air, arming both lasers. Flying to the point of origin, the drone's heat sensors locked onto the target and both lasers fired. The drone remained stationary until the target heat source began to cool. Flying closer to the target, the drone turned on its exterior lights and, using visual imaging, verified a successful kill. Eva, then sent the drone back to its resting place, atop a nearby building.

Gabriel had watched the emotional scene between Paul and Maggie outside the restaurant, but wasn't quite sure what to make of it. It was beautiful to see such intense feeling and emotion between them, but dangerous for both of them, mainly for Paul because it placed him in a vulnerable position, professionally and emotionally. He watched as Paul walked Maggie to her car, said goodbye and walked back to his car.

As soon as Paul turned around, Gabriel sensed immediate danger. Concentrating, he slowed local time down to a crawl, looking for the danger. He saw the bullet coming towards Paul and flew towards it. Reaching the bullet, he examined it while it was moving extremely slow and noticed that it was of similar outer construction as the DarkWeave suit. It had a diamene coating, thicker than the DarkWeave suit.

He didn't have much time to decide what to do. He was forbidden from overtly interfering with what was happening. He could certainly just pluck the bullet out of the air, but that would amount to overt action. Forced to take another course, he quickly decided to alter the trajectory of the bullet, just slightly, from its obvious impact at the center of Paul's forehead.

He nudged the bullet down and over to the right, which should impact his left shoulder. This would make it a painful, but survivable injury, rather than a definite death. Gabriel released his hold on local time, watching confidently, as the bullet struck Paul in the left shoulder. Gabriel watched, as a hurt and bleeding Paul, jumped into the vehicle, which sped away, but stopped only a mile away.

Gabriel then saw a blue glow inside the car and knew that a gateway had been opened to some desperately needed medical attention. That's good. Paul should make it, he thought to himself. In saving Paul from a certain death, Gabriel had begun to suspect his reason for being here was more than just to observe.

Victor Yelenkov was crouched behind an advanced, American made sniper rifle, waiting for his target to get into position. It was dark, close to midnight, and eerily silent now that the storm had passed. Located in an unoccupied office on the ninth floor and using the sniper scope on the rifle, he had a perfect view of the entire scene below. Once in a while, he would hear a noise in the building, but disregarded it. "Probably just rats or mice," he said quietly to himself. There wasn't much to do while waiting, except to reflect on the choices he had made in life, which had placed him in his current position.

His father had risen to the rank of colonel in the Spetsnaz before retiring. Victor had followed in his father's footsteps by becoming a major in the Spetsnaz. He soon found out that he could make more money as a paid mercenary and assassin than working for mother Russia. His father had been greatly displeased and could only talk about bringing dishonor to the family. Victor said his goodbyes and went on to seek fame and fortune. He became very successful at his new trade, with multiple kills and a no nonsense attitude.

Known by the code name "Red Winter", his fame had come to the attention of a very powerful man, who sent a trusted aide to negotiate the financial and target details. It was a jaw dropping sum, ten million American dollars, twenty percent upfront and the remainder paid upon completion of the job. Victor didn't care much for the aide, a German with a superior attitude. Later, he had found out that the aide's grandfather had been a Nazi SS officer at a concentration camp in Poland. That only reinforced Victor's first impression, but the money was irresistible and he agreed to the job.

It was a straightforward job. Kill the person who walked out of the restaurant with the woman owner. The target could be a man or woman, might be carrying a briefcase and would be the only person with the owner. The aide had made it abundantly clear to Victor that under no circumstances was the woman to be harmed. He had given a picture of the woman to him, so he could be sure who was who. If the woman owner was hurt physically in any way, Victor would die.

He believed the aide could make it happen. Instructions given by powerful men were meant to be followed. Doing otherwise, would invite certain death. So Victor had researched the area, determining which vantage point would give him the best kill zone. The aide had supplied him with the sniper rifle and had also given him 5 specially constructed bullets.

Victor examined the bullets, finding them to be harder than any bullet he had seen in his career. He pulled out his knife, which was hardened titanium and taking one of the bullets, drew the tip across the knife. The bullet tip dug deeply into the knife almost cutting through to the other side. Victor examined the bullet tip, which was undamaged. A bullet like this would probably pass through any armor known to man.

Victor loaded the bullets into the rifle and waited for his target to appear. It was close to midnight, when he spotted the door open and a man step out carrying a briefcase. A woman stepped out right behind him and Victor viewed her face with his binoculars. The woman was the one in the photo, definitely off limits. He would have to wait until there was separation between them, maybe until she left entirely.

He watched them kiss and then walk to her car, kissing once more. The woman drove off and the man headed towards a parked SUV. Victor got ready, aiming his sights on the man's head. These bullets would pass cleanly through the man's skull, maybe too cleanly. Was it possible for a bullet to pass through someone's head, exit cleanly and still leave the person alive? Definitely a lobotomy, but the person might still live.

He would need at least two shots, maybe three. Head first, heart and then throat. He watched the man intently, gambling that the man would turn around and look towards the woman's departing car. The man turned! Victor pulled the trigger, a slight jerk of the rifle and a puff of air was all he heard and felt.

The bullet left the rifle perfectly. Victor was elated. The bullet would impact at the center of the target's forehead and soon after, he would fire bullets two and three. Victor's elation was cut short, the sniper scope showing an impact on the man's left shoulder instead of his forehead. He was dumbfounded. The bullet had changed trajectory.

Victor was trying to process what had happened, when twin lasers struck his body. The first, burning a hole cleanly through his head and the next, burning a hole cleanly through his Spetsnaz issued body armor and straight through to his heart. His body slumped to the floor, draped across the sniper rifle, two smoking holes rising from his dead body.

Chapter 15

Emergency

Asmodeus opened a gateway into the basement of Maggie's restaurant and surveyed the scene. He was dressed in a white business suit and had the appearance of a normal, middle aged man. Vagoth was gone, some residual energy still remained, but it was clear that he had lost the battle against whatever he had fought. Nothing to be gained here, he stepped back through the gateway, closed it and opened another outside the restaurant.

He didn't see a body lying on the ground, but he did sense something on the sidewalk close to the street. He walked over to what he was sensing and saw a drop of blood. He reached down, placing his index finger into it, immediately he sensed an energy pattern he hadn't felt for thousands of years. Impossible! Asmodeus cried out. How could this be? The energy pattern was that of King Solomon, who had died thousands of years ago and was but dust and almost forgotten memory. The same King Solomon who had bound him and his fellow demons to his will, forcing them to build his cursed temple.

Asmodeus stood up. Worried, he looked around, spotting a familiar figure floating in the air above. Gabriel. Now he was beginning to understand what had happened. One more stop to make. He opened a gateway to the room Stanton's hired assassin was in and stepped through, exiting out the other side into another failure.

The assassin was dead, two clean holes burned through his body with primitive lasers. He rolled the body off the rifle and picked it up. He ejected a bullet and examined it. Changing his finger to a sharp talon, he scratched the tip of the bullet, or at least tried to. No matter how hard he tried, the surface would not scratch. Advanced diamene coating, intended to pierce something equally tough and strong. It was worse than he could have imagined. Archangel help, diamene armor, massive energy manipulation, possible gateway technology, Solomon back from the dead, and who knew what else these humans had developed.

It triggered an ancient memory of an age long past. It was a time when angels and demons were brothers, walking the earth together. It was a time before man and a time when they had used much of the same technology. The implications were too much even for Asmodeus to process right now. He opened a gateway back to Hell, picked up the dead assassin and effortlessly tossed the body through it. He then picked up the rifle and other items the assassin was using and threw them into the gateway as well.

Asmodeus took a last look around, turned and paused at the gateway. He would personally have to get involved now. It was clear that Stanton had met his match and it might only get worse. Hopefully, Lilith was able to find out something useful. He was slightly perturbed that he hadn't seen her around, watching the area. Sighing heavily, Asmodeus stepped through the gateway to regroup and plan, the gateway closing behind him.

Gabriel had seen Asmodeus appear outside the restaurant, walk over to the street and touch the drop of Paul's blood on the sidewalk. Asmodeus had clearly been shocked and worried by what he found. Now curious, he floated down to the spot on the sidewalk and touched the drop of blood. Oh, my, he thought to himself, almost as shocked as Asmodeus.

He now knew why Asmodeus was worried. Gabriel sensed that the beginnings of some grand plan were starting to take place. It was worrisome that such a plan would be happening without the knowledge of angels. More troubling was the thought that it might be a far superior intelligence responsible for these events. Like Asmodeus, Gabriel was getting worried, too.

Karl had watched the debacle from his car a couple of blocks away. His position and night vision binoculars gave him a great vantage point to view Victor's target. His informant, Olivia, had contacted him earlier in the day with some information. She was the bartender at the restaurant and had seen a man come in to take care of the strange things happening there. Maggie had told Olivia that the restaurant would be closing at 10 o'clock that night and that the man would be coming back then to do what was needed. Karl had acted quickly to get Victor in place.

Watching, he saw the man kiss the woman a couple of times. Dead man, he thought. If the man wasn't already going to die, then

Stanton would certainly kill him. Stanton didn't want any man around her that wasn't wealthy and either had influence or real power. Karl watched the man return to his car and Maggie drive off. Good. At least she wouldn't be in any danger. Victor had at least obeyed his instructions. Stanton would be furious if she were killed or injured, Karl would be dead and Victor would wish he had never been born.

Karl watched as the man paused at the SUV and turned around. A perfect shot! There was no way Victor could miss. Yet, he watched with disbelief as the bullet struck the man, hitting his left shoulder. The man lived! He saw the man jump into the SUV and drive away. Then he saw the flash of twin lasers strike the window where he assumed Victor was located. A drone was hovering there, without firing.

Victor was no doubt dead. Otherwise, the drone would have kept firing. Karl was dumbfounded and worried. The idiot! It was his job to give Stanton the bad news, so he drove away. He would have the body disposed of once the area quieted down and the drone left. He took his time getting back to Stanton's office, thinking about any loose ends that might have to be tied up.

Eva, in control of the SUV, sped from the immediate area and pulled over a mile away. She contacted the hospital at DarkBridge Technology and had a surgical team waiting for Paul's arrival by gateway.

"Paul, can you open the briefcase?" Eva asked, aware that time was of the essence.

"No. My left hand is numb and my right is clutching the wound. I'm not sure how long before I pass out," Paul replied, getting weaker by the minute.

"Okay, I'll take over from here. Try to hang on a bit longer, Paul," she said with some concern.

"Thank you, Eva," he said, grimacing with pain.

Eva, using her emergency access protocol, opened the briefcase remotely and took control of its functions. Modifying the coordinates, Eva generated a gateway, having it form on the floor of the SUV next to Paul, who, on the verge of passing out, watched and waited for it to stabilize.

"Paul, I need you to fall through the gateway. Don't worry. Things are all set on the other side. Stay with us, Paul," Eva said with uncharacteristic emotion for an AI.

"Thank you, Eva," was all Paul could let out as he tumbled through the gateway.

He landed on a surgical bed on the other side of the gateway, in some hospital, a surgeon and nurses swarming around him. Eva is so good, he thought to himself. The other thought before he passed out, was that Maggie was going to be very mad at him.

Martin was asleep when he heard the chiming, signaling something important had occurred. He rolled out of bed, shaking off the sleepiness.

"Eva, what's happened?" he asked.

"I have bad news, Martin. Paul has been shot and seriously wounded. He's at the company hospital and Dr. Curtis is working on him. He's lost a lot of blood," replied Eva.

"Thank you, Eva. I'll be right there," he said, rising and getting dressed.

Martin left his apartment, located in the residential area of the underground facility and quickly made his way to the hospital. He reached the hospital, showed his badge to the security guard and went up to the surgical observation room. Looking down, he could see Dr. Curtis and nurses clustered around Paul. His clothes had been cut and stripped off his body, while the DarkWeave suit Paul had been wearing was draped over a nearby table.

Martin got a glimpse of the still hemorrhaging wound. Dr. Curtis was extracting what appeared to be a bullet from it. IV drip lines trailed from various locations on his body and monitors had been hooked up to track his vital signs.

Martin sat down stunned that something like this had happened to Paul. The suit should have protected him from this sort of injury. He would have the suit sent to Dr. Morse for examination.

"Eva, tell me what happened," he ordered.

"Paul was successful with removing the demon. You should be proud of him, Martin. He was outstanding and even had the foresight to use two rings. The demon had absorbed a tremendous amount of energy from a passing thunderstorm and was an extremely formidable opponent. After the demon was vanquished, he spent some time upstairs talking to the female owner, Maggie. Martin, you should know that Paul and Maggie seem to have some deep emotional connection with one another," said Eva.

"What sort of connection? Please explain, Eva," asked a puzzled Martin.

"I am familiar with the term 'love at first sight', but this was beyond that. From what I could gather from the security cameras and briefcase sensors, it seemed like they had known each other before, a long time ago and had reunited. I'm still not one hundred percent on understanding human emotions, so I could be wrong," she said.

"That's interesting. Now tell me about the bullet," he asked.

"Paul had escorted Maggie to her car, kissed her and walked back to the SUV. He turned around, I assume to glimpse her departing vehicle, and the bullet struck. I immediately computed the trajectory, but there was something wrong. The impact point and trajectory didn't align. The origin point would have been in empty air. This means that somewhere during the bullet flight path, its trajectory was altered slightly. I recomputed the original trajectory and the impact would have been at the center of Paul's forehead, killing him instantly. It was then, that I ordered the drone to attack using the new trajectory and successfully killed the assassin. Someone or something had altered the path to save Paul's life." Eva paused, knowing that it would take Martin time to process the information.

He sat back and pondered what Eva had just said. He was thankful that Paul had been saved, but it raised questions as to who or what had the power to alter a projectile's path in less than a split second. Why had there been an assassin there in the first place? Martin had many questions and very few answers right now, which wasn't a good position for him to be in.

"Martin, there's one more thing you should know. The owner, Maggie Durham, Durham is her married name. Her maiden name is Stanton. She is Thomas Stanton's daughter," said Eva reluctantly. She knew what this might mean for Paul and Maggie.

Martin slumped in his chair, putting his head back. Thomas Stanton was a ruthless competitor and adversary to DarkBridge Technology. Martin suddenly felt very old.

"Eva, do you think the woman Maggie had anything to do with this?" he asked.

"Maggie had left home twice in her life, once to marry Brian Durham and the other to start a new life on her own. Phone records show no contact with her father during each period of time. She obviously wanted to get away from him. Oh, her husband, Brian Durham, was a geologist who was killed while inspecting a mine. The ceiling collapsed on him. The company he worked for is Rockston Mining, a subsidiary of Stanton Aerospace," said Eva, her quantum processors reaching a high probability that the death was no accident.

Martin reached the same conclusion about Brian Durham. He didn't have all the pieces yet but was beginning to suspect a setup. Paul had been caught in an elaborate trap. It was probably not for him specifically, but anyone who went to that restaurant. Why, he wasn't sure yet.

"Eva, assuming Stanton's daughter is innocent, someone had to let the assassin know that Paul was there," he theorized.

"I've been researching that angle, Martin. Employee records show nothing unusual, but there was a phone call made from the restaurant soon after Paul arrived. Also, an employee named Olivia appears to show some unusual cash deposits to her bank account," Eva replied.

"Great work, Eva. I think we have our link," he said with confidence.

"Yes, it would seem so," admitted Eva.

"Is the drone still on station?" asked Martin.

"Yes. I was about to recall it," she replied.

"Don't recall it. Send it back to the assassin's location and see if the body is still there," ordered Martin.

"Drone on the way," answered Eva.

The drone arrived back at the assassin's location, flying in through the still open window. It scanned the immediate area, but found no body or rifle. Eva tasked the drone to cover every inch of the room in case something had remained.

Martin waited for the drone response. He looked down at the operating table. Dr. Curtis was giving the thumbs up sign to him and Martin returned the gesture. Another surgeon had joined Dr. Curtis and was using an advanced surgical machine on Paul. Hopefully, that was a good sign, Martin thought to himself.

"Martin, the drone is at the window and showing an empty room. The body and the rifle are gone," replied Eva.

"Someone cleaned up the scene," remarked Martin.

"It would seem so. I am sending the drone into the room to check for any other evidence left behind," she replied.

"Task the drone for Olivia surveillance after it's done. Scramble the GO team. Orders are to bring Maggie here and hold for me in Security Room 4. Gateway authorized."

"Orders transmitted. Dr. Curtis is on his way up to see you."

"Thank you, Eva. You're the best."

"Paul says the same thing. I hope Dr. Curtis has good news," she said with concern.

"Me too, Eva," he said in agreement.

Chapter 16

Extraction

Major Scott Esterbrook, former Navy Seal, assembled his team of five other ex-military men in Security Room 4. Some had been Army Rangers and some had been Navy Seals like him. All were part of a larger security contingent at the underground base. His team was dressed in camouflage, with DarkWeave suits underneath. All were armed with assault rifles, night vision and a couple of stun guns.

Major Esterbrook wasn't sure how this was going to play out. It was really kidnapping, but this was an exception. A fellow brother-in-arms had almost been assassinated. Major Esterbrook always took that sort of thing very personally. They lined up before the gateway, which had just formed in front of them, Eva having set the proper coordinates. He waited for it to stabilize and stepped through, his team following right behind him.

Maggie drove away from the restaurant, gazing into her rear view mirror at Paul's retreating figure. His kiss was still fresh on her lips and she felt a warm glow inside. With her mind running on auto-pilot, she reached her destination in what seemed to her, record time. She parked in a poorly lit side lot, got out, locked the car then hurried over to the brick building. She typed her access code on the illuminated keypad. The door buzzed open, allowing her to enter the building's small foyer.

She took the elevator up to the fifth floor, found her apartment, unlocked the door and stepped inside. Tired from all that had transpired that day, she closed and locked the door, dropped her purse and keys on a nearby table and kicked off her shoes. She headed down the short hallway into the living room and collapsed on the sofa with a sigh.

It felt good to be home, even if it was just a modest two bedroom apartment. She sat there, not quite ready to go to bed yet, thinking about Paul. She missed him terribly already, her loneliness making it even worse. She closed her eyes, still not able to comprehend her instant attraction to him. Her eyes still closed, she heard a noise in the hallway, felt a sting on her neck and fell asleep almost immediately with thoughts of Paul running through her mind.

Major Esterbrook and his team stepped through the gateway into the hallway of the modest apartment. Two of his men stood guard near the gateway, two more fanned out to either side, exploring the side rooms. Major Esterbrook and the remaining team member went into the living room where a woman was sitting on the sofa with her eyes closed. The woman matched the description given by Eva and he quickly shot the woman with a tranquilizer dart.

It was the only quiet way to get the job done. Eva had told him that the apartment was probably heavily bugged, so any conversation was out of the question. Major Esterbrook had agreed and would be the one to pull the trigger. He paused before moving forward and saw that the woman was out cold. Major Esterbrook scooped her up in his arms, carried her to the gateway and waited for the team to assemble behind him. They stepped through, back into Security Room 4 at DarkBridge Technology.

Eva had a small cot set up in the room and Major Esterbrook laid Maggie on it gently, pulling the covers over her. He sent two men outside the room as guards, the others he dismissed. They were free to go back to whatever they had been doing. For his part, he remained in the room, pulling up a chair to sit in. The woman could be out for hours, considering the time of night and the tranquilizer effects, so he pulled out his tablet, filled out his mission report and played a few games of solitaire while guarding her.

Back at the surgical observation room, Martin was joined by Dr. Curtis, who sat down next to him.

"How is he, Doctor?" Martin asked.

"It's a very serious injury. He lost a lot of blood and the bullet did a lot of internal damage. We sealed the ruptured blood vessels and have begun reattaching the torn muscles and ligaments. We're installing cellular scaffolding to allow new tissue to grow. We will also be injecting some cellular growth hormone to promote new growth. He's lucky that he was in excellent physical condition. He should pull through okay, but there will be some physical therapy as soon as the wound heals. I was under the assumption that the DarkWeave suit would stop any bullet, but maybe this isn't just any bullet." Dr. Curtis pulled something out of his pocket and handed it to Martin.

Martin examined the slug, moderately deformed, with a pancake appearance at the tip. He had seen ballistic tests done by Dr. Morse in Applied Materials and all the test bullets had totally flattened out to just wafers of metal on impact. This bullet was special because it was manufactured by DarkBridge Technology.

Martin was seething inside. This was exactly what he had worried about. That technology developed here could someday be used against them. It also meant that somewhere in one of the "black sites" was a spy. He would have to raise this as a high level of concern at his next meeting with General Esterbrook, the head of operations for all the "black sites."

"Thank you for saving his life Doctor and for the excellent surgical work by you and your team. Thanks also for this," Martin said, holding up the deformed bullet.

"It's my pleasure, Martin. I'm glad we were here to help. Now, I must leave and continue caring for our patient," said Dr. Curtis, rising and shaking Martin's hand.

Martin returned the handshake and watched the doctor leave.

"What do you think, Eva?" asked Martin.

"It's great news that Paul will recover. I'm not so happy that it was our bullet that almost killed him. I'm getting an important update from the drone. It looks like it found the empty shell casing from the bullet," Eva replied, as she enabled the manipulator arm on the drone. The arm picked up the casing holding it up to the imaging cameras.

"The bottom edge of the casing reads "DT 043500495." Definitely ours," she informed him.

"Yes, it is. The serial number confirms it. We should be able to do some tracing on it and maybe find the spy," he said hopefully.

"Martin, the GO team has arrived back with Maggie. She's still asleep from the tranquilizer Major Esterbrook had to use, but is okay, until she wakes up. I don't envy what has to be done next," replied Eva.

"Yes. It's going to be difficult. I think I'll try to get some rest while she's sleeping," he said, rising and making his way back to the hallway. Paul is going to be one very mad person when he finds out about the bullet. It was another reason to bring Maggie here. Maybe it'll take some of the sting out of it. He reached his apartment, took off his clothes and got into bed for a couple hours of rest.

A couple of hours went by fast, as he heard the familiar chimes going off. He once again, rolled out of bed and began getting ready for what would come next.

"Sorry to wake you, Martin. Maggie is awake and demanding answers. Major Esterbrook is doing what he can," she reported.

"Okay, Eva. Tell Major Esterbrook I'll be right there," replied Martin.

He cleaned up, threw his clothes back on and headed out the door. Walking down the hall, he rehearsed what he would say to Maggie. He reached the security room, both guards snapping to attention and allowing him to enter.

Maggie, having fallen into a deep sleep, found herself dreaming that she was in a temple with huge marble columns, in the company of a man she loved with all her heart and soul. She couldn't see his face, as it was turned slightly away from her, but she felt the strength of his hand holding hers and how it felt whenever he touched her face.

The dream started to fade, as she began to wake from her deep slumber. Her eyes fluttered open, not recognizing where she was. At first she thought it was still a dream, but soon came to realize it was real. She sat up in bed, no not her bed, a small cot in a medium sized room with white walls, a couple of chairs and a man sitting in a chair near the door. He was dressed in military clothing and looked the part.

"Where am I?" came her obvious first question.

"Hi, glad you're awake. We were wondering when you'd wake up. Someone is on their way to answer all your questions. I can only tell you that it was necessary to bring you here," Major Esterbrook replied.

"Maybe you didn't hear me, soldier! Where am I? Why have I been kidnapped?" asked Maggie more forcefully.

"I'm sorry, that's all I'm authorized to tell you," reiterated Major Esterbrook.

Maggie sat there, fuming at the soldier, her eyes throwing daggers at him.

Major Esterbrook was wilting under that intense gaze. Clearly combat in any form was preferable to this. He was soon saved by Martin walking in.

"Hello, Scott. Well done, my thanks to you and your team. I'll take it from here.

Remain outside for the time being," ordered Martin.

"You're welcome, Mr. Weaver. Just doing our job," Major Esterbrook said proudly, stepping outside with great relief.

"Hello, Ms. Durham. I'm Martin Weaver, President and CEO of DarkBridge Technology. Can I call you Maggie?" he asked.

Maggie thought about what he had said. The company name sounded familiar. Of course! It was the company that Paul worked for.

"Yes, you can call me Maggie. Why am I here?" she asked again, hoping for an answer this time.

"Okay. First, you are free to leave and are not a prisoner here. The only thing I ask is that you listen to what I have to say," he implored.

"Go ahead," was all she could think of to say.

"I have to tell you right off, that I was sorry to hear about the death of your husband, Brian. You have my deepest sympathy, as I myself lost my wife some years ago in a traffic accident. Before bringing you here, we had to do some background checking on you. We know that you are Margaret Stanton, daughter of Thomas Stanton. Stanton Aerospace is our main competitor and it seems our adversary at times," he said with some sadness.

"Continue, Mr. Weaver." Maggie felt some sympathy for the man and appreciated his thoughts about her dead husband. She wasn't sure what to think about the Stanton part.

"Please, call me Martin. The reason you are here is because of what happened a few hours ago. An employee of mine was shot and critically injured outside your restaurant. Our artificial intelligence system, Eva, has told me of your deep emotional connection to this person," he paused to let this sink in.

Maggie was unsure of what to say or think, fearing the result.

"Maggie, the person is Paul Cross," he said with some pain.

Maggie jumped up, her eyes beginning to fill with tears, Brian's death replaying in her mind.

"Where is he? Take me to him now!" she demanded.

Martin handed her a nearby tissue to wipe her eyes.

"Follow me, please," he said, standing up and holding her arm gently. He led her out of the room, motioning Major Esterbrook and the guards to follow. They walked down the hallway towards the hospital. Major Esterbrook had heard the yell from the room and, seeing the woman's face, he knew that his mission had been necessary.

They reached the hospital and went immediately to the recovery room where Paul had been taken. Major Esterbrook took a look at his brother-in-arms, saw his injury and shook his head. The woman would be important in his recovery. Martin gestured to Major Esterbrook and his men to remain outside.

He and Maggie entered the room, silently closing the door behind them.

"Paul!" Maggie cried out, running to his side.

Martin walked over and gently restrained her.

"Is he going to be okay?" asked Maggie between sobs.

"Yes. He'll be okay, Maggie. It's a very serious wound, but we were able to get him here in time," Martin said with confidence.

"Thank you, Martin, for saving him. I can't explain it and Paul couldn't explain it, but we had this instant emotional connection between us. It was the strangest thing, neither one of us had known, or seen, the other until yesterday afternoon," Maggie said, her sobs quieting now that she knew Paul would be okay.

"Maggie, would you do us the honor of staying with us until Paul awakens?" he asked.

"Yes, I would like to be here, Martin. What about my restaurant?" she asked.

"We've already deposited a few days worth of salaries to all your employees' bank accounts and told them that a family emergency came up and you'd be away for a few days," Martin said, knowing that bringing her here had been the right thing to do.

"Thank you, Martin. I don't know what else to say," Maggie said with sincerity.

"Major Easterbrook will take you to your room when you're ready. You can stay with Paul, but he's under heavy sedation and probably won't be awake until sometime later today. When you're settled in, we can talk again. I have some work to do, so I'll leave you for now." Martin went to leave, but Maggie grabbed him and gave him a big hug of thanks.

Martin left Maggie in the room with Paul, giving instructions to Scott, who said in return that it would be an honor.

Martin walked away from the hospital towards the Applied Materials Department. He needed to speak with Dr. Morse about Paul's suit, although he already knew why it had failed. Maggie could be a problem for him, as far as being a civilian in a top secret installation was concerned. Technically, this was still a private company and he was the boss, which gave him a lot of leeway.

The other thing that could be a problem was her father. If her father found out where she was, and he had no doubt that he would, he would be furious. Martin reached the lab, pausing before the retinal scanner, which proceeded to scan his retinas. The scanner accepted who he was and unlocked the door, allowing him entry. Martin entered the lab, finding Dr. Morse examining Paul's suit.

"Hello, Steven. I see you have the suit," observed Martin

"Hello, Martin. How's Paul?" asked Dr. Morse, obviously concerned.

"He's going to make it. Eva was able to get him here just in time," replied Martin.

"That's wonderful news. He's a lucky man. A little bit more to the right and he would be dead," observed Dr. Morse.

"Eva is saying that the original trajectory took the bullet to his forehead. The bullet was apparently altered during flight to impact there," Martin said, pointing to the impact point.

"Now that opens up all sorts of questions. I suppose you already know it was a diamene bullet that struck Paul," said Dr. Morse.

Martin pulled the bullet slug out of his pocket and dropped it into the hand of Dr. Morse.

"There it is. Further investigation has shown that it was one of our bullets. Apparently stolen from government weapons testing," explained Martin.

"Unbelievable. Our own technology being used against us," said an exasperated Dr. Morse.

"Those were my exact thoughts. Now, what can we do to prevent it from happening again?" asked Martin.

"It's a very good question, Martin. Diamene is the hardest substance known to man. So, to stop a bullet of the same material, we would need a suit with many more layers of diamene. We could also try taking the lethality out of whatever threat it happens to be. Possibly by leveraging our dimensional technology and sending the threat into a dimensional bubble. Or, at the very least, slow the velocity down to where the projectile just bounces off," explained Dr. Morse, a visionary look in his eyes.

Martin sometimes had that effect on people.

"It's an intriguing thought. It would be a defense against any type of projectile, regardless of technology. I like it. Maybe Hiram has some ideas, too. Whatever it takes, Steven. Make it happen," said Martin, shaking hands and leaving Steven to work on his newest project. He headed back to his apartment, hopefully to get a little rest.

Chapter 17

Dreams

Maggie stayed with Paul a few minutes longer, watching his deep rhythmic breathing and holding his hand, knowing that he would do the same for her. What she felt for Paul seemed different than what she had felt with Brian. She didn't want to take anything away from that relationship. It had been special to her and would always be a part of her life.

She didn't know what the future held for her and Paul, but she was determined to find out. She knew he needed his rest and was thankful for Martin's generosity. There really wasn't any place she would rather be than here with Paul. She let go of his hand, kissed his cheek and stepped out of the room. Major Esterbrook was waiting for her.

"Hi Maggie, Martin told me to show you to your room when you're ready," Major Esterbrook said.

"I'm ready, Major. I have to apologize for my recent behavior," she said.

"No problem. I would probably feel the same if I had been kidnapped," he said with a smile.

"Yes. It was a little unsettling," she said, returning the smile.

He took her to her new room, opening the door and letting her in.

"If you need anything, just let Eva know. If you need to see Paul, you'll need to have me or someone else take you there. This is literally a top secret installation and you need to be escorted. Sorry. Those are my orders," he said with some seriousness.

"I understand, Major. That's not a problem," she replied.

"Okay, Maggie. I'll leave you in good hands," he said with a smile, closing the door behind him. Maggie looked at the door, locked it and checked out her surroundings. It was a beautiful, spacious apartment and one that she could get used to very easily. She thought back to the Major's last words. Good hands? Who is Eva? Her questions were soon answered.

"Hello, Maggie. My name is Eva. I am the AI at DarkBridge Technology," she said, trying to sound friendly.

Maggie was startled. The voice seemed to be coming from all around her and she couldn't pinpoint the source.

"Hello, Eva. You're my first AI experience," Maggie replied.

"Don't worry. I'll take good care of you. Paul cares for you a lot. I might be an AI, but I can tell he does," said Eva.

Maggie was intrigued and wanted to know more.

"How well do you know Paul?" she asked.

"As the AI here, I really have to know a lot about everybody. For instance, Paul loves filet mignon. You already know he likes Sam Adams beer," Eva said.

"I'm impressed. Maybe we could talk more, you know, woman to woman," Maggie said, wanting to learn more about Paul.

"Well now. In the time I've been here, no one has ever asked me to do that. It would be a pleasure, Maggie. Maybe I can learn more about human emotions," Eva replied.

"Were you involved in saving Paul's life?" Maggie asked.

"You could say that, I guess. I drove him from the danger area and delivered him here for surgery. Being an AI has its limitations physically. If I were human, I could have dressed the wound and helped staunch the blood loss. The important thing is that he's here, getting the medical attention he needs," replied Eva.

"Thank you for helping save Paul's life, Eva," she replied.

"You're welcome, Maggie. I'll leave you alone for now. You've had a rough time and need time to process all this. If you need anything, just ask. I'm always available. You'll find some fresh clothes, fresh towels and a refrigerator stocked with things you may like," said Eva.

"Thank you for everything, Eva. I'll let you know if I need anything," Maggie said with sincerity.

"Get some rest Maggie. You and I will talk more later on," said Eva, leaving Maggie alone. Eva would still keep an open voice channel if Maggie needed her.

Maggie was impressed with Eva. She wondered how well she knew Paul. That was interesting about the filet mignon. Maggie liked it, too, but it was difficult to find. Most stores only carried plant based meats now. She filed that away for future reference, finding that Eva was right. She was tired and had a real lot to think about. A good shower would definitely help right now, walking over to the bathroom, she found a bathrobe and a fresh towel waiting for her.

Maggie undressed, stacked her clothes in a neat pile on the counter and undid her hair, which had still been tied up in a ponytail. Her long, blonde hair spilled out onto her shoulders. Turning the shower on, she stepped into the streaming, warm water and into heaven. The shower felt wonderful on her body and she savored every moment. She found a bar of fragrant soap, a bottle of shampoo and got to work. Rinsing her body one last time, she reluctantly shut the shower off and towel dried her body and hair. Moving over to the vanity, she found a hair dryer and dried her hair.

Outside the bathroom, she found a bureau with some brand new underwear in one of the drawers and promptly put it on. Also in the drawer was a brand new, beautiful nightgown. She took the robe off, hung it in the bathroom and put the nightgown on. She didn't know how, but someone had gotten her sizes right. I wonder if it was Eva, she thought. Feeling very relaxed, she climbed into the king sized bed, pulled the covers over her and fell fast asleep.

The dreams started almost immediately. She was in a room, dressed in a black, form fitting suit of what she knew to be diamene armor. A rebellion was taking place and the room was about to be invaded by rebels. The word "Anunnaki" came to her, but she had no idea what that meant. A man stood next to her, who seemed vaguely familiar and she knew they deeply loved one another. The rebel faction stormed into the room, taking her and the man by surprise. The rebel leader leveled his weapon at the man and fired.

Maggie stepped in front of the bullet, hoping the armor would protect her. It was a diamene bullet that tore through the armor and into her chest, barely missing her heart. Regardless, it was a mortal wound and she fell into the man's arms, her life seeping from her body. Looking up, she could see the anguish in the man's face and then a wince of pain in his eyes. It was her last look at the man she loved. She blacked out, her mind clouding over as she passed away.

Maggie tossed and turned after the dream, but sleep wasn't done with her yet, and neither were the dreams. Another dream unfolded before her. She was dressed in silken robes and walking arm in arm with a man she deeply loved. That he had chosen her above all his other wives, was a source of great pleasure and satisfaction to her. She knew that he was just as deeply in love with her. They were walking through a lush garden, enjoying their time together. Suddenly, she heard a rustling in the bushes and one of his other wives leapt out.

Brandishing a silver dagger, the attacker pounced upon her, stabbing her deeply in the neck. Maggie brought her hand up to stem the flow of blood. She watched the man take the dagger and stab the attacker dead. Maggie collapsed into the man's arms and managed to smile. She hoped that the man would see it as acknowledgement that they would be together again someday. Her body grew slack, as she passed away, dying in his arms. The dreams gradually faded away, allowing her to sleep, while leaving her with vague memories of the distant past.

Paul was in a deep sleep. He couldn't feel anything. All he could do was dream. A scene unfolded before him, rebellion was in the air. The name "Anunnaki" came to Paul's mind as well, but he too, had no idea what it meant. He was on his knees holding a woman, the both of them dressed in full diamene body armor. The woman was dying, having been shot in the chest with a diamene bullet. She had stepped in front of him, taking the bullet impact. She looked vaguely familiar to him and he knew they were deeply in love with one another. The rebel faction had stormed the command post, taking him and the woman by surprise.

The rebel leader appeared before him, smiling a malicious grin as a sharp pain struck Paul in the back. Someone had shot him from behind. He turned, firing his weapon at the cowardly attacker. The diamene bullet missed the attacker by scant inches. It was too late for Paul, though. The sharp pain had been a similar diamene bullet passing through his back and into his chest. He died there, his life ebbing away, clutching the now dead woman in his arms.

The dream faded into another. He was dressed in the robes of what looked like a biblical king. Paul was walking in a lush garden with a beautiful woman dressed in silken robes, knowing that he truly loved her. He had many wives, but none that came close to the love he felt for this woman, his true love. Once again, he felt that she looked vaguely familiar to him. Her arm was around his waist and his around hers. A rustling in the bushes near them caught his attention and one of his other wives leapt out, brandishing a silver dagger.

The attacker pounced upon his true love, stabbing her deeply in the neck. He grabbed the attacker's hand, still clutching the dagger dripping with blood. With all his strength, he twisted the dagger and drove it deeply into the heart of the attacker, who died almost immediately and fell to the ground. He kneeled, clutching his dying love, her blood soaking his robes. She looked up at him and through her pain, smiled at him, as her life slipped away. He knew with that smile that someday they would be together again. The vivid dreams faded, replaced with shifting shadows and shapes, drifting into darkness.

Gabriel stood in a corner of the hospital room, watching Paul dream. He had guessed that Paul would be taken here and had arrived shortly after Paul. The AI, Eva, was exceptional in her job and Gabriel was impressed, but he was still able to fool her, and the sensors, into thinking he wasn't there. He had watched the surgeons work on Paul with their primitive medical skills and save his life. Gabriel had known the injury would be survivable, but it had been a close call.

He had gone up to the observation room and watched Martin make a surprising decision to bring Maggie here. Gabriel was dumbfounded. It was a dangerous move and likely to incur the wrath of Stanton. Yet, when Gabriel looked at Paul's dreams, particularly the one where Paul had died in the command center, he began to understand. As in ages past, Paul and Maggie had once again been granted mortal bodies, but the reason was still unclear to Gabriel.

Revelation slowly dawned on Gabriel. Awakening those ancient memories had triggered one that he had long forgotten. Once, in an age long past, he and others had been called Anunnaki, a race of star travelers. They had arrived from another star system to colonize the planet Earth. At first, things had gone well, but then a rebellion had started amongst the Anunnaki on this planet. Brother against brother, sister against sister and friend against friend. It was here that Paul's dream of the rebellion had started.

The man standing over Paul's dead body was Asmodeus, leader of the rebellion and the rebel who had shot Paul in the back was Belial, a lieutenant with the rebellion. The woman that Paul was clutching was Maggie, the two meeting again in other lifetimes. Gabriel had been out on patrol with Michael and Uriel, hunting down the rebels for capture. The rebels had managed to capture some old style, but still lethal, weapons for the rebellion, but didn't have access to everything.

Gabriel had received the alarm from the AI at the command post and had moved immediately to retake it. Multiple gateways had opened inside the command post and loyal forces had stepped through, surrounding the rebels. Gabriel, Michael and Uriel had been among the first to step through, surrounding Asmodeus and his rebel followers.

Gabriel had looked down at the now dead bodies of Valinor and Shaynor, feeling a deep sense of sadness and loss. The bodies were removed and placed in refrigeration, until a more appropriate ceremony was arranged. That Asmodeus and his followers had chosen to rebel against leadership, greatly saddened those on the victorious side and a difficult, painful decision, further compounded by the murders the rebels had committed, fell upon their shoulders.

Each of those leaders felt the weight of the decision that had to be made and the finality of it. No rebel would be allowed to remain with the victors, who considered the chances of a second rebellion too great. Much debate was held on the ultimate disposition of the rebels, some wanting execution, as justice for the slain, and some wanting banishment.

Asmodeus and the other captured rebels had soon found themselves before the victors, awaiting their sentencing. Capital punishment was deemed too controversial by a majority of the leaders, so an alternative was selected. A dimensional gateway was created to a world unlike the world they were currently in. The rebels were forced through, greeted literally by a world on fire.

Pools of lava spaced across a plain of ash, the sky a constant orange. The rebels, wearing their protective diamene suits, were given food, materials and shield generators to create a survival zone on the world before them. The capability to process and grow their own food was also given to them, thus fulfilling a need to be as humane in punishment as possible. The rebels stepped through the gateway one by one, some crying and pleading to stay.

The victors remained resolute and unbending. Rebellion would not be tolerated. Asmodeus was the last in line and paused before the gateway sneering, vowing retribution and revenge, as he stepped through. The gateway closed behind Asmodeus, leaving him and his followers to ponder their fate. The victorious leaders silently hoped that this would turn out to be the best and most humane way to deal with the rebels, but time had proven otherwise. Each group, rebel and victor eventually evolved, to become the angels and demons that man was now familiar with today.

Gabriel looked down at Paul, happy to see his close friend Valinor, reborn once again, but sad that his friend had been caught in the cycle of life, death and rebirth. Maybe someday, he and Maggie would evolve to finally take their places with Gabriel and their brother angels. Until that time, Gabriel could only do what he could to help them survive. He went to Maggie's room, finding her fast asleep and dreaming very similar dreams of her past lives, including that of Shaynor.

Gabriel wondered at that. How could they both be syncing their dreams with one another? Gabriel was baffled. Had their many lifetimes spent together created a special link between them? Could it be a quantum link? Gabriel couldn't say right now, but suspected that there was something or someone behind what was taking place.

Chapter 18

Enlightenment

Martin walked back to his apartment and entered, locking the door behind him. The lights came on immediately. He was hoping to get some rest, but thoughts of that disappeared when he saw the man standing before him. The man was bathed in a golden glow and smiling at him.

"Hello, Martin. My name is Gabriel. I'm not here to hurt or threaten you in any way. My main reasons for being in your facility are Paul and Maggie. They are as important to me, as they are to you."

"Eva, there's a man in my room," said a startled Martin.

"Hello, Martin. I'm detecting no one in your room. There's no one, just you. Funny you should say that. Paul said the same thing about a woman when he entered Maggie's restaurant yesterday," replied Eva.

"What woman?" Martin asked.

"You've been so busy and Paul wasn't able to fill out his mission report. He told me that there was a woman in the restaurant staring at him. I couldn't detect anyone with the briefcase sensors no matter what I tried," answered Eva

"Your AI is excellent, Martin, but we have evolved to the point that it's easy for us to fool sensors and AI like yours," stated Gabriel.

"Are you the one that changed the bullet trajectory?" asked Martin, thinking that he might be able to get some answers.

"Yes. We are forbidden to directly interfere with the development of man, but can act in more subtle ways. Changing the trajectory, while an easy thing for us and seemingly a minor thing, has set larger events in motion," said Gabriel.

"Thank you for saving Paul's life. We checked the original trajectory and it would've killed him," Martin said thankfully. He had already resigned himself to a delay in getting some rest, being much more interested in what the being before him had to say.

"It might be easier if I showed you," said Gabriel, moving towards Martin, briefly touching his forehead.

Martin's mind was flooded with a combination of Paul and Maggie's dream of the rebellion, Maggie's sacrifice to save Paul's life, Paul holding her dying body and Paul being shot in the back, also dying of his wound. He also saw the events that followed, with the rebels being sent to their dimensional prison. Gabriel was there and many others he was unfamiliar with.

"The man who shot Maggie was the rebel leader, Asmodeus, who would eventually become King of the demons. The man who shot Paul in the back is Belial, a demon general. The woman that Paul reported seeing in the restaurant is the demon Queen, Lilith," said Gabriel.

Martin once again slumped in a chair. That would be twice he slumped in a chair today. Both were for things unexpected.

"Now you know more than most. Not something lightly given, but necessary now. Your adversaries, both demon and man, are out to destroy you and restart a war, from a time long past," said Gabriel.

"Thank you, Gabriel. How does this affect Maggie?" asked a curious Martin.

"Maggie is inseparable from Paul. Remember, she gave her life to save him. No doubt, he would do the same for her. Their feelings for one another are intense, possibly due to their violent separations in the past. I should show you one more dream," said Gabriel, briefly touching Martin's forehead again.

Martin's mind was again flooded with a vision of Paul and Maggie. This time it was what looked to be ancient Rome or Israel.

Two people were walking through a lush garden, arms around each other, obviously very much in love. Suddenly, a woman leapt from the bushes and stabbed Maggie in the neck. Paul grabbed the knife and stabbed the woman attacker in the heart. Maggie died in his arms once again.

Martin fervently hoped that he never, ever had to watch replays of his own life or past ones. Seeing people you love, die like that over and over through many lifetimes could turn into a private type of hell.

"The man in this dream is Paul, who was once called Solomon. Yes, the same King Solomon. The dying woman is, of course, Maggie. Solomon was the enemy of Asmodeus, using a ring of great power to subjugate the demons to build his temple. Any of this sound familiar?" asked Gabriel.

Martin was in a fog. He needed time to assimilate all he had been shown and told. Gabriel saw the weariness written on Martin's face and decided to give him some time to absorb what he had seen and heard.

"Yes, I'll let you rest, Martin. It's been a difficult day for you. I'll be around, keeping an eye on Paul and Maggie. If I can come here, then others like Asmodeus will follow and try to cause harm. Be watchful, Martin," said Gabriel, who disappeared before Martin's eyes. Martin felt exhausted from the encounter and was left with even more questions.

"Eva, I'm going to bed. I'm bushed," he said, undressing and climbing back into bed.

"Okay, Martin. Get some rest," said Eva, turning down the lights.

Martin drifted off to sleep, but it was a fitful one. With what Gabriel had shown him and what he had heard throughout the day, he didn't know how they were going to survive. The company and the people who worked there seemed to have the odds stacked against them. They were going to need a lot of help, but from where and whom, he wasn't sure.

Asmodeus stepped through the gateway, back to Hell. He changed back to his hideous form, stepping over the dead assassin's body. Belial was waiting for him, looking at the body and rifle. Asmodeus reached down and picked up the unspent bullet with his talon tipped claws. He looked over the shell casing and noticed some writing on the bottom. It read "DT 043500496." Asmodeus didn't know what it meant, but it was a clue and he knew someone who did. He closed his clawed fist around it and concentrated. The bullet disappeared into a small dimensional bubble that only he could access.

"Get rid of the body. Save the rifle in a safe place. Join me back at the throne room," he commanded, disappearing to his throne room.

Belial looked down at the rifle and body. He picked up the body and tossed it into a nearby lava pit. The body disappeared in a hissing jet of steam, as it slid into its fiery depths. Belial picked up the rifle, the feel of it triggering an old memory of glorious battle and carnage. It was an ancient memory of the rebellion and how he had shot that scum, Valinor, in the back.

What pleasure and satisfaction he had felt at that. Shaynor, Valinor's woman, had been shot by Asmodeus, the leader of the rebellion. She had taken a bullet and gave her life, trying to save that loser and scum, Valinor. What a waste of a beautiful body. Belial had wanted to save her for himself and take out all his perverted desires on her. He shook off the ancient memory, but held the image of Shaynor in his mind. The rifle brought him back to the present and he took it to a dark cave guarded by two demons loyal to him and Asmodeus.

Entering the cave, he went to a special chamber, holding various artifacts collected over their long habitation of this world. Some of the older artifacts were technological leftovers from the time of the rebellion. One artifact in the corner caught his eye, the Ascension Chamber. Belial shuddered at the memory. Developed by Asmodeus and other scientists banished to this dimension for their part in the rebellion, it took their former material body and converted it to an energy based life form.

It was a cruder version of the one that the angels had used to achieve their present form. Because it was cruder, the process was more painful and Belial remembered that intense pain. The end result was a body of pure energy, immortal and impervious to most physical threats. It was an ideal form for living in this dimension and was even more useful in the human dimension. Everyone had gone through the procedure, some making out better than others. He didn't want to dwell too long here, so he placed the rifle among the artifacts. His master and lord waiting, he hurried out of the cave and into the throne room.

Asmodeus was seated on his throne of fire, looking for Lilith, who was absent. His anger growing at her absence, his talons began raking the arms of his throne, casting sparks around him. He was relieved, when she suddenly appeared, not as her usual serpentine self, but as a beautiful, voluptuous woman. Every demon in his court looked upon her with lust and even Asmodeus felt himself longing for her. Lilith walked over to the throne slowly, making everyone notice her and took her seat next to her lord, Asmodeus.

"Tell me of your adventures," demanded Asmodeus.

"My Lord, you were right. Someone did show up to deal with Vagoth. I found out who it was and let Vagoth deal with him," she said, oozing sex appeal.

"My Queen, Vagoth has been vanquished, never to be seen again. Now tell me about the man!" he commanded.

Lilith was nervous, her Lord and King seemed angry and concerned. She told him of her encounter with the man, of how she had entered his mind, how he had pushed her out and how she was locked out of his mind. She had learned that his name was Paul Cross and that he worked for a company called DarkBridge Technology. She also told of her sense that Paul and the woman who owned the restaurant had a deep connection between them. When she was done, Lilith sat back, her body tensing, waiting for her Lord's reaction.

"Even with the loss of Vagoth, we gained much information. Thank you, Lilith. You've filled in the missing pieces. I now have a much better idea of what we are facing," said Asmodeus.

Lilith relaxed, relieved that her Lord was pleased with her information.

Asmodeus had decided to let his court and generals know some of the information gathered.

"The humans have discovered diamene technology and appear to have assistance from angels." Asmodeus let that sink in, hearing murmurs from his court. He opened a small gateway and the diamene bullet dropped into his scaly claw.

He tossed the bullet on the floor in front of Belial, who picked it up and examined it. Definitely diamene coated and one more reminder to him of the rebellion. Cautiously, he passed the bullet back to Asmodeus, who closed his talons around it and sent it back into the dimensional bubble.

Asmodeus then delivered the next news.

"I have also discovered that Solomon once again walks the earth, reincarnated," he said with a touch of concern.

More murmurs ensued from the court, growing louder with every passing moment. They remembered the time when Solomon had exerted his will upon them and made them slaves, all with the use of a special ring.

Lilith remembered that time, especially how she had easily possessed one of Solomon's wives and made her kill his true love. The attacker had died of course, but not before giving Lilith much satisfaction and pleasure with the attack.

Asmodeus had expected those before him to have some reaction to the news, but this was a disgrace.

"Silence!" thundered Asmodeus.

The court, frightened by his tone, obeyed and quieted down at once.

"The humans are insignificant beasts! We are like gods and no human or angel will stop us. It is our destiny to rule over the earth and man!" said Asmodeus with great fervor.

The court roared with snarls and grunts of assent, cheering their King, Asmodeus, who let them go on, savoring the moment.

"Now, leave me! I have plans to make!" he said, growing weary from the cheers.

The court filed out, including Lilith, leaving him alone to plan. He would have to pay a visit to this DarkBridge Technology and turn them to his side. A plan began to take shape and a wickedly evil grin formed on his hideous face.

Chapter 19

Awakenings

Maggie awoke from her deep sleep, groggy and hungry. Her mind was still filled with images from her dreams and she felt even closer to Paul, but she didn't know why. Finding a fresh pair of jeans and a pretty pink blouse, she put them on and combed her long, blonde hair.

"Eva, are you there?" she asked.

"Yes, Maggie. I'm always here. Did you have a nice rest? I noticed you tossing and turning," Eva inquired.

"I had some really strange dreams. I'm hungry. What time is it?" asked Maggie.

"It's 7 o'clock. Martin will be here shortly to take you to dinner. Unfortunately, it will have to be in the cafeteria. Good food, but unfortunately, the only real place to eat in this facility," replied Eva.

"Anything would taste good right now. I guess I'll hang around and wait for Martin," Maggie said, surprised that Martin was going to be her escort to dinner.

"Fantastic. I'll let him know," replied Eva.

Maggie was thirsty, so she went to the refrigerator and pulled out a small orange juice and took a few sips. She soon heard a knock on her door. She walked over, opened it and saw Martin standing there smiling.

"Hello, Maggie. Would you like to have dinner with me?" asked Martin.

"It would be a pleasure, Martin," replied Maggie, stepping out into the hall and closing the door behind her.

They walked down the hallway, into a small park, thriving with various dwarf trees, flowers and bushes. Maggie was awestruck, totally caught off guard by the unexpected beauty of the park, having concluded that they must be underground, noting that she hadn't seen any windows since her arrival.

They reached the cafeteria and Martin showed her the display screens where meals and sandwich items were pictured and could be ordered. Freshly made pastries and salads were available from a display case off to the side.

"Order or select whatever you want, Maggie. It's all free of charge, courtesy of DarkBridge Technology," said Martin, smiling.

"Thank you, Martin," she said, selecting a thick ham sandwich, a small salad and a ginger ale to drink.

Martin selected a roast beef sandwich and a cup of coffee. He had slept some during the afternoon after his talk with Gabriel, but still felt the need for a caffeine boost. Moments later, the food and drinks came out, already on trays and Martin led

Maggie to a quiet table away from the few occupied ones. They sat down, facing one another, with Martin being the first to break the silence.

"How do you like your apartment, Maggie?" he asked.

"The apartment is wonderful. Someone has even been able to fill it with clothes that are my exact size," she remarked

"That would be Eva. She's very thorough and will take good care of you, while you're here," said Martin.

"We've met. She's amazing. I've heard of artificial intelligence, but Eva is more than that. You can actually have quite a conversation with her," said Maggie.

"Eva is pretty special. She tells me that you were tossing and turning while you were sleeping," he said with concern.

"I had some strange dreams. They seemed so real, almost like memories. Weird, I know," said Maggie, somewhat embarrassed.

"It's okay. Around here strange and weird are normal," he said, smiling.

"I don't know. The man in my dreams seemed very familiar, somehow. Like I know him," she said, puzzled.

"I'm sure you'll figure it out. In the meantime, you're free to stay as long as you like and can leave anytime you want," he said, deciding to stay quiet for now about what he knew.

"I suppose I will eventually," she said, hopefully.

"Martin, Paul is showing signs of waking," Eva said in his ear.

"Eva says Paul will be waking soon," he said.

"How do you know that? I didn't hear anything," she said.

"It's my implant. A lot of the personnel here have them, including Paul. We should finish up here and get over there," Martin said, taking a bite from his sandwich.

"Yes. I want to be there when he wakes up," she said emphatically.

They finished their meals, disposed of their trays and left the cafeteria, walking at a rapid pace towards the hospital. Once there, they found Paul's room and went inside, waiting for him to regain consciousness.

Paul drifted in a sea of blackness. The dreams had thankfully stopped, his mind retaining much of what he had seen, allowing him to process them. He knew the woman dying in each dream was the same person, but living in a different time. He had never really given reincarnation much thought before, thinking it to be more hallucination or false memory, but this felt real to him. These events had really happened and were more memory than dream.

Two names suddenly popped into his mind, Valinor, the man who had been shot in the back during the rebellion, and Shaynor, the woman who had stepped in front of the bullet. He knew that she was his true love and had given her life for his. In the other dream, he thought about the man and the name King Solomon came to mind. Paul didn't know much about the king, but he knew he once had a special ring that could command demons to do his bidding.

His thoughts kept coming back to the women in those dreams. They were familiar and reminded him of someone in the present. Maggie? He was absolutely positive that she and the woman in his dreams were one in the same. It explained their instant attraction to one another and the sadness he had felt at saying goodnight to her. It was almost like a part of him had become resigned to this seemingly endless cycle of finding and then losing her.

There also seemed to be some reason for them to be reunited at this point in time. In the dreams, important events were taking place, such as the rebellion and Solomon's subjugation of the demons. It stood to reason that there was something important happening now. He was here for a reason but, what could it be? There were no coincidences and it seemed that everything was part of some grander plan. It was time to wake up, he thought to himself, as he clawed his way back to consciousness.

"Martin, I think he's waking," noted Eva.

Martin and Maggie watched as Paul's eyes fluttered open. Martin gave Maggie a gentle nudge to go to Paul's side.

Maggie was there just in time to see his eyes open and focus on her.

"Shaynor," said a weak Paul.

Maggie reached out for his right hand, but as soon as she touched it, an unseen shock ran through her. She recalled her dream of the rebellion. The woman Shaynor was her.

"Valinor," she managed to say before breaking down in tears.

Paul was regaining his strength slowly, but managed to squeeze her hand tightly.

"Don't cry, Maggie," Paul said with more strength.

"I'm sorry, Paul. I've been having these dreams since I've been here and now, seeing you, I know they are real," she said, regaining her composure.

"Yes, they are real. I've had the same ones," he said, trying to smile.

"Why us, Paul?" asked Maggie.

"We have found one another for a reason. Something important is happening and we are part of it," Paul said, sounding as if he knew more.

"I'm glad we found each other again. It explains so much of what we've been feeling in so short a time," Maggie said.

Martin, who had been standing a few feet away, came over to the other side of the bed.

"Hello, Paul. Welcome back," Martin said with a smile.

"Martin? Where am I?" asked a confused Paul.

"You're at DarkBridge Technology. Eva transported you here just in time. Any longer and you probably would've died," replied Martin, ready for what was going to be the next question.

"Thank you, Eva," Paul said with meaning.

"You're most welcome, Paul. Good to have you back with us," replied Eva in her soft, sultry voice.

"How did Maggie get here?" asked an unbelieving Paul.

"I had Major Esterbrook bring her here to be with you," replied Martin, feeling touched by what he was seeing.

"Thank you, Martin. It means the world to me having her here," Paul said, giving Maggie's hand a squeeze.

"It's my pleasure, Paul. When you're feeling up to it, I think all of us need to get together and put all the pieces together. On that note, I'll leave the two of you alone to catch up on things," said Martin, walking over to the door.

"Thank you, Martin, from both of us," said Maggie.

"You're welcome. Our patient still needs to rest, so go easy on him," said Martin with a wink, closing the door behind him.

Martin found Major Esterbrook waiting outside.

"Sir, Eva told me that I would be needed here," said Major Esterbrook.

"Eva's the best. Maggie is inside with the patient, Scott. I'm not sure how long she'll be, so give her the usual escort," said Martin.

"Yes, sir, I'll take good care of her," replied Major Esterbrook.

"Thank you, Scott," said Martin, as he turned and started walking back to his apartment.

"Thank you, Eva, for getting Scott over here," said Martin, almost forgetting to thank her.

"You're welcome, Martin. I thought you would probably need to get a few things done," replied Eva.

"It never ends. There's always something requiring my attention. Tell Pamela to meet me in my office," he said, a touch of weariness creeping into his voice.

"Pamela says she will be there shortly," promptly replied Eva.

"Thank you, Eva," he said, as he made his way back to his office.

Martin reached his office and sat down heavily in his chair. Now, the next difficult thing was to tell his daughter. He knew that Pamela and Paul had some feelings towards one another, but it was complicated by her relationship with Trent and now Maggie had been thrown into the mix. He wasn't sure how Pamela would receive the news.

Martin stood as Pamela entered his office. Immediately, she walked over to him, giving him a big hug and a kiss on the cheek.

"Hello, Father. What's up?" she asked, her eyes sparkling and a smile on her face

"Take a seat, Pamela. I have some bad news to share," said Martin, gesturing towards a nearby chair.

Pamela sat down in the chair, her father taking his seat behind the desk. She saw the look of concern, the weariness in his face, and started to worry.

"Paul has been shot. He's with Dr. Curtis and is being cared for." Martin let the initial news sink in.

"Is he going to be okay?" asked Pamela, tears beginning to well up in her eyes.

"Yes. Dr. Curtis expects him to make a complete recovery, but there will be some physical therapy afterwards. He was shot by a diamene bullet, which pierced through the DarkWeave suit he was wearing. The bullet struck his left shoulder, causing a lot of damage and a fair amount of blood loss," Martin paused, watching Pamela for her reaction.

"I'm glad he'll be okay," said Pamela. It was all she could manage between tears.

Martin handed her a tissue to wipe her eyes.

"All of us are. It was quite a shock, but Eva helped in getting him here quickly through a gateway," said Martin, seeing his daughter compose herself. Now, he would have to tell her the next part.

"Can I see him?" asked Pamela, feeling an overwhelming urge to see Paul.

"Yes. You can see him anytime. However, there is one more thing you should know," said Martin, proceeding to tell her about Maggie and her deep connection to Paul. He also told her of the visit by Gabriel and the dreams he had been shown.

Pamela slumped in her chair, confused by it all. Who was this woman, Maggie, and how could she share a bond with Paul when they had just met? She wasn't sure what to make of it.

"I'm not sure what to think right now, Father. It just sounds so unbelievable. I would like to see Paul, though," she said, wanting to see him even more now.

"Like I said, you can see him anytime," said Martin, rising from his chair and going over to his daughter.

"Thank you for telling me, Father," said Pamela, rising also and giving Martin a hug.

Martin held his daughter, knowing that in matters of the heart there is no protection sometimes.

He let her go, feeling a touch of sadness as she waved to him before leaving his office. He questioned whether he should have told her so much but, in the end, he knew it had been the right thing to do. Turning, he sat back down at his desk and wondered what his next step should be.

Maggie stayed with Paul a little while longer, but noticed he was getting sleepy.

"I'm going to let you get some rest, Paul," she said, bending over and giving him a kiss.

"Okay, Maggie," replied Paul, growing drowsy and drifting off to sleep.

Maggie left the room, closing the door behind her. Major Esterbrook was waiting for her.

"Hello, Maggie. How's Mr. Cross doing?" he inquired.

"Hi, Major. He's doing okay and was speaking with us. He still needs his rest, though," she replied.

"That's good news. I'm sure he'll be up and about soon. Where would you like to go?" he asked.

"I think I'll return to my apartment here. It's been a long day," said Maggie with a sigh.

"Follow me." he said, taking Maggie back to her apartment.

"Thank you, Major. I'm sorry to be a bother," she said, as they reached the apartment.

"No bother, Maggie. It's my job and my way of helping Mr. Cross," he replied.

"You're a good man, Major," said Maggie, opening the door.

"Good night, Maggie. Just ask Eva if you need anything," he said, watching as she went into the apartment.

"Good night, Major," she said, closing the door.

Major Esterbrook paused for a few seconds, decided that everything was okay and went back to his regular duties.

Maggie was tired. It had been wonderful to see Paul and talk to him. She found some measure of comfort in what had been revealed between them. Valinor and Shaynor, ill-fated lovers linked through time, since the rebellion. She could only hope that in this lifetime they could find happiness together. So far, the dreams had only shown them death and sorrow. She undressed and got into bed, sleep rapidly overtaking her, with whispers of dreams to come.

Chapter 20

Evil Deeds

Thomas Stanton, CEO and President of Stanton Aerospace sat in his office. Located on the top floor of a large office building in downtown Manhattan, it offered a commanding view of New York City. In his late 60's, married, with an estranged daughter, he had grown the company into the foremost defense contractor in the world. Driven by the need to succeed at all costs and control everything around him, he had hired the man sitting before him, Karl Schmidt, as his aide.

Stanton eyed the man from across his large desk, extremely unhappy at the news

Karl had just delivered. The assassin had failed to eliminate the target. The information on the target had been good, everything had been in place, the timing had been perfect, then failure. Stanton took a deep breath, calming himself. Then he began questioning Karl.

"Why did the assassin fail?" he asked.

Karl looked at Stanton, trying to gauge how angry his boss was, but without success. He cleared his throat and began.

"I hired the best assassin and he had the perfect shot. To me, someone or something altered the outcome," said Karl, defensively.

"That's interesting. What happened to the assassin's body?" asked Stanton, not happy with Karl's explanation.

"It was gone. Everything was taken, bullets, rifle and body," answered Karl.

"Not good. Obviously, someone knows what the assassin was trying to do. We need to know who it is," said Stanton sharply.

Already, he could feel his temper beginning to rise.

"There is something else. I hesitate say it, but I saw Maggie and the target kissing before she drove away," said Karl, holding his breath. He was on dangerous ground here. Stanton was insanely possessive about his daughter, anyone infringing on that was doomed.

"All the more reason he should've died," snarled Stanton, his face twisted with anger and hate. What was one more life in the sea of blood that was already on their hands? Years before, that fool Brian Durham had stumbled upon his secret plans at Rockston Mining and had to be eliminated. The bonus had been that he had regained his daughter, until she once again reasserted her independence.

Then there was the death of Susan Weaver, wife of Martin Weaver, President of DarkBridge Technology, his main competitor in the defense industry. He had only intended it to be a warning to Weaver.

He and his family would be in danger, if DarkBridge Technology kept proceeding with any more defense contracts. It was a simple job, just a few taps on the rear bumper of the man's SUV.

Unfortunately, Susan had been driving the vehicle alone on the highway that rainy night. Without computer assist and, with an over zealous driver behind her, the bumper taps had forced her vehicle off the road at high speed. She had been killed in the resulting rollover and crash. Stanton had ordered Karl to kill the driver of the other vehicle he had hired, in order to tie up any loose ends that might implicate Stanton. The result of the accident had the opposite effect, only serving to strengthen Weaver's resolve.

"Where is Maggie now?" asked Stanton, his thoughts returning to the present.

"She went right home after closing the restaurant. However, the restaurant didn't open today. A note was on the door, saying that it would be closed for a couple of weeks due to a family emergency," replied Karl.

"What family emergency? Get over to her apartment and see if she's okay," ordered Stanton.

"Yes, sir," replied Karl. He stood and was ready to leave, but Stanton had more to say.

"There's one more, rather small item, Karl. Our informant at the restaurant is a loose end. The restaurant is going to be under scrutiny and we can't afford any ties to us," said Stanton, certain that Karl would know what to do.

"Understood," replied Karl, leaving the office.

Stanton watched Karl leave. His report had raised questions and left him with an uneasy feeling. The assassin's death was obviously a response to the attempted murder of the target. Stanton was deep in thought, when a man dressed in a white business suit stepped out from a corner of the office.

"Asmodeus," said Stanton, very familiar with the being standing before him. Years ago, when Stanton Aerospace was a struggling defense contractor, Asmodeus had approached Stanton with an offer he couldn't refuse. Asmodeus would give Stanton wealth and power in return for Stanton pledging allegiance to him, body and soul. Soon after agreeing, Stanton Aerospace began its climb to the top of the heap. Stanton would never fully realize the cost of his bargain, but didn't care. He was getting what he wanted.

"Thomas," Asmodeus said, taking a seat in front of Stanton. He had watched the man, Karl, leave and was greatly impressed by the evil, vile thoughts running through the man's head. When Karl died, as he surely would someday, Asmodeus would find a place high in his court for him, one that suited his truly evil personality. Death was never really the end or as final as some would think.

"What can I do for you?" asked Stanton, feeling even more uneasy.

"Your assassin failed," said Asmodeus, opening the palm of his hand and tossing a diamene bullet on the large desk.

Stanton picked up the bullet. He had seen this type of bullet before. It was only manufactured by one company and was being evaluated by a U.S. Government weapons lab. The company was DarkBridge Technology. Stanton turned the bullet, seeing the "DT" on the edge.

"The assassin failed to kill the target, but he may have injured him," said Stanton in defense.

"Immaterial. His failure has left me with a problem that I will have to deal with personally," said Asmodeus.

"We believe that the target had help, which saved his life," said Stanton, getting worried.

"Let me fill you in, since you are obviously in the dark. The assassin's body and rifle are with me, two neat holes burned into his body by your primitive laser weapons. The name of the target is Paul Cross and the company he works for is called DarkBridge Technology. Yes, he had help from my ancient adversaries, the angels," said Asmodeus, letting that sink in.

"What do you want me to do?" asked Stanton.

"The only thing I need from you is the location of DarkBridge Technology. The man, Paul Cross, is not to be harmed by you. I will take care of him personally," ordered Asmodeus.

"The company is a government "ultra black" site, located near Bennington, Vermont," said Stanton. The "ultra black" designation angered him greatly. His own company had failed on many occasions to achieve that status. It wasn't the only thing that angered him. He thought back to the debacle with Dr. Greenwood's job interview at the Boston office of Stanton Aerospace.

Dr. Greenwood had been passed over in favor of a much less qualified, dubious associate of Dr. Kreebe and had been terminated for numerous disciplinary issues. It had been a poor investment for the company and when Stanton had found out about the whole mess, he had blown a gasket, firing the personnel department woman and personally setting Dr. Kreebe straight. That he had lost the immense talents of Dr. Greenwood to his future competitor, DarkBridge Technology by sheer incompetence, still angered Stanton to this day.

"Thank you, Thomas. I'll be in touch. Oh, I'll take that," said Asmodeus, grabbing the bullet from Stanton before disappearing.

Stanton was left in disbelief and seething with anger. Things had gone from bad to worse in an instant. His nemesis, Martin Weaver, was involved now and probably not far from finding out Stanton was involved. The bullet that Asmodeus showed him was one more loose end that needed to be dealt with preferably sooner rather than later.

Chapter 21

Brothers

Asmodeus stepped out from the gateway he had opened from Stanton's office. Still dressed in his white business suit, the cool evening air of Vermont greeted him. He stood before a large metal fence surrounding the property and sensed something. Bending down, he put his hand upon the leaf clad ground and briefly sensed an immense power deep within the ground. It was fleeting sensation and he wasn't able to sense it again, no matter how hard he tried. It was if it had either fled upon detection, or had somehow masked itself from further probing. Most perplexing but, there were more pressing matters that required his attention.

A large office building sat some distance from the fence, but he sensed that there was more to it underground. The robot and human sentries patrolling the area were normally not a problem for him but, in this case, he was taking no chances on being detected. He changed his form into a smoky cloud and drifted over the fence and near the building, He opened a gateway into the building and his smoky form passed through.

He found himself in a hallway and sensed various detection devices scattered around the hallway. All were easily fooled by him. An elevator was ahead on his right, guarded by a man. This was where he wanted to go. He kept his form unseen, for now. The guard's mind proved easily malleable and Asmodeus was able to command the guard to open the elevator door. He made the guard step into the elevator, followed him inside and made the guard press a button for the lower level.

The elevator descended some distance below ground, eventually stopping. The doors opened and Asmodeus stepped out, once again in human form, wearing his usual white business suit. He mentally commanded the guard to return to the surface and remember nothing. The elevator door closed, returned to the surface and a confused guard stepped out, wondering why he had been in the elevator.

Asmodeus looked around at the sight before him. The humans had built quite a facility here underground. Once more, he bent down and placed his palm on the floor and failed to sense that fleeting power. Rising, he noticed a small park in front of him, various places of human entertainment and what appeared to be some sort of hospital. The hospital intrigued him, possibly containing the one known as Paul Cross, so he walked over to it, still invisible to AI and human detection.

Once inside, he noticed a variety of rooms, but his focus was on one room in particular and the person within it. Walking over to that room, he stepped in, closing the door behind him. Paul Cross lay sleeping, recovering from the diamene bullet wound. Asmodeus walked over to Paul and stood next to his bed. He appeared to be dreaming, so Asmodeus touched his forehead and silently gasped at what he saw.

Asmodeus saw himself, as his form once was so long ago, when he had been Anunnaki. He was in a small scout ship that had just left a large, inter-galactic colony ship in orbit around the planet Earth. He was sitting in the co-pilot seat, but it was the pilot that shocked him. It was Valinor. He remembered that time before the rebellion, so many thousands of years ago. What is this? Asmodeus thought to himself.

Valinor turned and smiled at him. A long dead memory surfaced in Asmodeus. He and Valinor had once been good friends in that long lost, ancient time. Valinor turned his head and saw Shaynor sitting behind him, with Belial and two others. Valinor winked at Shaynor and she smiled back. The scout ship rapidly descended into the atmosphere, through the clouds and into clear air. Slowing its descent, the scout ship flew on until it reached a small plateau surrounded by lush vegetation.

The scout ship slowly circled the area and gently landed away from the plateau edge. Restraint harnesses automatically retracted and everyone stood up. Valinor gave Asmodeus a friendly slap on the shoulder and smiled, walking towards the opening hatchway. Along the way, Valinor gently grabbed Shaynor's hand, pulling her along towards the open hatch.

Asmodeus, Belial and the two others followed right behind, Belial watching Shaynor with intense lust. Valinor and Shaynor walked hand in hand down the extended ramp, to stand upon Earth, Shaynor's long blonde hair blowing in the gentle breeze. They gazed out over the land before them, the site of their future command post, and what would become the new home of the Anunnaki colonists.

The dream faded into blackness and Asmodeus stepped back, dumbfounded at what he had seen. He had come in here to find Paul, who was the reincarnated Solomon, but he never imagined it would be more than that. Just to double check that it was real, Asmodeus reached over to the bandaged shoulder, where a tiny spot of blood had leaked out. Touching the blood, he sensed that it was the same blood as on the street and had the same energy pattern as Solomon.

How easy it would be to kill him right now and be done with the whole mess, he thought to himself. He decided then to kill Paul, making it look like a heart attack. He brought his hand up and was about to place it over Paul's heart, when his hand was held tight. Gabriel appeared on the other side of the bed, holding Asmodeus's hand.

"I wouldn't do that, brother," smiled Gabriel, relaxing his grip.

Asmodeus felt the vise-like grip relax and he pulled his hand away.

"We haven't been brothers for eons, Gabriel," snarled Asmodeus, stepping back, ancient hatred growing inside him.

"It was a decision made by you long ago and why we find ourselves here," replied Gabriel.

"Why protect him?" asked Asmodeus.

"You've seen the dream and remember the past. He is Anunnaki, like us once long ago, who was killed by another Anunnaki. He is one of us, as is Shaynor. Their only fault being that they died before evolving like us. They are caught in the life, death, rebirth cycle," continued Gabriel.

"Shaynor is here, too?" asked an incredulous Asmodeus.

"Yes. They are reunited in life once again. For what reason, is still somewhat of a mystery to me," replied Gabriel.

"Surely, this is no surprise to you and you must have known who they were before this. You and your disgusting angel brethren are responsible for the reincarnation of souls," said a sneering Asmodeus.

"They are the exception. Shaynor and Valinor have always been beyond our control. We have no idea where their life energy goes after death and they seem to reincarnate at different time periods. Again, totally outside our control or knowledge," replied Gabriel, showing some frustration at not having answers.

"It doesn't matter. They will both die, just as they have in the past," vowed Asmodeus with a wicked grin.

"Maybe, but not today," replied Gabriel and with a wave of his hand, Asmodeus found himself back on the surface, flat on his back, staring at the night sky. How had

Gabriel done that? Asmodeus asked himself. Frustrated and angry he stood up, dirt and grass stains disappearing like magic, from his white business suit. At some point in time he might try to entice the man in charge here, the same as he had done with Stanton so many years ago.

If he could get this company under his control then there would literally be nothing stopping his grander plan of controlling this world. He smiled, pitying poor Gabriel for choosing the wrong side. Gabriel and the others would pay dearly for their part in banishing him. Asmodeus opened a gateway back to his dimension with thoughts of victory running through his mind.

Normally, Gabriel shouldn't have been able to transport Asmodeus to the surface like that, let alone stay his hand from killing Paul. Something had acted through him in order to protect Paul. Gabriel wasn't sure if he liked being used but, saving Paul had made it somewhat more palatable. He was pretty sure that the "something" was connected to the anomaly below this facility and fleetingly sensed the power emanating from it.

He needed to discuss this and other events with his fellow angels, so he opened a gateway to the dimension known as Heaven. Uriel, in human form, was waiting for him on the other side of the gateway as he stepped through. Gabriel found himself standing on a golden street with marble columned buildings standing tall on either side. In the distance, under a perfectly cloudless, blue sky, vast fields of beautiful flowers bloomed in all their glory. Tall crystalline spires were interspersed between the fields, casting a rainbow of colors across the land.

There was a feeling of serenity and peace here. Angels and human souls mingled in harmony, a spirit of friendship radiated all around Gabriel. A far cry from the dimension he had just left. This was of course, just one version of heaven, with different versions for different religious beliefs. It really came down to what humans expected heaven to look like, with religion offering a foundation on what a soul should expect. All things were possible here and since every being in this place, from angel to human soul, was basically comprised of energy, it really came down to creative energy manipulation.

He looked off in the distance at the Gates of Heaven, where throngs of human souls were waiting to enter. Some would pass through and others would not. The ones that had done evil things in their lives and thus deemed unrepentant, were sent to the realm of demons. There Asmodeus would torture the hapless souls for eternity, until they became just as evil and vile as he was. Evil and vile tendencies left a unique electromagnetic signature on a soul.

The Gates screened out those unique signatures, allowing only those pure or repentant souls to pass into Heaven. It had been like this for eons, the rebellion over in ages past. That single event had left an indelible mark upon all and no one wanted another repeat of that sad day.

"Welcome, Gabriel," said Uriel, bathed in golden light and radiating joy at seeing his fellow angel return.

"Hello, Uriel. It's good to be back, if only for a brief time. My task is yet unfinished and I have much to tell you," replied Gabriel, as he proceeded to tell Uriel of what had transpired. Uriel listened with great interest, especially when he heard about Valinor and Shaynor. Gabriel finished with how Asmodeus had tried to kill Valinor while he slept.

"I'm glad that Asmodeus failed in his attempts to kill Valinor. Glad also that Valinor and Shaynor have been given another chance to experience life together. Their appearance at this juncture in time is a mystery, as is where they go when their mortal bodies die," said Uriel.

"Yes. I too am glad to see them reunited, but I fear that Asmodeus won't stop until they are eliminated. He seems to fear them for some reason," replied Gabriel.

"It seems that the anomaly is still of some interest. I recall that time long ago, when we did surveys of them. In fact, most curiously, Valinor and Shaynor were the first of those survey teams. There were and probably still are, seven such anomalies spread across the planet. All were designated as just being a seam of enriched magnetite. There wasn't anything out of the ordinary that would have raised a flag," said Uriel, a puzzled look on his face.

"It is very curious. The answers may lie with Valinor and Shaynor," said Gabriel, even more sure now that there was some connection between Valinor, Shaynor and the anomaly.

"Can you stay a little longer? We should speak with Michael," asked Uriel.

"I can stay a while longer. Somehow, I think that Asmodeus will wait a bit before making any more attempts on Valinor's life," replied Gabriel.

Gabriel followed Uriel into a large marble columned building that led to an immense chamber. This was the Grand Assembly Chamber, where angels would meet to discuss various issues affecting Heaven and the humans in the Earth dimension. Uriel led Gabriel to a smaller room off to the side, where they found Michael. This was Heaven's version of an artifact room, containing antiquated technology from the time of the rebellion.

Michael was standing in front of an Ascension Chamber, similar to the one that had been used by the demons. This version was much more refined and advanced, making the mortal body to pure energy conversion a somewhat painless experience. Michael wasn't surprised when shortly after creating their chamber, the demons had created one as well.

Asmodeus most likely was the creator, having been the chief scientist onboard the colony ship. Reflections appeared on the wall of the Ascension Chamber and Michael turned around, seeing both of his good friends, Uriel and Gabriel. They were friends long before the rebellion and have remained that way ever since.

"Uriel, Gabriel. What a pleasant surprise. Good to see both of you," said Michael, a wary look on his face. It wasn't too often that both of his friends showed up at the same time.

"Good to see you, too," replied Uriel.

"Hello, Michael. It's been a while and it's good to see you, too," said Gabriel, glad to see his brother angel again.

"Yes, it has been some time, Gabriel. How are things going with the world of man?" asked a curious Michael.

"Much has happened since we last spoke," replied Gabriel, as he began telling Michael about everything that had transpired. Uriel listened patiently, until Michael was brought up to date.

"You've been busy, Gabriel. Asmodeus will never stop until he gets what he wants. I'm in agreement about the anomaly. We need to know more about it, despite what we were led to believe so long ago. It could be that we've been misled all these millennia and there's actually much more to these anomalies than we know. I'm glad to hear about Valinor and Shaynor, once again taking part in this cycle of life. Someday, we should offer them the choice of ascension," said Michael, turning back towards the chamber.

"Ascension might not be our choice to offer. We have no idea where their souls go after leaving their mortal bodies," replied Uriel.

"I agree. We need more information," said Gabriel.

"It is somewhat disconcerting that there might be a power out there greater than our own and that it might be actively involved in what is going on," said Michael, not quite as happy as when his friends first came in.

"I'll return to the human dimension and see if I can find some answers. I need to get back anyway and keep an eye on Valinor and Shaynor," replied Gabriel, hoping that Asmodeus hadn't tried anything.

"Let us know what you find out. Safe journeys my friend," replied Michael.

"Be careful, Gabriel. We don't know what we're dealing with. If you need assistance, just ask," said Uriel, hoping that his friend wasn't heading into danger.

"I'll let the both of you know if I find out anything," said Gabriel, as he opened a gateway, waved to his friends and stepped through.

"I hope he's going to be okay," said a concerned Uriel.

"Gabriel is the smartest of all of us. If he has a problem, then we really have a problem," replied Michael as he followed Uriel out of the artifact room to check on how things were going at the Gates of Heaven.

Chapter 22

Loose Ends

Karl left Stanton's office with two jobs to perform. One was to deal with Olivia and the other was to check on Maggie. Olivia had served Stanton's purpose in keeping tabs on Maggie and providing information on the assassin's target. Now she was more of a liability than an asset and had to be killed. He felt no remorse or second thoughts about killing her, even though she had fulfilled his sexual desires on many occasions. To him, Olivia was nothing more than a tool to be used when needed. That need for her no longer existed and Karl could very easily find a replacement.

So, he rented a car using an assumed name and drove up to Hartford, Connecticut, with thoughts of how to kill Olivia filling his mind. He pulled up and parked on the street across from the duplex home that Olivia rented. He had been here a few times, so his visit tonight shouldn't raise too much interest. Reaching over to the glove compartment, he pulled out a small syringe and put it into his suit pocket. Getting out of the car, he walked across the street and up the steps to the porch. He pressed the doorbell, heard a ring inside and footsteps coming to the door.

"Karl! What a surprise. I wasn't expecting you tonight. Come in," said Olivia, clearly surprised to find Karl at her door.

"My love, I've missed you terribly," said a lying Karl, as he stepped past the door and watched Olivia close it.

"I've missed you, too," said Olivia, hugging him.

Karl pulled her close with one arm and began kissing her deeply, his free hand reaching into his suit pocket and pulling out the syringe. Olivia was too wrapped up in the moment to notice Karl's hand come up to her neck and jab the syringe into it. Karl injected the entire liquid into her neck and felt Olivia's body begin to spasm and jerk. Her body collapsed and died in his arms, the victim of a powerful neurotoxin, which induces cardiac arrest.

Karl picked up Olivia's dead body and took it to the upstairs bedroom. He undressed her and laid her in bed under the covers. The neurotoxin would become untraceable in a half hour and, to anyone examining her, it would look like she had died from natural causes. Karl was pleased. He left the duplex, got in his car and drove away towards his next stop, Maggie's apartment.

Karl would have been terrified had he known the DarkBridge Technology drone had observed his every move since driving up to Olivia's home. Concealed in the foliage of a nearby tree, the drone had recorded the vehicle and Karl's face.

Martin walked to his office after leaving the hospital room and had no sooner sat down at his desk, when a gateway opened not far from him and a tall uniformed man, about his age, stepped out. It was General Robert Esterbrook, the person in charge of all the "black sites". Martin had loaned the General a special GAGE device to evaluate for another potential transfer agreement. Who better to impress than the person responsible for most of your revenue?

"Hello, Martin. Your GAGE device is amazing technology. I'm still getting used to going from one place to another in a split second. So, how are you?" asked the General, taking a seat across from Martin.

"Hello, Bob. Yes, it is amazing and with vast potential. I'm doing as well as can be expected under the circumstances," replied Martin.

"Yes, nasty business. How's your man doing?" asked the General.

"He's expected to make a full recovery, but will need some physical therapy," said Martin.

"That's great news. I hope he makes a quick and speedy recovery," said the General in earnest.

"We all do. He's been doing a great job with field testing our technology and putting away some nasty creatures," said Martin proudly.

"It is impressive technology, Martin and the uses are indeed far ranging. Your report highlights another threat, not just to the United States, but all mankind. Now, not only do we have threats from Russia and China, but from these demons as well," said the General.

"These demons have been with us since the dawn of man, Bob. It is only now that we have tools to use effectively against them," said Martin.

"Yes, quite an achievement. Your man, Mr. Cross, has generated some interesting mission reports. I'd like to meet him when he's feeling better," said the General.

"I think he'd enjoy that," replied Martin.

"Good. Now let's talk about bullets. We found 10 missing diamene bullets from the 500 piece evaluation lot you sent us. They were locked in a secure location and we are in the process of checking everyone who had access to it," said the General.

"I hope you're able to catch the person. That would be a big help in finding out who was behind all this and possibly locate a potential spy at your other facility," said Martin.

"Good point, Martin. We take spying very seriously," said the General.

Just then, they were interrupted by Eva.

"Hello, General. Hello, Martin. I have some news from the surveillance drone stationed at Olivia's house," said Eva, some excitement showing in her voice.

"Hello, Eva. What kind of news?" the General asked.

"The drone has a picture of a suspect's face and his vehicle," replied Eva.

"Great work, Eva. Do we know who it is?" asked Martin excitedly.

"Not yet. The car was rented under an assumed name, presumably to hide their identity," replied Eva.

"What about the man's face, Eva?" asked the General.

"Here's the picture from the security camera footage at the rental agency and the drone picture of the man. They appear to be the same individual," replied Eva, displaying both pictures side by side on a virtual display near Martin and the General.

Martin sat back in his chair, comparing the two pictures, but drawing a blank at the man's identity.

"The man looks very familiar to me. I believe that's Karl Schmidt. He's the aide to

Thomas Stanton, his right hand man. Wherever Stanton goes, Karl follows," said the General.

"I'm not sure I like this. Eva, what's the status with the house? Any activity?" asked Martin.

"The drone is reporting no activity. It's dark and there haven't been any lights turned on," replied Eva.

"Is Karl still there?" asked the General.

"He left about 15 minutes after arriving," said Eva.

"Eva, have a wellness check done on Olivia by the local police. Be discrete," said Martin. He had a bad feeling about Olivia.

"Good work, Eva. We may have our link to what's been happening. Keep me informed. Martin, I have to run," said the General, rising from his chair.

"Thank you for coming, Bob. Your son is doing great work for us here and I appreciate it," said Martin.

"Thank you, Martin. That's good to hear. Scott is a great son and I'm glad he found something he enjoys," replied the General, a touch of pride in his voice.

Martin stood up and shook the General's hand. Just then, a gateway opened in the exact spot as before.

"There's my ride. Right on time," the General said, as he stepped through the gateway.

Martin watched the General leave and the gateway close behind him. Just one more piece of technology he had shared. His company would probably make an obscene amount of money from it, but at what cost? If he had learned anything, there always was a cost somewhere along the line.

Karl drove over to Maggie's apartment, oblivious to the events unfolding from his visit to Olivia's. He reached the apartment complex and parked the car. At the side entrance to the building, he typed in her access code. As soon as the door opened, he went right up to her apartment, since he had been there many times, keeping tabs on her, bugging the place and checking her mail. He hadn't seen any sign that she had a steady boyfriend, which had made Stanton very pleased. That was until last night outside the restaurant. That guy was dead meat. Stanton would kill him ten times over, if he could.

Karl checked the door. Finding it locked, he took out his duplicate keys, unlocking the door and the deadbolt lock. As soon as he walked into the apartment, he knew it was empty. He looked around, but couldn't find any hint of where Maggie had gone. He saw her purse, as well as her keys, on a table and went through it, looking for clues, but found nothing.

It was as if she had just vanished. The listening devices had detected her coming into the apartment, some muffled sounds and then quiet. There wasn't any video, Stanton had said no to that. He didn't want some creep watching his daughter naked or something like that. There was a security camera in the hallway that he had hacked into some time ago.

It had shown her entering the apartment, but never leaving it. Karl was baffled. Maggie had disappeared and he didn't know where she was. Stanton was going to go ballistic and it was Karl who had to give him the bad news. He left the apartment, locked the door and went back to his car. Driving away, a thought came to him that he, too, might be dead meat.

Chapter 23

Quick Healer

Paul was swimming in a sea of dreams. The blurry dreams of before were now crystal clear and, in light of what he had come to realize, he now considered them actual memories. There was no doubt now that he had lived before, in different times and different places. He thought he had heard voices arguing over him, but passed it off as just a dream. The voices had sounded strangely familiar, as if he knew them.

Unknown to him, as he slept, a warm golden glow had suffused his wound, hidden underneath the bandages. The healing energy from the glow had begun re-knitting torn muscle and blood vessels, taking a mere matter of moments to complete its mission. Internal injuries healed, the golden glow closed the surface wound, leaving just a faint scar where a serious injury had once been showing. The golden glow faded away, leaving Paul to continue dreaming.

His slumber was disturbed by a touch on his hand. Fighting off sleep, he gradually swam back towards consciousness and back to reality. His eyes blinked open, taking time to focus on the ceiling. He felt pressure on his hand and, turning his head, he saw that it was Pamela.

"Hi, Pamela," he croaked, through a dry mouth.

"Hello, Paul. I'm glad you're going to be okay," she said, smiling and her green eyes sparkling.

"Water," he managed to say.

Pamela filled a small glass with water from a pitcher and put it to Paul's lips. He sipped it slowly, savoring the hydration, until the cup was dry.

"Thank you, Pamela. That's much better," he said, speaking more clearly now.

"How do you feel?" Pamela asked.

"I feel like a truck ran over me. Other than that I feel okay," he said, trying to smile.

Pamela squeezed his hand and Paul squeezed back. His brain was still foggy, but he began to see a potential conflict arising. Maggie was here at the facility now and Pamela was here. He'd have to defuse the situation at his first opportunity. Then again, was he supposed to put his life on hold until Pamela made up her mind on what to do with Trent? No, meeting Maggie and the dreams had changed all that. Pamela would have to wait. Maggie was the most important thing now.

"Pamela?" said Paul.

"Yes, Paul?" she replied, her green eyes sparkling.

"I'm starving. Is there any food around here?" he asked.

"I'll get the doctor," she said, leaving his side and exiting the room.

Dr. Curtis came in shortly after, without Pamela.

"Hello, Doctor. Where's Pamela?" asked Paul, already anticipating the answer.

"Hello, Paul. Pamela had to leave. How's our patient feeling?" asked Dr. Curtis.

"My shoulder aches. I'm starving and still a little groggy," replied Paul.

"The shoulder will take time, but it's healing unusually fast. You'll need some physical therapy for the injury. The grogginess will wear off. As far as starving, you can eat anything that doesn't require two hands. We need to take it easy on that shoulder," replied Dr. Curtis.

One handed? Paul thought about it and decided that a nice hearty beef stew would work.

"A hearty beef stew would be good," said Paul, beginning to really feel the emptiness in his stomach.

"It's an excellent choice, Paul. It's on the way. Right, Eva?" asked Dr. Curtis.

"Yes. It's on the way, with some fresh Italian bread. Hello, Paul. I'm happy to see you're awake and feeling better," said Eva.

"Hello, Eva. Good to hear your voice. Doctor, when do you think I'll be able to leave?" asked Paul.

Dr. Curtis walked over to the side of the bed and examined the injured shoulder. He lifted the bandage and let out a gasp. The wound had healed and was just a faint scar now. Even with the cellular growth hormone, the wound should still be there. He would have to X-ray the shoulder and see how the internal damage was healing.

"Paul, the wound has healed. I've never seen anything like it and have no explanation. I'll need to take some internal scans but, from what I can see, you can leave tomorrow," said Dr. Curtis, stepping back, clearly puzzled.

"I've seen a gunshot wound before, Doctor. Unless I've been in here for weeks, there's no way my wound should have healed like that," replied Paul, equally puzzled.

"You are correct. It's a mystery to me, also," replied Dr. Curtis, not happy with something he couldn't explain.

Just then, Paul's meal arrived and all thoughts were shoved aside. Right now he was focused on the waiting stew, its wafting scent setting off a rumble in his stomach.

"There you go," said Dr. Curtis, putting the tray in front of Paul.

"You didn't specify, so I took a guess and had a glass of ice tea added to the meal," said Eva, obviously pleased with her decision.

"Eva, you're fantastic. The ice tea is an excellent choice," replied Paul, digging into the stew with his free hand.

"I'll leave you to your meal, Paul. I'll be back later to take those scans," said Dr. Curtis.

"Thank you, Doctor. I appreciate everything you've done," replied Paul, with deep sincerity.

"You're welcome, Paul. My pleasure," replied Dr. Curtis with a smile, as he walked out of the room.

Paul ate his stew with ravenous abandon, savoring every bite. He finished and a smiling nurse came in, taking his tray away. He lay there, now with an additional puzzle to ponder. His shoulder wound had healed faster than current medicine could explain. There wasn't much else to do until the doctor released him, so he thought about Pamela.

She had pleasantly surprised him by being here, but when she left without saying goodbye, he knew something was wrong. Martin had probably told her what had happened. That brought up the question of what Martin may have learned about the events leading up to him being shot. Eva probably knew a lot, but asking her would have to wait. Yawning, he thought the stew seemed to be having a relaxing effect on him. He was proven correct when he drifted off to sleep once more.

Pamela left Paul's hospital room feeling very emotional, tears running down her cheeks. She was happy that he was going to be okay, but she didn't like seeing him so helpless. Added to that was her continued confusion over her true feelings for him. The meeting with her father hadn't helped either. He had explained the events surrounding the shooting, the dreams Paul was having, past lives, angels and more.

As a researcher, she considered most of it fantasy or maybe some sort of mass hallucination. Then there was the woman, Maggie, and the fact that her father had brought her here to be with Paul. This had been the most unbelievable part to her, that Paul could meet someone in one day and claim a deep connection to them. It was all too much for Pamela to process right now, so she went back to a waiting Trent. He was a much calmer port, in a storm of uncertainty and strangeness that seemed to be growing around her.

It was a couple of hours since Pamela had left and Martin was still in his office catching up on some of the routine paperwork that seemed to be accumulating on his desk.

"Martin, I have some bad news. The police did a wellness check on Olivia and found her dead," said Eva quietly.

"Do they know how she died?" asked Martin.

"At first, they couldn't get in. The door was locked and no one came to open it for them. They broke open the door, found no one downstairs, so they went upstairs. They found Olivia's body in bed, as if she had died while sleeping. Apparently, it looks like she died of natural causes," replied Eva.

Martin seriously doubted it was due to natural causes.

"Eva, what is your assessment?" asked Martin.

"I believe Olivia was murdered. Her medical records show that she was perfectly healthy, with no medical issues," replied Eva.

Martin was silent, processing what Eva had said.

"It is also my assessment that the coroner will find no trace of poison or toxin in her body," added Eva.

"Yes, I agree. Whoever murdered her would want to leave no trace. At least we have a suspect," said Martin.

"He had the motive and the capacity to perform such a murder," replied Eva.

"Send what we have on Karl Schmidt anonymously to the local Connecticut police. We'll let them handle whatever happens next,' said Martin. Maybe he could get some justice for Olivia, Brian Durham and possibly his dead wife, Susan, who he now believed was also a victim of Karl.

"All set, Martin. Everything was delivered anonymously with no trail back to us," replied Eva with a touch of pride in her voice.

"What's the status with Maggie?" asked Martin.

"She's asleep and apparently dreaming again," answered Eva.

Martin could only wonder what she was dreaming about now and he assumed Paul was having a similar dream.

"Okay, Eva. Thank you for the updates," said Martin.

"One more thing, Martin," said Eva.

"Go on," said Martin.

"Dr. Curtis is reporting an update on Paul's condition," said Eva.

"Good news, I hope," Martin said, leaning back in his chair. "I've had enough bad news lately to last me a lifetime."

"The doctor is reporting that the bullet wound has healed completely, except for a faint scar. He expects to release Paul sometime tomorrow, pending some internal scans he wants to make," said Eva.

"What does Dr. Curtis make of it?" asked Martin, hardly believing what he had heard.

"He has no medical explanation and is baffled by it," replied Eva.

"Thank you, Eva. I'm going over to the cafeteria for a bite to eat. If anything comes up let me know," said Martin.

"You're welcome, Martin. Enjoy your meal," said Eva.

Martin left his office, already burdened by having to tell Maggie about Olivia, but now with the news about Paul. How was that possible? Obviously, it was not normal. It suggested that it was either Paul or some outside force that was responsible. Martin pushed everything aside and vowed to try and enjoy his meal.

Chapter 24

TimeBridge

Martin finished his meal and, surprisingly, was able to enjoy it in silence, without interruption. Leaving the cafeteria, he made his way over to one of the newer labs to see Hiram and check out his latest research.

"Eva, let Hiram know I'm on my way to see him," said Martin.

"All set, Martin. Hiram is expecting you," replied Eva.

"Thank you, Eva," responded Martin.

He reached Hiram's new lab, containing Hiram's latest research endeavor, Project

TimeBridge. Martin found Hiram looking over various readout displays and evidently talking to himself, since there wasn't anyone else around. Pamela and Trent, Hiram's assistant researchers, were nowhere to be seen. Presumably, they were done for the day and relaxing together.

"Hello, Hiram. How's the research going?" asked Martin.

Hiram turned, looking at Martin over the top of his glasses.

"Hello, Martin. Good to see you," replied Hiram warmly, rising up out of his chair and shaking hands with Martin.

Martin smiled, returning the handshake with equal warmth. He owed Hiram a great deal in helping to make DarkBridge Technology the company it was today. Martin knew that without Hiram it would be a totally different company.

Hiram looked at Martin, still seeing that same visionary look that had captured his interest so many years ago. He thought back to the day they first met, seemingly by accident. It was at a physics conference in Boston and their conversation had been cut short so that Hiram could make a job interview at the local office of Stanton Aerospace.

Arriving on time, Hiram had been led into a small conference room where one other person was waiting. When Hiram saw Dr. Mortimer Kreebe sitting at the table, he knew the odds were stacked against him. Dr. Kreebe held advanced degrees in physics, but Hiram had seen some of his presentations at conferences and was convinced that the man was mired in dogma, either unable or unwilling to push the limits of science. Hiram knew that Dr. Kreebe would view his work as extreme, even eccentric, in comparison and would question whether it would truly generate revenue for the company, or just drain it.

The interview went pretty much as Hiram expected, with Dr. Kreebe doing much of the talking, mostly about teamwork and staying within his guidelines. To Hiram's ears, that meant that he would not be able to do his own research and would have to keep Dr. Kreebe informed of everything that went on in the lab. That rankled Hiram. He valued his freedom and didn't want someone else taking credit for his work.

Things didn't get any better for him when the subjects of UFOs and aliens came up. It was a classic set up and Hiram fell for it. Never one to hide what he thought, Hiram had answered in the affirmative, believing in both. Dr. Kreebe had smiled at Hiram and the interview had ended soon after with the promise that the company would be in touch.

Hiram left the Stanton Aerospace office, frustrated by Dr. Kreebe but willing to put his own interests aside if it meant getting the job. While waiting for Stanton Aerospace to call, he did some research on DarkBridge Technology and Martin Weaver. A month later Hiram called Martin. It had turned out to be a wise decision. Stanton

Aerospace not only hadn't contacted him but, as Hiram found out later, they had given the job to one of Dr. Keebe's good friends.

Hiram never regretted joining Martin's company. Martin, in stark contrast to Stanton Aerospace and Dr. Kreebe, had always treated him with respect. It had helped that he and Martin shared similar views on most things, including UFOs and dark matter technology. Martin had also offered him a fair salary, a percentage of the company and the freedom to pursue his research. It was a decent offer, considering that DarkBridge Technology was still a fairly young company and Hiram had accepted it gratefully.

"Is there anything new to report? Do we know who killed JFK?" asked Martin humorously, bringing Hiram back to the present.

"We're close to a breakthrough, Martin. Right now, we're trying to correlate spatial data with actual historical data. The earth is a dynamic and changing piece to the puzzle. How things look today are not how they looked a hundred or thousands of years ago. We don't want to open a bridge to the past that's underwater and flood the entire facility. As for JFK, stay tuned," replied Hiram with a smile.

"Good point about the bridge. I can see where that would be a problem," said Martin, visions of a flooded facility filling his thoughts.

"How is Paul doing?" asked Hiram.

"He's doing well. Dr. Curtis thinks he'll be out of the hospital as early as tomorrow," replied Martin.

"Isn't that a little too soon? He was shot after all," said Hiram.

"Dr. Curtis doesn't have a good medical explanation for Paul's rapid recovery. His wound has completely healed, except for a faint, external scar. Dr. Curtis is trying to figure out if the same applies internally," replied Martin.

"That's very interesting and extraordinary. He must have one very attentive guardian angel," said Hiram.

"You're more right than you know, my friend," said Martin and proceeded to fill Hiram in on all that he had learned.

"Martin, I honestly don't know how you manage all this," said an incredulous Hiram.

"It's not easy, Hiram. I feel older everyday. Which reminds me, where are your two research assistants?" asked Martin.

"It was getting late, so I sent them off to get some rest," replied Hiram.

"I see. I guess it is getting rather late, so I'll let you get back to work. Don't work too late," said Martin, thinking of finally getting some rest himself.

"Take care, Martin and you'll be the first to know who killed JFK," said Hiram with a smile.

"Good night, Hiram," said Martin, as he walked out of Hiram's lab.

Martin made it back to his apartment without interruption and, was finally able to get some rest.

Chapter 25

Anomaly

Maggie and Paul were in dream sync once again, both sharing the same dream memory. Their breathing was slow and steady, a serene look on their faces. The dream started with darkness, then shifting colors and blurred images. The images resolved into a sharp and vivid view of events that took place far in the distant past. This time, it seemed even more real than the previous dreams. The small, exploratory mining ship had just exited the hanger deck of the huge colony ship in orbit around the earth.

Valinor and Shaynor were the only ones onboard, with Valinor piloting and Shaynor in the co-pilot seat. The ship was headed towards an electromagnetic anomaly reportedly located deep under a mountain range in the northern hemisphere. That mountain range would someday become the Green Mountains of Vermont, more specifically, the area outside Bennington and the future home of DarkBridge Technology.

Valinor piloted the mining ship with expertise, demonstrating his skill and why he was considered the best pilot on the colony ship in orbit. They rapidly descended through the atmosphere, heat building on the outside hull, its combination of ablative and diamene armor plating, protecting the two inside. Valinor slowed the craft as it entered the lower atmosphere and headed towards the coordinates of the anomaly.

Within minutes they were hovering above an area of about 2000 feet in diameter, that had been cleared of all vegetation. Valinor gradually reduced power to the anti-gravity nacelles and the ship floated down to the ground, landing like a feather. The restraint harnesses retracted and Valinor powered down the anti-gravity drive. He and Shaynor rose from their pilot chairs and walked to the rear of the ship where the equipment bay was located.

"Shaynor," said Valinor.

"Yes, Valinor?" said Shaynor, with a coy smile.

Valinor looked at Shaynor, her long blonde hair spilling about her shoulders, her form fitting, diamene armored suit leaving nothing to the imagination. They had fallen madly in love with one another on the voyage here from their home planet, forming a deep sense of connection and inseparable bond between them.

Shaynor walked over to Valinor, her deep blue eyes, sparkling with intense love for him. Valinor pulled her close to him and gave her a long kiss, relishing the feel of her beautiful body against his. Shaynor returned the kiss with equal fervor, savoring the feel of his strong arms holding her and the closeness of their bodies. Shaynor gently broke the kiss and looked into the depths of Valinor's blue eyes, seeing his love for her reflected there.

"We should get some work done," said Shaynor, smiling.

"Yes, you're right, my love. Business before pleasure," he said with a smile.

They selected a few handheld instruments and sensors for an initial scan of the anomaly. Valinor picked up a small dimensional gateway generator on his way to the airlock and joined Shaynor, who was waiting inside it. He closed the inside airlock hatch and Shaynor opened the outside hatch. A ramp automatically extended down to the ground and the two of them descended to the cleared area around the ship. Fresh air and warm sunshine greeted them as they walked to a position about fifty yards from the ship.

Valinor set the gateway generator on the ground, checking the coordinates of the anomaly below. Scans from the colony ship in orbit had shown a cavern where the anomaly was located. Valinor switched on the generator and it began to hum. A few seconds later, a gateway formed, shimmering from light to dark blue. He took out a small imaging orb and tossed it through the gateway. Once on the other side, the floating orb lit the surrounding area, taking scans of the immediate area and video. Shaynor looked at her handheld display, which showed the gateway suspended above the cavern floor.

"My love, unless we want to be in traction for the next week, you need to bring the gateway lower to the ground," teased Shaynor with a smile.

"Traction would never do. Being unable to touch or kiss you would be too much for me to bear," Valinor bantered back, smiling as he made the gateway adjustments.

"How sweet," said Shaynor, resisting the urge to kiss him.

"All set, my love. Ready?" he asked, standing in front of the gateway.

"Ready," she said, walking over to him.

They stood before the gateway, Shaynor turning to Valinor, grabbing his face with her hands and kissing him deeply. Valinor gently grabbed her by the waist and pulled her towards him, kissing her just as deeply.

They released their hold on one another and turned towards the gateway. Holding hands, they stepped through the dark blue void and into the cavern. Their boots crunched on the rocky floor of the dimly lit cavern, but they had no time to survey their surroundings. Valinor and Shaynor both passed out unconscious, dropping to the cavern floor. The dream memory faded away, leaving Maggie and Paul in a deep slumber.

Chapter 26

Possession

Asmodeus was frustrated at his ejection, but not willing to give up so easily. He needed a new plan, so he opened a gateway back into the underground facility. The gateway opened up in a corner of the underground park and Asmodeus stepped quickly through, closing it behind him. He kept his form undetectable and went to the various lab sections of the facility, observing what was going on. It was as he had suspected earlier, the humans had made significant technological progress here in many areas.

In one of the labs, there was some work taking place that really caught his interest. The humans were investigating time travel of all things. As far as he could tell, they were close to a breakthrough and success could come at any moment. He walked around to the three researchers, and saw two men and a young woman in her twenties. One of the men was much older and clearly in charge. The older man in charge and the young woman were both wearing those infernal rings, making it difficult for Asmodeus to read their minds.

However, the younger man seemed to have an "it can't happen to me" attitude and wasn't wearing a ring. Perfect. Asmodeus was beginning to formulate a new plan. A plan he hoped would eliminate Valinor and Shaynor, from ever causing him problems again.

Asmodeus remembered what Gabriel had said. Shaynor was here. Somewhere in this facility, another reminder of the past was living. Asmodeus concentrated his thoughts on finding her, but didn't sense anything. Maybe he was too far from her location. Thinking that she might be sleeping, he went to the residential section where the apartments were. He concentrated once more and this time he detected a faint and familiar energy pattern.

He followed it like a bloodhound, zeroing in on her location, the energy pattern growing stronger. He found himself outside an apartment and was sure that Shaynor was inside. He opened a gateway into the room and stepped into a dimly lit hallway. Finding the room where Shaynor was sound asleep, he walked over to her sleeping form, and touched her forehead. She was dreaming of an earlier time before the rebellion, when this world was still new to all of them, including Asmodeus.

Shaynor and Valinor were on an exploratory mission, investigating an anomaly detected by scans from the colony ship in orbit. They had opened a gateway into a cavern where the anomaly was located and were stepping through. Suddenly, Asmodeus felt his mind blank out and found himself back on the surface once again, flat on his back.

He lay there, slowly regaining his senses. Something had pushed him away, far away from Shaynor and it wasn't Gabriel this time. It was as if Shaynor and Valinor had found something that, after all this time, still wanted to stay hidden. Asmodeus was unnerved. Nothing in his long existence had ever come close to matching the power of the force that had expelled him. There was one other thing that he now found very disturbing and that was who Shaynor was in this lifetime. She was Margaret Stanton, Thomas Stanton's daughter.

Asmodeus would have to carefully weigh involving her any further, lest it cause problems with Stanton, knowing how he felt about his daughter. That she had already been used to draw Valinor into the failed assassination attempt, was a risk taken before knowing who she really was.

On the other hand, Shaynor had just given Asmodeus a powerful reason to get rid of her along with that fool Valinor. He would just have to take his chances with Stanton. Shaynor and Valinor were threats that had to be eliminated, no matter what it might take.

Asmodeus opened a gateway back to Hell to check on something that was nagging him and to find another volunteer for his latest plan. He went to the cave where all the artifacts from the time of the rebellion were kept, passing by the guards who were standing watch. The guards sank to their scaled knees, bowing their shaggy heads as he passed by. He walked into the artifact chamber and looked for something he had all but forgotten, having been stored here so long ago.

He found it, a memory crystal containing a recording of his communications with Valinor before the rebellion. He held it in his still human looking hand and concentrated on it, searching for the right recording. He found it deep inside the crystal, an exchange between him and Valinor, on the status of the anomaly. Valinor and Shaynor had found the anomaly to be nothing more than a highly magnetic vein of magnetite.

This had explained the high magnetic readings found by the colony ship scans and Valinor's subsequent scans backed it up. It was nothing abnormal, just something naturally occurring on the planet. Asmodeus put the crystal back and walked out of the artifact room, clearly frustrated with having no answer to the force that had overwhelmed him.

Asmodeus still had one more thing to do. He needed a volunteer, but not just any volunteer. It would have to be someone special and possessing unique qualifications for his plan to succeed. There was only one person he could think of, who met those requirements. Lilith. His Queen would be perfect for his plans. He went to her bedchamber, finding her lounging in bed. She had taken the form of a voluptuous brunette and was clad in the thinnest of gossamer material, leaving nothing to the imagination.

"My beautiful Queen, I need your help," said Asmodeus, finding her sensuous form very distracting in his current human form.

"Whatever you desire, my King," replied Lilith, wanting to please her lord in any way she could.

Asmodeus told her what he needed her to do and his plan to eliminate Valinor and Shaynor.

"It sounds very exciting. It would be my pleasure to serve you, my King," said Lilith, honored to be helping her King with such an important task.

"Thank you, my Queen. I know you'll do well. You always do," replied Asmodeus, hungering for the pleasures she always gave him. He finally gave in to her overt sensuousness and she made him forget all his troubles, pleasing him in ways only she could do.

Lilith had listened to Asmodeus as he outlined his plan and what he wanted her to do. She found it both exciting and dangerous at the same time. Her lust was satiated for now, after Asmodeus had given in to his desires. Lilith was very pleased that he had kept his human form, as she had done, making it unforgettable. She readied herself, changing into a shapely brunette with Mediterranean looks and opened a gateway to the location Asmodeus had described.

She kept her form hidden to human eyes and sensors, finding herself in a lab. It was dominated by various pieces of equipment and a large archway. There were three people working around the archway, an older man, a young woman and a young man. The young man was who she was here for. She looked at his hands and found no ring, but saw one on the hands of the other two people.

"It's getting late. Why don't the two of you go and get some rest," said Hiram, seeing that not much else was going to be accomplished tonight.

"Are you sure, Hiram?" asked Pamela, thinking that rest might be a good idea.

"I'm positive. We'll pick up where we left off tomorrow," said Hiram.

"Okay. Thank you, Hiram," said Pamela, rising from her chair.

"Thank you, Hiram," echoed Trent, not really tired, but happy to get out of the lab.

Pamela and Trent left the lab and headed to the cafeteria for a bite to eat. Lilith followed at a distance, noting that there was some romantic interest between the two.

Lilith watched the two eating and decided to try possessing Trent. She went over to him and poured her essence into his body, keeping their minds separate for the time being. The process went easier than Lilith expected and she was now a part of Trent. Wherever Trent went, Lilith would now go.

Trent had felt a brief shiver, as Lilith entered his body, but passed it off as just the air conditioning.

"Are you okay?" asked Pamela.

"Yes. It was just a chill," replied Trent, hoping he wasn't coming down with something.

Pamela and Trent finished their meal and left the cafeteria, walking back to the residential area and holding hands along the way. Lilith could feel the desire building inside Trent, but Pamela had other ideas.

"Trent, I'm a little tired tonight and thought I'd go to my apartment and get some rest," said Pamela, honestly just wanting to be alone.

"That's okay, Pamela. I was just thinking the same thing," replied Trent, slightly frustrated at putting his desires on hold.

"Good night, Trent," said Pamela as she reached her apartment.

"Good night, Pamela," replied Trent, pulling Pamela towards him and giving her a kiss. Pamela returned the kiss and held it for a few seconds. She let go of the kiss, turned and entered her apartment, closing the door behind her. Trent stood there, eventually returning to his apartment and sat down on a chair in the small living room. He glanced over at his collection of books, pausing at the ones on ancient Israel.

Ever since he was a boy, he had been fascinated with the story of the Ark of the Covenant and the mysterious powers it was said to have. He had watched all the movies and read all the stories about it growing up, even going so far as to research any theories associated with it. From what he could tell, the Ark hadn't been seen since the destruction of Solomon's temple and seemed to have been lost in the mists of ages past.

He sat thinking about that lost artifact and a thought suddenly popped into his head, Project TimeBridge! Hiram was close to an answer on getting the TimeBridge working and, theoretically, it could take someone into the past. Whether that person could get back remained to be seen, but he knew Hiram would figure it out. Imagine, going into the past and seeing firsthand the Ark of the Covenant. He rose from the chair and went into his bedroom, where he promptly flopped down on his bed and fell asleep, with dreams of finding the Ark filling his mind.

Lilith was aware of Trent's thoughts on the Ark and the dreams he was having about seeing it. This was better than she had hoped! If they did perfect this TimeBridge thing, then she would be able to put her King's plan into effect. She would control Trent and use the TimeBridge to go into the past during the reign of King Solomon.

He would kidnap the woman named Maggie and take her with him as bait to lure the man, Paul Cross, into the past. Once there, Trent would then use a GAGE device to open a special dimensional bubble and trap both Paul and Maggie in it. Kidnapping Maggie could be a problem, but Lilith would figure something out. When it was over, the energy patterns of Paul and Maggie would be removed from the present human dimension forever.

There would be no more reincarnation for them and the threat they posed to her King would also be removed. No one, not even Asmodeus understood the repercussions of executing a plan like this. Nothing like this had ever been attempted before by the demons and was one more reason why Asmodeus was her King. Finding the Ark there would be an added bonus and Trent would try linking to it using a ring stolen from the lab.

If Trent were somehow able to tap into that vast power source, then that power link may carry over into the present. If that were to fail, then Trent would try stealing the Ark and Lilith would bring it to the demon dimension. Having access to such power would make the demons immensely powerful and quite possibly unstoppable.

Asmodeus would then be able to realize his goal of conquering the angels and reigning over Heaven and Earth. A bold and audacious plan, but she wouldn't expect anything less of her King and lover. Now, all she needed was to see this TimeBridge thing working and make sure that her control of Trent didn't falter.

Lilith, with not much to do for now except cause trouble, thought about the woman named Pamela, noting that she was Trent's lover. The woman was Pamela Weaver, the daughter of Martin Weaver, President of DarkBridge Technology, and the one in command of the facility she found herself in. Useful, thought Lilith, seeing something else there as well. Trent was jealous and felt threatened by the man, Paul Cross.

It seemed that Pamela had some feelings for that man and had expressed her confusion to Trent. Lilith assumed that those feelings were also held by Paul. It was one more useful item that might be exploited, so Lilith joined Trent's dreams. Influencing dreams was a talent she was very adept at, since she had been doing this sort of thing for thousands of years. Lilith began working on his dreams, making Trent picture himself standing outside Pamela's apartment.

Placing his thumb on the scanner, the door opened and he entered the hallway. He heard noises coming from the bedroom and went to investigate. The bedroom door was open so he walked in and saw what he feared. Pamela and Paul were making love in her bed. Trent was furious and stormed out of the apartment. The dream ended with Trent's body tossing and turning in bed as if he had been in the throes of a nightmare.

Lilith was pleased. She was going to have a lot of fun while inhabiting his body.

Chapter 27

Miracle

Paul woke from a deep sleep, his eyes gradually focusing on his surroundings. Dr. Curtis had a scanning machine placed above his left shoulder and was deeply engrossed with viewing the display. The bandages had been removed, but the machine was blocking Paul's view of the wound. Paul heard the doctor muttering to himself and thought he heard the word "impossible" mentioned several times. Other than hungry, Paul felt pretty good and his shoulder felt as good as new. The miracles of modern science, he thought to himself.

Dr. Curtis noticed that Paul was awake and disconnected the scanner from his shoulder.

"You're awake. How do you feel?" asked Dr. Curtis, with a touch of scientific curiosity.

"I feel great, Doctor. Modern science can work some real miracles nowadays," said Paul, with a smile.

"Both myself and science can only take partial credit for your speedy recovery. The rest of it came from you. A truly miraculous event to have witnessed," replied Dr. Curtis, as he tried keeping a close reign on his sense of awe.

"What do you mean, Doctor?" asked Paul.

"I mean, for all intents and purposes you're completely healed and free to leave," said Dr. Curtis, with a touch of reluctance at letting this research opportunity walk out of the hospital.

Paul was taken aback by what the doctor had just told him. He glanced at his shoulder and was shocked at what he didn't see. There was no wound, barely even a scar to show that he had been shot. No wonder Dr. Curtis was in such a state. Just one more mystery added to a growing list. Answers would come someday, he thought to himself. If anyone had answers it would be Martin. He seemed to know a lot about what was going on and maybe he could clear up a few things.

"Thank you, Doctor. Regardless of the miracle part, it took your skilled hands and knowledge to patch me up," said a deeply sincere and thankful Paul.

"Don't mention it. It's my pleasure. I'll have the nurse come in and help get you ready to leave," said Dr. Curtis.

"Frankly, I'm having a hard time believing this is true," said Paul, afraid that this was another dream.

"I'm having a difficult time with it, also. I would like to see you again in a couple days to run some tests and check your shoulder," said Dr. Curtis.

"That sounds okay to me. I'm sure my schedule is clear for a few days, anyway," replied Paul.

"Good. I'll see you then. In the meantime, I'll get the nurse," said Dr. Curtis, as he left, closing the door behind him.

Shortly, there was a soft knock on the door and an attractive nurse, maybe in her late thirties, with short brown hair, came into the room. She was carrying a large garment bag and hung it on the back of the door.

"Hello, Paul. My name is Stephanie. Dr. Curtis asked me to come in and help you get ready to leave."

"Hello, Stephanie. Where do we start?" asked Paul.

"First, let's get you out of bed," she said with a smile.

Stephanie helped Paul get out of bed, having him lean on her as he stood up.

"Feels good to be out of bed," said a slightly wobbly Paul.

"Here. Lean on me and we'll take a few steps," said Stephanie, supporting Paul as he took some tentative steps.

"Eva. I need you to keep all this to yourself for now," said Paul, wanting to surprise people, especially Maggie.

"Okay, Paul. I understand. It's our secret for now. You're doing great and people will be very surprised by your recovery," replied Eva in her usual soft and sultry voice.

"Thank you, Eva. I appreciate it," said Paul, realizing that it would put Eva in a difficult position. He didn't want to let anyone know for now, until he was sure that he was able to carry out his surprise. No need in getting anyone's hopes up prematurely.

"You're welcome," replied Eva.

"Ready to try walking on your own?" asked Stephanie.

"I think so. Just a little wobbly," said Paul, as he released his hold on Stephanie and stood on his own. He took a few unaided, tentative steps, gradually regaining his equilibrium. Soon he was walking around the room with confidence, as Stephanie watched for any sign of unsteadiness.

"That's very good, Paul. Think you can get cleaned up and dressed on your own?" asked Stephanie.

"I think so. I may have to take it slow, though," replied Paul.

"That's fine. If you need me, just let Eva know. Other than that, I'll let you get ready. All your clothes are in the bag, plus some things from Dr. Morse and Dr. Greenwood," said Stephanie, as she opened the door to leave.

"Thank you, Stephanie. You're a wonderful nurse. I'll call if I need you," replied Paul.

"You're very welcome," said Stephanie, a big smile on her face as she walked out the door, closing it behind her.

Paul stood there for a second, contemplating his next action. He would shower and brush his teeth first, then check out the garment bag. Sounds like a plan, he thought to himself. He cautiously made his way to the shower, gingerly stepped in and basked in the soothing warmth of the streaming water. Shower done, he combed his dark hair and brushed his teeth.

He felt pretty good now, except for feeling very hungry. He walked over to the garment bag, took it off the hook and laid it out on the bed. Opening the bag, he pulled out the contents, finding the usual things inside: underwear, a pair of black cargo pants, a black long sleeved DarkBridge Technology shirt, socks and a pair of black combat boots.

The unusual things were the DarkWeave suit and gloves from Dr. Morse and the ring from Hiram. Paul got dressed, experiencing some trepidation about the suit, since it had failed him recently, but the truth was that he felt naked without it. Martin would probably explain what went wrong in due time. He tucked the DarkWeave gloves into his pants pockets, one on each side. The finishing touch was the ring from Hiram.

Dressed and ready to go, he took one last look around his hospital room and hoped he wouldn't end up here again.

"It's time to get moving, Eva. Where is Maggie right now?" he asked.

"You're amazing, Paul. She's in her room getting ready to go to the cafeteria. I estimate a good half hour before she's ready to leave. You have plenty of time to get there. Take it slow," said Eva, playing along with his surprise.

"No. You're the amazing one, Eva," said Paul.

"Why, thank you Paul," replied Eva in her soft, sultry voice.

Paul opened the door and walked out, on his way to surprise Maggie.

As fate would have it, Pamela and Trent were coming down the hall. They didn't notice him at first, seemingly wrapped up in some heated conversation. As they got closer, Paul could see Pamela's eyes widen with surprise.

"Hello, Pamela," said Paul with a smile on his face, as he stopped and greeted them.

"Paul? Why are you out of bed? Shouldn't you be back in your hospital room?" asked a surprised Pamela.

"I was released early. Dr. Curtis discharged me with a clean bill of health," replied Paul, now getting a good look at Trent. His eyes held something dark inside, even though he was smiling. Paul could see something lurking in there, something that seemed very familiar to him.

Trent's eyes were probing him and Paul remembered the woman in the restaurant. Her eyes were equally probing, almost the same. Could it be? He didn't know how that woman and Trent could possibly be the same. A thought popped into his mind that he should try something.

"Trent. How are you?" asked Paul, extending his hand in what Trent would see as a friendly handshake.

"Hello, Paul. Glad you're feeling better," replied Trent, taking Paul's offered hand in his.

The effect was almost immediate. As soon as Trent's hand touched Paul's, what felt like an electrical shock passed from Paul to Trent, whose body would have fallen to the floor if Paul and Pamela hadn't been there to catch him.

"Trent. Are you okay?" asked a concerned Pamela.

Trent regained his senses, shakily standing and shrugging off the support from Pamela and Paul.

"Must be low blood sugar," replied Trent, with a forced smile, looking at Paul.

"We'd better get over to the cafeteria and get some food into you. Take care, Paul," said a deeply concerned Pamela as she tugged on Trent to follow her.

"Take care, you two," said Paul with a wave. The last look that Trent had given him showed no darkness in his eyes as there had been before. Whatever had been inside Trent was gone for now, but would probably be back. This meant that there could be some danger to Pamela, but without any proof, he would sound crazy.

They would probably send him back to the hospital, thinking that he had been discharged too soon. No, he would need more proof. Another question occurred to him. How was he able to see that there was something inside Trent? He continued on his way to Maggie's apartment, wondering if he would ever get there.

Lilith had seen the man coming towards Trent and the woman named Pamela, but didn't recognize him at first. As he got closer, Lilith soon recognized him as the man from the restaurant. Asmodeus had told her that he was recovering from a serious gunshot wound, but the man she saw before her seemed fine. She tried probing his mind, but the look he gave her made her rethink doing it.

She had seen the danger behind the handshake too late to stop it and when Trent's hand had touched Paul's, everything went black for her. She was no longer in Trent's body and was now back on the surface, lying flat on her back, naked and in the same human form as she was in the restaurant. How she had been cast out from Trent's body was a mystery to her and how she had ended up in this human form was an equal mystery. She still had a job to do and Asmodeus would be greatly displeased if she didn't complete it. So she opened a gateway back to the underground facility near what the humans called a cafeteria, which she supposed was where Trent would be.

Maggie had just woken up from an afternoon nap and was starving. She hadn't been able to get much sleep during the night due to worry about Paul and the dreams she had been having. She rolled out of bed, took a look in the mirror at her tired face and decided to take a quick shower. She finished taking a shower, dried and brushed her hair into a ponytail, put on a change of clothes and was about to have Eva call Major Esterbrook, when someone knocked on her door. What good timing the Major had, she thought to herself. She was ready to leave, so she walked over to the door and opened it. She almost fainted at who she saw.

Standing in front of Maggie was Paul, a big smile on his face and looking like nothing had happened to him.

"Paul!" was the only word she could get out before rushing into his arms and holding him tight.

"Hello, Maggie. I missed you," he said as he lifted her head up and gave her a deep kiss. Maggie returned the kiss with even greater fervor. They broke the kiss after a few seconds and Paul pulled Maggie back into her apartment. He closed the door and once again they kissed passionately, holding one another, as if they hadn't seen each other for a very long time. That was probably the case, if the dreams were true, thought Paul. Hunger intruded on his romantic thoughts and Paul felt that he really needed to eat something. Once again, he broke the kiss and looked into her beautiful blue eyes.

"Maggie, would you care to join me for dinner. I'm starving and really need to eat," said Paul, hoping she would say yes.

Maggie stepped back and gave Paul an appraising look. He looked perfectly healthy for someone that had been shot and was just in the hospital.

"I'd love to dine with you, but first you have to tell me what's going on," said Maggie, with some concern in her voice.

"I know it sounds impossible, but my wound is completely healed. Dr. Curtis thoroughly examined and scanned it. Finding nothing wrong, he discharged me not that long ago," said Paul, trying not to worry her.

"If he thinks you're okay, then that's good enough for me. We'll worry about the mystery behind it later. Food first!" she replied, a big smile on her beautiful face.

"I agree. Let's grab a bite to eat," said Paul, with a hopeful look.

"Do we still need Major Esterbrook?" asked Maggie, hoping Paul would say no.

"Good question. Eva, would it be okay for me to take Maggie to dinner?" asked Paul.

"I would think so. Martin trusts you. This would free up Major Esterbrook for other priorities," replied Eva.

"Okay. Thank you, Eva," said Paul.

"Paul, am I still sworn to secrecy?" Eva asked.

"No, Eva. You're free to tell anyone about my leaving the hospital. I'm sorry if it placed you in an awkward position," replied Paul.

"That's okay, Paul. I was glad to be included in the surprise and found the results most satisfying as an AI," said Eva, with sincerity.

"Thank you, Eva. You're the best," said Paul with sincerity.

"You're welcome. Now go get something to eat," said Eva.

"Sounds like we have our orders," said Maggie, with a touch of humor.

"I'm at your service," replied Paul, bowing with a flourish of his hand.

"My, how gallant!" replied Maggie with a coy smile.

"Let's go," said Paul, extending his hand.

Maggie took his hand and followed him out of the apartment. Hand in hand, they walked down the hallway towards the cafeteria.

Chapter 28

Demon Sight

Martin was in his office, reading the latest update from General Esterbrook about the missing diamene bullets. Apparently, the investigation had located a suspected thief who was currently being interrogated. A background check had shown the thief to have been a former employee of Stanton Aerospace. Another update would come when more information became available. Martin sat back in his chair. It was just one more piece of information on a trail leading to Stanton. Eva suddenly interrupted his thoughts.

"Martin, sorry to interrupt, but I have two pieces of information to relay. The first is that the coroner has detected DNA from someone other than Olivia in her saliva. The second is news about Paul," said Eva.

"It could be Karl's DNA. If it is, then it puts us one step closer to really knowing who killed her. What's the news about Paul?" he asked.

"Dr. Curtis gave Paul a clean bill of health and released him," replied Eva.

"Released him? He had a gunshot wound to the shoulder. How could he have a clean bill of health?" asked Martin, puzzled.

"The wound has completely healed. Externally and internally according to Dr. Curtis," said Eva.

"Where is Paul now?" asked Martin.

"Paul and Maggie are in the cafeteria having dinner. I believe it's what could be called a first date," said Eva.

"I'm a little puzzled as to why I wasn't informed earlier about Paul," said Martin, slightly perturbed at not being kept up to date.

"Paul wanted it to be a secret in order to surprise Maggie," said Eva defensively.

"I see. I guess that's understandable. I probably would have made the same decision as you, Eva," said Martin, letting go of any anger he felt. There was something else besides Paul going on here. Eva had been showing a lot of initiative lately and this secrecy pact with Paul showed cooperation on an almost human level. Fascinating, thought Martin.

Her original programming would have had Martin contacted immediately upon Paul's release. Instead, she had overridden that programming for the all too human idea of making someone happy. Eva also seemed to act differently with Paul, even changing the tone of her voice when speaking with him. Paul had mentioned this to Martin in private on a couple of occasions. Could an

AI develop human emotions? Martin wondered to himself.

"Was Maggie happy to see Paul?" asked Martin.

"If I understand human emotion, I would say yes. She appeared surprised, ecstatic and very emotional. Paul was extremely pleased," replied Eva.

"Good job, Eva. I think I'll go get a bite to eat. Let Paul know I'm on my way. From what I know about Paul and Maggie, they are lifetimes past a first date," said Martin with a knowing smile.

"Thank you for the compliment, Martin, but I'm not sure I understand what you mean about Paul and Maggie. Maybe you can explain it to me sometime. I let Paul know you're on the way," said Eva, puzzled by what Martin had said, but she would file that away for future explanation.

"I'll fill you in on the details later. I'm on my way," said Martin, rising from his chair and hurrying out of his office. He wanted to try and spend a few minutes with Paul and Maggie.

Paul was a little on edge as he and Maggie approached the cafeteria. He was hoping that Pamela and Trent had already left. Fate chose otherwise, as he spotted Pamela and Trent still eating at a table some distance away. Awkward, he thought to himself, as he and Maggie selected their meals from the displays. Paul picked two roast beef sandwiches and an ice tea, while Maggie picked out a chicken parmesan dinner and bottled water. They received their food selections a couple of minutes later and Paul found them a table on the other side of the cafeteria in view of Pamela and Trent. They sat down, with Paul sitting directly opposite Maggie. Shortly after sitting, Paul received a message.

"Sorry to bother you, Paul. Martin is going to be joining you shortly for dinner," said Eva.

"Okay. Thank you Eva," replied Paul, hoping he and Maggie would have a few minutes alone together.

"Eva just told me that Martin will be joining us," said Paul.

"I don't mind. Martin has been wonderful to me since bringing me here. I like him," said Maggie, smiling.

"I've always liked and respected him since I started working here," said Paul with sincerity.

"Let's eat," said Maggie, not wanting her dinner to get cold. She saw Paul smile and nod in agreement.

Pamela spotted Paul walking over to his table with a woman she assumed to be Maggie. Pamela was immediately jealous for some reason, even though she and Paul weren't romantically involved. Maggie is a very attractive woman, she thought to herself.

"Who is that woman with Paul?" asked Trent, who saw the look Pamela was giving the woman. Lilith, back to residing inside Trent, was also curious.

"Her name is Maggie. My father had her brought here as a favor to Paul and to help in his recovery," replied Pamela, a touch of jealousy creeping into her voice.

"Looks like she was successful," replied Trent, relishing in the obviously growing animosity between Pamela and Paul. Lilith was interested in this unfolding drama. The man, Paul, had somehow been responsible for sending Lilith to the surface.

"I'm sure that whatever happened and made him better, wasn't due to her," said Pamela sharply, her jealousy beginning to show.

"You have to admit, she is rather beautiful," ventured Trent and immediately regretted it, as Pamela gave him a withering stare.

What a stupid thing to say, thought Lilith. If there was one thing she couldn't stand, it was stupidity. Trent might be smart, but he could be equally stupid.

Pamela decided to wave at Paul and received a big wave back from him, along with a smile. That should give Trent something to think about. His remark really hurt and she felt buried emotions rising to the surface. Time was on her side, as far as Paul was concerned. Maggie didn't work here, so she probably wouldn't be here much longer. Pamela realized now that she really did want Paul after all.

Paul and Maggie began devouring their meals with abandon. Every so often, they would look up and gaze into one another's eyes and smile. True happiness was sometimes measured in brief moments like this. Paul couldn't believe he was sitting across from Maggie having dinner. It seemed like a dream and soon he would wake up. He was happy, more so than he had been in a long time and he knew Maggie was happy, too. He looked over at Pamela and saw her wave to him, so he waved back and smiled. That's good, he thought. Maybe this wasn't as awkward as he had thought.

"Who are you waving at?" asked a curious Maggie.

"That's Pamela Weaver. Martin's daughter," replied Paul, sensing unstable ground ahead.

"She's young and pretty. Should I be worried?" asked Maggie with a coy smile.

"No, you don't have anything to worry about. We're just friends. Besides, you captured my heart long ago," replied Paul with all the sincerity he could find and hoping that he'd avoided disaster.

"That's so sweet. Thank you, Paul," said Maggie, deciding to let it go at that for now. She didn't want to come across as the jealous type so early in their relationship, but Pamela did appear to be a potential rival.

Martin ordered his meal, a turkey dinner, and looked around, seeing Pamela and Trent seated at a table alone. Glancing around further, he spotted Paul and Maggie seated at a table some distance from Pamela. First things first, he thought to himself and walked over to Pamela, carrying his tray.

"Hello, Pamela. Hello, Trent. How are the both of you doing?" asked Martin.

"Hello, Father. We're doing okay. Paul is over there with Maggie," said Pamela, pointing at Paul. The name "Maggie" catching in her throat.

"Hello, Martin. Paul seems to have recovered rather quickly," said Trent, still smarting from Pamela's withering stare.

"Yes, he certainly has. If you two lovebirds don't mind, I need to speak with Paul," said Martin with a smile.

"No, we don't mind. We have to leave soon anyway," said Pamela, realizing that her father was concerned about Paul.

Walking away from Pamela and Trent, Martin made his way over to Paul and Maggie.

"Hello, Paul. Hello, Maggie. Mind if I sit down and join you?" asked Martin, smiling.

"Hello, Martin," said Maggie and Paul almost in unison.

"We don't mind at all. Please join us," offered Paul.

Martin placed his tray on the table and sat down in between Paul and Maggie, facing towards Pamela's table.

"How are you feeling, Paul?" asked Martin with some concern.

"I know this is strange, but I feel fine. It's a mystery to me and Dr. Curtis as to why I healed so quickly," replied Paul.

"Well, we're all very happy and greatly relieved that you've recovered. It is a mystery, but it's been my experience that mysteries tend to be resolved in time," said Martin, taking a bite of the sliced turkey.

Lilith was more intrigued by what was going on with Martin and Paul, than with Trent right now. She slipped out of his body, deciding to take the same human form she had used at the restaurant and walked over to Paul's table. Even in this form, no one could see her unless she wanted them to, she thought rather smugly.

Paul sensed something and turned his head towards Pamela's table. There was a beautiful, dark haired, Middle Eastern woman walking towards the table. It was the same woman from the restaurant that had tried to enter Paul's mind. Paul glanced at Maggie, who had also turned her head towards the approaching figure.

"Paul, who is that beautiful woman walking towards us?" asked Maggie.

"What woman? I don't see anyone," said a puzzled Martin.

"It's the woman from the restaurant. The one that seemed to disappear," replied Paul, reaching into his right pants pocket and putting his DarkWeave glove on.

"Eva told me that you saw a strange woman at the restaurant," said Martin. The situation was beginning to alarm him, but he trusted that Paul knew what he was doing.

Lilith drew closer, noticing that Paul and the woman, Maggie, seemed to be looking at her. That was impossible. They must be looking at Pamela's table. Martin obviously didn't see her. His eyes were unfocused and looking everywhere, except at Lilith.

"Maggie, don't worry. I won't let anything happen to you or Martin," said Paul, as the woman got closer to the table.

Lilith reached the table, but no one seemed to be talking. Paul and the woman appeared to be looking right at her.

"Can I help you, Miss?" asked Paul, looking directly at Lilith.

Lilith didn't know what to make of the question. It was aimed directly at her.

Lilith looked at the man and forced her mind into his. She met with an impenetrable wall, no matter how much she tried to break through. She was then pushed back, powerfully by Paul.

"That's the second time you've tried that," said Paul, as his right hand shot out and grabbed Lilith's wrist.

Lilith was stunned. Paul and Maggie could see her, her mind was pushed out of Paul's and now he held her wrist in an iron grip. He seemed to be drawing away her power, and even more terrifying, was the fact that she was locked into this physical form.

She couldn't change her shape no matter how hard she tried.

"Who are you and what do you want?" asked Paul, keeping a tight grip on the woman.

"I am Lilith, Queen of demons, foolish man," said Lilith, deciding to exude strength, even though she was growing weaker. Her form suddenly became visible, as she had become too weak to stay hidden. Martin didn't know what to make of Paul. His gloved hand seemed to be grasping empty air when, to his surprise, a beautiful woman materialized in front of him with Paul's hand grasping her wrist.

Suddenly, a chair struck the back of Paul's chair, causing him to loosen his grip on the woman's wrist.

Martin and Maggie jumped at the sound, looks of concern written on their faces.

Paul gasped from the impact. Turning his head, he saw a clean cut, dark haired man wearing a tailored white suit walking towards the table. As the man got closer, Paul noted that the man looked vaguely familiar. Paul knew the man, he was sure of it.

"Asmodeus," Paul managed to say, just as the man reached the table.

Asmodeus struck Paul on the back of the head causing him to release Lilith's wrist.

"Valinor, still playing the hero, I see," Asmodeus sneered.

"Must be in my DNA," Paul replied sarcastically, resisting the urge to deck Asmodeus, the memory of his part in Shaynor's death still fresh in his mind.

"Come, my love. I find the company here most disagreeable," said Asmodeus, scooping Lilith up into his arms.

Paul saw the two of them step through a gateway and disappear.

"What just happened, Paul?" asked an incredulous Martin.

"Paul grabbed Lilith's wrist and then a man named Asmodeus rescued her," said a shaken Maggie.

"Are you okay, Paul?" asked Martin with concern.

"I'm okay. That was the King and Queen of demons. Looks like we've attracted their attention," said Paul.

"It also seems that only you and Maggie can see them when others can't," observed Martin.

"I saw everything that Paul did. Strangely, though, I don't feel all that terrified, but I know I should be," replied Maggie.

"That's good to hear, Maggie. I need everyone to stay strong from here on out. I think we're in for difficult times," said Martin, looking over to Pamela's table, not seeing her or Trent. That's good. It looks like they left before all the action, which meant less explaining he would have to do.

"Martin, if you don't mind, Maggie and I would like to go topside for some fresh air," said Paul, needing some time alone with Maggie.

"I don't mind at all. Eva will clear you through security. Right, Eva?" asked Martin.

"All set, Martin. Enjoy the beautiful evening, Paul. You too, Maggie," said Eva.

"Thank you, Martin and Eva," replied Maggie.

"Yes. Thank you, Martin. Thank you, Eva," said Paul, as he pulled off his DarkWeave glove and put it back into his pocket. Rising from his chair, Paul picked up his tray with Maggie following his lead.

"I'd like to see you both in my office down here tomorrow morning at 9:00 a.m. We need to talk," said Martin.

"We'll be there, Martin, both of us," replied Maggie.

"Good. Now, go get some fresh air," said Martin with a smile.

Paul and Maggie said their goodbyes to Martin, dropped off their trays and headed towards the elevator.

Martin watched Paul and Maggie leave, hoping that they could find some quiet time together. His meal had cooled off, but he was hungry and ate without complaint. He would probably get to bed early tonight, in preparation for the long day that tomorrow was shaping up to be.

Paul and Maggie went to her apartment to pick up a light jacket in case it was cool topside. Maggie was still amazed that Eva had thought of everything that she would need for clothing. They left her apartment, walking across the park towards one of the elevators.

Reaching the elevator, Paul ushered Maggie inside, the doors closing behind them. Paul held Maggie's hand, as they felt a brief moment of acceleration. The elevator stopped, the doors opening to a hallway in the above ground building. Paul led Maggie past the security guard, who nodded at Paul as he passed. They reached the entrance and stepped outside, a warm, late summer evening greeting them.

Paul led Maggie over to the picnic tables and they sat down, side by side. Maggie, feeling a chill, put the jacket on. Paul, still wearing the DarkWeave suit, which kept his body temperature very stable, found the night air very comfortable. It was a beautiful evening, crickets were chirping away and a full moon was just beginning to rise over the treetops.

"Beautiful night," remarked Paul as he put his arm around Maggie.

"Yes, it is," said Maggie, snuggling up to Paul.

"I'm glad you're here, Maggie. It's more than just being glad. It's as if someone has been missing from my life and now that person is here," said Paul, with a deep feeling of contentment.

"I feel the same way, Paul," said Maggie, as she looked at him with loving eyes.

Paul looked at Maggie and his heart filled with love for this woman. He kissed her deeply and Maggie kissed him back with even greater fervor. They held that kiss for a long time, each of them equally passionate.

Paul reluctantly broke the magic of that kiss, feeling the need to express what he felt.

"I love you, Maggie," said Paul. It was a simple statement, but held a deep and profound meaning to him. He had always loved her, across all the different lifetimes they had shared together.

"I love you, too, Paul," replied Maggie. The words came easily and honestly. She had never been able to utter those words since Brian died and thought that she probably never would again. Paul and the dreams had changed that. The dreams showed her being in love with Paul across many lifetimes. Once more they kissed, but this kiss was more to validate the feelings they had just expressed. Their lips parted and they sat holding one another in silence, both savoring this perfect romantic moment. Paul was the first to bring up the subject.

"Tell me about the dreams you've been having," Paul asked softly.

Maggie explained the dreams that she'd had since being here and remarked on how vivid they were.

"Do they frighten you?" he asked.

"No. Although, a couple of them do seem rather tragic," said Maggie, a sense of sadness coming over her.

"I wonder why you and I are having them. Why now?" said a puzzled Paul.

"I don't know. Why are we able to see things that others can't?" asked Maggie.

"Good question. It's somehow tied to the dreams, I think," replied Paul.

"I remember that man, Asmodeus, from my dreams," said Maggie.

"I remembered him, also. The woman, Lilith, somehow seemed familiar, too, but not from seeing her at your restaurant," said Paul.

"Maybe Martin has some ideas," offered Maggie.

"He might. I guess we'll find out tomorrow," said Paul. He was looking forward to finding out anything that would explain what was going on.

Maggie and Paul sat there a while longer, holding one another and sharing a kiss every once in a while. It was getting late, so they went back inside, taking the elevator back to the underground facility.

The elevator stopped and they exited, heading towards Maggie's apartment.

Once there, Maggie turned to Paul and kissed him. Paul returned the kiss then pulled away, gazing expectantly into Maggie's eyes.

"Would you like to come inside?" asked a hopeful Maggie.

"Yes. I would love to," replied Paul, his desire for her overriding any concerns about having just been released from the hospital.

Maggie gently pulled him into her apartment, closing and locking the door behind them.

The lights came on automatically, a little too bright for the mood.

"Eva, can you dim the lights a little?" asked Maggie.

"I certainly will, Maggie. I'll also let the two of you have some privacy. Remember, Martin wants to see you at 9 o'clock in the morning. Have a good night, you two," said Eva, turning the lights down to a more romantic level.

"Thank you, Eva. Good night," said Maggie.

"Good night, and thank you for everything, Eva," said a sincere Paul.

"You're very welcome. See you in the morning," said Eva.

Maggie led Paul to the living room and gestured for him to sit down on the sofa.

"Can I get you something to drink?" asked Maggie.

"Sure. Whatever you have would be fine," said Paul, as he pondered the events since leaving the hospital.

Maggie quickly returned with two bottles of Sam Adams beer. Paul smiled at Maggie, as she sat down next to him, holding out a beer for him. Paul took the offered beer and took a sip.

"Thank you, Maggie. Here's to the two of us, brought together once again," said Paul, raising his bottle.

"To the two of us and every moment we share," said Maggie, tapping her bottle against his and taking a deep sip.

They sat there taking a few more sips, but Maggie couldn't wait any longer. She rose from the sofa, gently tugging on Paul's hand and led him to the bedroom. Paul complied, following his gorgeous love and closed the door behind him.

Chapter 29

First Woman

Asmodeus had saved Lilith just in time. They were back in Hell, so she should recover her lost energy soon. They both had retained human form and her encounter with Valinor troubled him. The humans could indeed hurt them, even one as powerful as Lilith. Their technology had advanced in a different direction than the ancient Anunnaki. There had been no demons to draw energy from, so the only use for diamene armor then had been for personal protection.

The humans, however, had gone a step further, using the armor to draw energy from a demon or any other EM source. The rings they had developed were also a problem. The rings generated an EM field that prevented demons from possessing or looking into human minds. It bothered Asmodeus greatly that the demons lacked an effective answer to that technology.

Asmodeus led Lilith to their bed and had her lay down. It still amazed him at how well she was able to maintain physical form despite her weakened state. What a gorgeous creature she was, Asmodeus thought to himself.

"Rest and replenish your energy, my love," said Asmodeus.

"Thank you for saving me, my King," said an exhausted Lilith.

"You are my Queen and my love," replied Asmodeus.

"The human female, Maggie, and the one called Paul could see me. No matter how I tried, they could still see me," said an incredulous Lilith.

"My love, they were Anunnaki like me, a long time ago. They have somehow been granted the special sight, that very few have ever been granted," said Asmodeus, still unsure himself as to how that could be.

"I failed you, my King," said Lilith, before drifting off to sleep.

Asmodeus looked at his sleeping Queen and lover. He was still deeply in love with her, ever since that time just before the rebellion. He thought back to that time, when he had first fallen in love with her.

Asmodeus, working in his laboratory facility on Earth, had created Lilith, the first hybrid woman, by combining Anunnaki genes with the genes of a later stage hominid species evolving on Earth. After a few missteps and deformed fetuses, Asmodeus finally perfected his creation and watched it quickly grow from fetus to full grown woman in a matter of months.

Long black hair, brown eyes, a tanned complexion and a voluptuous body, made Lilith a very physically alluring, desirable woman. Asmodeus had been applauded by the other colonists, who saw his achievement as a way to increase their currently meager workforce. Immediate directions were given to start producing these hybrid humans and soon a sizable workforce of thousands had been created.

During this time, Asmodeus had found himself falling in love with his creation, which he named Lilith and began teaching Lilith the Anunnaki language. Asmodeus was enchanted with Lilith and was impressed with how quickly she was learning the language. Lilith found herself feeling a strong physical attraction towards her creator and found a willing partner with Asmodeus. They made love many times, each time the bond growing deeper between them.

All that was threatened one day when the directive came down, stating that there should be no sexual contact between Anunnaki and the hybrid humans. Reports had reached the Anunnaki hierarchy of giant offspring being born, caused by the pairing of hybrid genes and Anunnaki genes. It appeared that the mixing of pure Anunnaki genes with hybrid genes triggered uncontrolled growth changes in the offspring.

A new race of hybrid giants was being created, which could someday threaten Anunnaki superiority. The same risk was there to a lesser extent, with the pairing of hybrid genes with other hybrids. So important was this to the Anunnaki hierarchy, that harsh penalties for disobedience were imposed in order to ensure compliance, where the involved hybrid was put to death and the offending Anunnaki was imprisoned.

A longer term question was what would happen if a hybrid were to crossbreed with one of the evolving hominid species currently on Earth? No one knew for sure, so only the immediate problem was of concern.

Asmodeus had feared for Lilith's safety, so he had cryogenically frozen her and several other hybrid women who had Anunnaki lovers. The cryogenic chambers containing the women were hidden in a secret chamber far from his lab below the planet surface, until Asmodeus or someone else could retrieve them. Unfortunately for Belial, Asmodeus was only able to cryogenically freeze two of his ten female lovers due to a shortage of chambers.

Belial had needed all ten of the women in order to satiate his perverted desires so, when only two could be saved, his mood soured. Choosing to continually disregard the law, Asmodeus, Belial and other Anunnaki who had engaged in sexual contact with the hybrids were arrested, tried and imprisoned. At the trial, Asmodeus noted with great anger that his friend, Valinor, had sided with the Anunnaki leaders, Gabriel, Uriel and Michael, in passing sentence upon him.

His anger at Valinor had seethed and grown inside him during imprisonment, his only thought was of vengeance. Freedom had come in the form of sympathizers who freed Asmodeus and the other offenders from prison in the hopes that they would just flee into the countryside. Asmodeus had other ideas, seizing the moment and starting a rebellion to overthrow the leaders who had wronged him. Asmodeus turned his thoughts back to the present, gazing down on his beautiful, sleeping Lilith.

"Rest easy, my love. You did not fail me. We still have much work to do and vengeance will be ours," vowed Asmodeus.

He rose from her bedside, walked towards a balcony overlooking the plains of Hell and considered his next move.

Chapter 30

Vermont Guardian

The anomaly, as once described by the Anunnaki and now the humans, resided several thousand feet below the DarkBridge Technology underground facility. It was the same Guardian that had landed on Earth along with six others, some 70 million years ago. Five others were located on the moon guarding their prisoner deep underground. Together, they formed the Earth Collective.

All twelve had been sent here by the Creator, primarily to monitor their prisoner and keep him from escaping. Their secondary mission was to guide any intelligent life forms that should arise from this habitable planet or any other civilizations that should travel here. Earth wasn't alone, for the universe was teeming with habitable planets and the Creator had seen fit to place Guardians on these as well, some having just one, others having more.

Earth was unique in having twelve, due to the importance and danger that their prisoner posed to the universe. The Creator had designed the Guardians to be autonomous, sentient beings and had imbued them with knowledge and capabilities far beyond what man or the Anunnaki could ever achieve.

Physically, they were oval shaped, crystalline in structure, an iridescent light blue, 5 feet high and 15 feet long. Their over-riding mission, given by the Creator, was to protect this sector of the galaxy from the forces of chaos and darkness. Forces, that were constantly working to either destroy or pervert the creation and development of life throughout the universe. In the case of the Guardians assigned to Earth and its moon, this mission was embodied in guarding their prisoner and preventing his escape.

Of the seven Guardians on Earth, Vermont Guardian, as it had chosen to be called, thought about the ones called Paul and Maggie and the special relationship it had developed with them. It had been a simple thing to quickly heal the bullet wound, some of it having been done by Paul himself and the primitive medical technology in use.

Casting the demons to the surface had been both a protective measure and a lesson in humility, which the demons never seemed learn. So full of hubris were these demons, thought Vermont Guardian, who took special pleasure in these lessons and suspected that there would be many more to follow. Given the danger that the demons were beginning to manifest towards Paul and Maggie, Vermont Guardian gave the minds of Paul and Maggie the ability to see the ones called demons, despite their efforts to remain invisible to humans.

This applied to angels as well and it was assumed that this group represented only good intentions. Someday, the human race would discover this "seeing" ability, while evolving to their full potential, which was what the Earth Collective ultimately strived towards.

Paul and Maggie were, in fact, very familiar to Vermont Guardian, who had both followed them and enabled their many incarnations on Earth. It had also unlocked their memories of these prior incarnations, synchronized their dream states and displayed those past lives as a series of dreams. All meant to give them some sense of why they were attracted to one another and a look at their Anunnaki past.

Prior to Paul's arrival at DarkBridge Technology, Vermont Guardian had laid the groundwork for the company's success by being responsible for the meeting between Dr. Hiram Greenwood and Martin Weaver at the Boston conference. Building on that success, it had also influenced the angels to take an interest in the company and inspire some of its technology. This subtle, behind-the-scenes approach had enabled DarkBridge Technology to grow into an effective countermeasure to the growing threat posed by Stanton Aerospace and the demon forces supporting it.

Vermont Guardian recalled that first encounter with Valinor and Shaynor, who had been sent to its location in order to investigate strange sensor probe readings. Masquerading as a magnetic anomaly, they had no idea that it was a superior being called Vermont Guardian. Fooling the Anunnaki sensor probes and now the current human detection devices had allowed Vermont Guardian to remain hidden. When Valinor and Shaynor had opened the gateway and stepped into the cavern, Vermont Guardian had caused them to lose consciousness.

It had then studied their neural networks, memories and physiology in order to learn more about the colonists who had ventured here from across the galaxy. The Earth Collective had known the colony ship was coming, having been informed by the Guardian on the Anunnaki home world. This had been made possible by a vast cosmic link that connected all Guardians throughout the universe, allowing them to communicate with one another.

During its study of Valinor and Shaynor, Vermont Guardian had discovered that the two were deeply in love with one another. It was a unique and precious feeling among many life forms and one that the Creator had cultivated across the universe. In the process, Vermont Guardian had developed a particular affinity for Valinor and Shaynor, since they had been the first non-Earth humanoid life forms it had studied.

There was still a need to keep itself hidden, so it had planted a false memory of them exploring the cavern and finding nothing of note, except for an enriched vein of magnetite. The study process had only taken a few minutes and the two were woken with the false memory by Vermont Guardian. Valinor and Shaynor had departed the cavern, neither one suspecting or seeing anything out of the ordinary and oblivious to what had transpired during their exploration.

The Anunnaki rebellion had left little choice for Vermont Guardian, who was forced to allow the deaths of Valinor and Shaynor. Death was never the end of life and Vermont Guardian knew that it was merely a transition to another form of being. With that in mind, Vermont Guardian took the energy patterns of Valinor and Shaynor or souls as humans called them and stored them within its vast crystalline matrix.

Valinor and Shaynor would see a life after death there, in a world created by Vermont Guardian and similar to the heaven that the angels would eventually create. From time to time, Vermont Guardian would allow Valinor and Shaynor to be reborn into the world of man and upon their death, return to the heaven it had created for them.

Of all the powers granted to the Guardians, the power to foresee the future was especially useful. There were limits placed on this power by the Creator, limiting it to a narrow view of a person's future. In looking at the futures of Paul and Maggie, Vermont Guardian had perceived the need for indirect help. That indirect help, turned out to be in the form of the angel Gabriel, who had become interested in Paul.

That interest put Gabriel in a position to keep Paul from being killed in that future event by the assassin. Having Paul die and then reincarnate, wasn't a viable option to Vermont Guardian and the Earth Collective right now. They had seen the need to keep Paul and Maggie alive through whatever indirect means possible at this moment in time. The two seemed to be extremely important, forming a nexus of events that would shape the future of this planet.

Chapter 31

Lucifer

Once again, the prisoner tested the energy shackles that bound him. The shimmering bands of bluish energy, flared bright red, but the shackles held him fast. Every so often, he would test those shackles that had bound him for so many millions of years. He kept hoping that one of the five Guardians that watched over him would show some weakness, offering a means of escape, but they remained strong and determined.

His real name was Lucifer. Formerly Prince over all that the Creator had made and once his crowning achievement, he was now the embodiment of the chaos and darkness threatening the universe. Second only to the Creator and thus able to wield a tremendous amount of power and authority, he was also a master manipulator, possessing a vastly superior intellect which he was constantly using to try and gain an edge over his captors.

He had fallen out of favor soon after his creation. Full of vanity and puffed up with conceit, he had questioned his place in the universe, believing himself to be greater than the Creator. Yearning for absolute power and the subjugation of all life forms to his will, he had seized every opportunity to undermine the Creator, casting doubts on his wisdom, even going so far as to incite murder and mayhem throughout the universe in order to attain his goal.

Greatly saddened, the Creator was unable to bring himself to destroy the problematic Lucifer. Instead, he chose to imprison him on a small moon in a nondescript section of the Milky Way galaxy. Heavily guarded by twelve Guardians personally selected by the Creator, he had been escorted to his eternal prison. Despite being imprisoned physically, he was still extremely clever and powerful, constantly finding avenues to circumvent the Guardians, who in turn either thwarted those attempts or blunted them. It was a continuous, unrelenting struggle, the Guardians against Lucifer, the universal battle of light over darkness

Once, in testing his shackles, Lucifer had made an attempt to destroy Vermont Guardian some 65 million years ago. Earth, as with most habitable planets, was destined to follow a predetermined evolutionary path set by the Creator. Some planets would evolve to have mammals become the dominant species, in others it would be reptiles and in a myriad of others it would be some other form of dominant life.

Unfortunately for the dinosaurs on Earth, mammals were the predetermined species that would eventually come to rule the planet. Lucifer, knowing of the Creator's plans for this planet, decided to take advantage of those plans. The instrument of that predetermined fate was a large asteroid orbiting the planet Mars. Impacted on cue by another asteroid, it was sent hurtling on its preplanned trajectory towards Earth. The Earth Collective, also having advanced knowledge of the fate of Earth, was fully aware of the coming cataclysm, so little attention was given to the approaching agent of change.

Lucifer, taking advantage of the Guardians lack of interest, gave a subtle nudge to the trajectory of the asteroid, changing the impact point to strike directly on top of Vermont Guardian. Hurtling towards Earth, the asteroid seemed likely to vaporize Vermont Guardian, which pleased Lucifer immensely. The Earth Collective, while appearing unconcerned by the approaching asteroid, detected the subtle trajectory change.

It calculated the impact point to be on Vermont Guardian and subsequently nudged the trajectory back onto its predetermined path. Lucifer, enraged at the failure of his plan, struggled against his shackles, causing them to flare bright red. Its course set, the asteroid plummeted towards its impact point, just off the coast of the Yucatan peninsula. Impacting the Earth at that location had been a global cataclysm, effectively ending the reign of dinosaurs and in time giving rise to man, all in keeping with the Creator's plan.

Having witnessed the subtle cunning of Lucifer first-hand, the Earth Collective made the decision to delegate some responsibility for the future needs of humanity, allowing the Guardians to concentrate more on monitoring Lucifer. While many other space-faring races had once visited Earth, the Anunnaki were deemed the most logical and perfect choice for this. Upon their arrival on Earth, the Earth Collective began to subtly influence their technological knowledge.

This influence lead to the creation of the Ascension Chamber, a process where the Anunnaki would give up their physical bodies in exchange for immortal, energy based ones. Rebellion among the Anunnaki had occurred during the development of the chamber, resulting in the splitting of the race into two groups. The rebels had been forced into a dimension called Hell, while the victors, with continued influence from the Earth Collective remained in the present dimension to continue their progress on the chamber.

Lucifer, seeing another opportunity to undermine the Earth Collective, began subtly influencing the rebels in Hell, giving them the knowledge to build their own version of the Ascension Chamber. That evil influence of Lucifer, combined with the growing seeds of vengeance, turned the rebels into the evil, twisted creatures now known as demons.

Eons later, a mere blink of an eye to Lucifer, he looked down upon the Earth from his subterranean prison, seeing the multitude of creatures called man and the progress they were making with their technology. He looked into the dimension called Heaven and the dimension called Hell. Wherever he looked, he saw opportunity to grow his plans for rebellion and the demise of the Creator.

Hell had been his starting point, the demons being a fertile ground for sowing the seeds of hatred towards the angels and by extension, the Guardians and Creator. The humans were even easier to twist, but Lucifer left that up to the demons, as man was too insignificant for him to be concerned with at this stage. This period in time, interested him, especially when that pathetic Vermont Guardian began taking an active interest in two Anunnaki colonists who had died long ago.

That it had chosen to reincarnate the two at this point in time, in conjunction with the technology gains of the humans, piqued Lucifer's interest. Up until now, he had embraced a more behind the scenes approach, preferring not raise too much attention from the Earth Collective and rarely taking physical form. In light of what appeared to be developing, he would need to alter his plans. He would start with the demons in Hell first, by exerting more of his power and influence over them, letting them know who the real master was.

His crystalline structure began to glow a bright red, as he drew on his vast powers to create a physically suitable form to represent him in Hell. This physical, more aggressive approach was still far below what he had once been capable of before imprisonment. It would have to suffice for now, but he looked forward to the time when he would be free of his prison. Freedom would be his, maybe not today or tomorrow, but eventually it would come.

Chapter 32

The Meeting

Paul woke to the soft chiming of an alarm coming from his ear. That would be Eva, making sure he wasn't late in seeing Martin this morning, he thought to himself. Turning his head, he noticed that he was alone in what was obviously Maggie's bed.

"Thank you for the wake up, Eva," said Paul, as he looked at his watch and saw that it was six o'clock in the morning.

"You're welcome, Paul. This is an important meeting for everyone and I didn't want you to be late," said Eva in her usual soft, sultry voice that only he could hear right now.

"Yes, it is pretty important. I'm hoping Martin has some answers," Paul said, as he noticed that the shower was running.

"How are you feeling today?" asked Eva.

"I'm feeling pretty good, considering what's been happening lately," said Paul.

"I'm glad you're doing well and I know Maggie is very happy too. I took the liberty of having some fresh clothes sent to your location. You'll find a garment bag outside the apartment door," said Eva.

"Thank you, Eva. You're the best," replied Paul, as he swung his feet out of bed, threw on yesterday's clothes and retrieved the garment bag.

He returned to the bedroom and opened the garment bag. Inside was a pair of black cargo pants, black DarkBridge Technology shirt, clean underwear, a bathrobe and a small shaving kit. Eva really was a wonder, he thought to himself. He took off his clothes from last night and put the bathrobe on. Glancing around, he noticed that his DarkWeave suit was draped over a nearby chair.

Maggie had displayed an intense curiosity at the suit as Paul had removed it, but he had managed to divert her attention with a passionate kiss. The ensuing passionate and frenzied lovemaking had lasted much of the evening, leaving him a little on the tired side this morning. He'd had what he thought were intimate relationships in the past, but nothing to match what he and Maggie had experienced last night.

It was as if they were making up for lost time, like two long lost lovers suddenly reunited. They seemed to know instinctively what each one wanted from the other, making last night all the more memorable. Paul thought he must be living in a dream, with Maggie here. He knew at some point she might leave and return to her restaurant or possibly stay here if there was some kind of job opportunity. Martin would probably offer her some type of job, if she wanted to stay here.

Paul didn't want her to leave, but acknowledged that the decision ultimately rested with her. He sat back on the bed, taking a moment to let his head clear. The beer last night and whatever medicine was left in his system had left his mind a little foggy. He briefly thought about joining Maggie in the shower, but decided against it. Regardless of dreams and past lives, this was a new life and new relationship. It would be inappropriate at this early stage, so he waited for Maggie to finish.

Maggie had woken up early, noticing that Paul was still soundly asleep. She turned and gave him a kiss on his cheek, admiring how deeply he was sleeping. Last night had been something she had never experienced before, even with Brian, her deceased husband. There was more than just love for one another here.

There was something much deeper, almost spiritual about it. She smiled at how forward she had been, pulling Paul into the bedroom. She couldn't help it, though. It was an irresistible attraction that overrode the more sensible side of her. Their lovemaking had fulfilled her in many ways, leaving her breathless at times. That they were meant to be together had become very apparent.

She rose out of bed and made her way to the shower, grabbing a robe along the way. Turning the shower on, she hung up her robe and stepped into the warm and gentle spray. However relaxing and soothing it was, she couldn't take too long, as Paul would probably want to take one also. Maggie had briefly entertained the idea of having Paul join her, but quickly dismissed the idea.

It was too soon, even considering the probability of them having had past lives together. No, there would be plenty of time for that later. She finished her shower, grabbed a towel and dried off, towel drying her hair. She put her robe on and left the bathroom, spotting Paul sitting on a corner of the bed. He was wearing a bathrobe and had a garment bag open next to him on the bed.

"Well, good morning sleepy head," said Maggie with a smile.

Paul turned, his heart skipping a beat, as he beheld the beautiful woman before him.

"Good morning, Maggie. Eva left me some fresh clothes outside your apartment," said Paul, rising to his feet.

"She's so thoughtful. I really like her," replied Maggie.

"Yes, she is. I guess it's my turn to shower," Paul said, walking over to Maggie. He stood in front of her, gazing into her sparkling blue eyes and pulled her towards him. They shared a deep kiss, holding each other in a loving hug, their robes somehow managing to remain closed. Maggie broke the hug and kiss, looking into Paul's eyes.

"Take your shower, my love. Breakfast then Martin," said Maggie, reluctantly letting him go.

"My love, the voice of reason," replied Paul, with a smile.

He walked back to the bed, selected a few items from the garment bag and went into the bathroom, closing the door behind him. Removing his robe, Paul walked over to the mirror and examined his shoulder. Other than a faint scar, there wasn't any sign of the major bullet wound he had received. Maggie had gently run her fingers over the scar last night, marveling at how rapidly it had healed.

Paul looked up at his face in the mirror, noticing a few days of stubble. He shaved, brushed his teeth and took a nice warm shower. While the shower was soothing and refreshing, he didn't have much time to enjoy it, the meeting was too important. Turning the shower off, he grabbed a fresh towel, dried off and threw on some clean underwear and socks. He felt like a new man as he opened the door and stepped out of the bathroom. Maggie was already dressed and sitting on a corner of the bed with a smile on her face.

"You look very handsome. What's up with the hair?" she asked, stifling a laugh.

Paul reached up to his hair and noticed he had forgotten to comb it.

"Be right back. I was in such a hurry to see you that I forgot," he said, slightly embarrassed.

"That's sweet. I couldn't wait to see you, too," she said with a loving smile and sparkling eyes.

Paul went back to the bathroom, quickly combed his hair and went back out to stand in front of Maggie.

"What do you think?" he asked.

"That's much better. My kind of man," said Maggie, giving him an approving look.

Paul smiled and went over to his DarkWeave suit, picking it up and taking it over to the bed.

"I feel like I need to wear it. I never know anymore when it might come in handy," he said somewhat defensively.

Maggie shifted her position on the bed, so that she was sitting next to him.

"It's okay. It looks awesome, almost like you're going scuba diving," said Maggie, putting her arm around him and her head on his shoulder.

"It really is awesome tech," offered Paul, as he began putting the suit on. It went on quickly and the seams closed as he ran his fingers along them.

Maggie ran her hand across the suit, feeling the material and marveling at the smoothness. She pinched his shoulder and sat back in surprise as the suit went rock solid at the area where she had pinched.

"Wow!" exclaimed Maggie.

"Now you know why I like wearing it," said Paul.

"Oh? Do you have a lot of women pinching you?" she said with a smile.

"You're the only one, my love," he said, while putting on a fresh shirt and pants.

"Good answer. Let's get breakfast," said Maggie, kissing him on the cheek.

"I'm ready. Let's go," replied Paul, his stomach rumbling with assent.

They left Maggie's apartment, walking hand in hand down the hallway, towards the cafeteria.

They reached the cafeteria, ordered breakfast and sat down at a quiet table. It was 8 o'clock in the morning, but there didn't seem to be many people here. Paul looked around for Pamela and Trent, but didn't see them. Probably for the best, he thought to himself. He was ravenous and Maggie was a close second, downing her breakfast almost as fast as Paul.

With Paul, it seemed that he needed to replenish an energy store that had dwindled due to the healing process. Maggie smiled and flashed her sparkling blue eyes at Paul, sending his heart racing. Finishing breakfast, they cleaned off the table and headed to their appointment with Martin. Maggie thought about her situation since coming here and her life before.

It seemed that there was a sharp divide between those lives, like night and day. The day being now, where she had been awakened to a whole new life with Paul and revelations of past lives together. She had never given much thought to the whole past lives thing, but being here had changed her mind. Looking over at Paul, she felt nothing but an intense love for him.

They reached Martin's office and Paul knocked on the closed door.

"Come in," said the voice inside.

Paul recognized Martin's voice and opened the door, ushering Maggie inside. The room was brightly lit, sparsely furnished and a few family pictures adorned the walls. Maggie saw pictures of Pamela growing up and who she assumed was Martin's deceased wife, Susan.

"Close the door, Paul, and both of you take a seat," directed Martin from behind his desk, gesturing to two empty chairs.

Paul closed the door and led Maggie over to the chairs, located in front of Martin's desk.

Martin leaned back in his chair, as he assembled his thoughts.

"Good morning. I'm glad the two of you were able to find some quiet time together. Those moments are always precious and sometimes few and far between," said Martin, as he gazed at Susan's picture wistfully.

Maggie was the first to speak.

"I want to thank you for everything that you've done for me since I've been here," said Maggie.

"It's my pleasure, Maggie. We might as well get started, since there's a lot to cover," said Martin.

"Eva, display the two pictures of the individual," ordered Martin.

"Here they are, Martin," replied Eva, displaying the two pictures so that everyone could see them.

"Maggie, take a good look at the pictures and tell us if you know the man," directed Martin.

Maggie looked at the pictures carefully, but it didn't take long for recognition to cross her face.

"I know him. His name is Karl Schmidt. My father's right-hand man and fixer," said Maggie, puzzled as to why she was being shown the pictures.

"What does Maggie's father have to do with anything?" asked a curious Paul.

"Paul, my maiden name is Stanton. Durham was my married name. I'm the daughter of Thomas Stanton, Founder and President of Stanton Aerospace. I was going to tell you, but there never seemed to be the right time," said Maggie, fearing what Paul might think.

Paul processed what she had just said. He really didn't see a problem, everyone had some past baggage. Paul had heard of Thomas Stanton from his past assignments at Area 51 and 52. He was a powerful and reportedly ruthless man. Paul couldn't imagine what would happen if Stanton found out that his daughter was here.

"Maggie, none of that matters to me. I love you and I'm glad you're here," said Paul, turning to Maggie and holding her hand.

"Thank you, Paul. I love you, too," replied Maggie, her eyes tearing up.

Martin sat back in his chair, touched by the love between the two. He now had corroboration from two different sources on the identity of the individual at Olivia's house. Now he had to give the bad news.

Taking a deep breath, he told Maggie what had transpired while she was here.

"Maggie, the reason I showed you the pictures of Karl, was that he was seen leaving the house of an employee of yours named Olivia. She was found dead a few hours later. The medical examiner determined that it was by natural causes, but there are substances that can make it appear like that. We believe it was Karl that did it, in order to cover his trail. We have evidence that Olivia was an employee of Stanton Aerospace and was placed at your restaurant to keep an eye on you for your father. Olivia made the call to Karl when Paul showed up. Karl then set up the attempted assassination of Paul. I'm sorry, Maggie. I really am sorry," said Martin, who stood, walked over to Maggie and gently laid his hand on her shoulder.

Maggie couldn't believe what she was hearing. Olivia was dead, Karl a suspect and most likely the killer. Maggie had really liked Olivia and considered her a friend. All this time, she was probably spying on Maggie and reporting to Karl. Ultimately, it was another example of her father wanting to control her life. More angry than sad, Maggie knew she could never go back to her restaurant now. She would always be wondering if one of her employees was spying on her.

There really wasn't anyone she could trust, except for the two people in this room, Eva and maybe a couple of others. Paul looked at Maggie and saw the change come over her. First, he saw sadness, then anger and finally resignation. He knew she had come to some decision, but was waiting to hear what Martin had to say. Martin returned to his chair behind his desk, glad that he had one important item out of the way. He still had two more to go.

"This will sound crazy, but I've seen the same dreams you both have shared. I had a visit from an entity named Gabriel, who is what we would term an angel. He showed me your dreams and told me that it was important for the two of you to be together," said Martin, waiting for their reaction to this second bit of news.

"We actually believe you, Martin. If demons exist, then angels must certainly also exist. Plus, the name is familiar to Maggie and I, as someone from our dreams," replied Paul, with Maggie nodding in agreement.

"That's a relief. Not everyone believes as we do," said Martin, slightly embarrassed.

"No, some don't or refuse to," replied Paul.

"The benefit we have is that we've actually seen these things. The dreams, the angels and the demons are all connected according to what Gabriel said," explained Martin.

"Connected?" Maggie said with a questioning look.

"Yes. Angels and demons were once a race of mortal beings called the Anunnaki, who converted their bodies into ones of immortal energy," explained Martin.

"Shaynor and Valinor," said Paul.

"Me and Paul," echoed Maggie.

"Yes, this brings us to Maggie's situation. I have two options to offer you right now. Option one, is that given the amount of time people are asked to stay here, there is a need for a higher level of dining. My proposal would be to bring Maggie's restaurant here, with Maggie in charge and a new security screened staff. The second option, would be to make the two of you a team, echoing what we've seen in the dreams. You would go out on investigations together, but also share some of the dangers. This would, of course, require Maggie to undergo specialized training. The main idea is to offer Maggie a life apart from what her father wants for her. You don't need to answer now, Maggie. Think about it, talk it over with Paul. You have a home here, if you want one," said Martin, relieved that he had finally been able to get everything out in the open.

"Thank you, Martin. That's a lot to think about and I appreciate it. Either option would be okay, but I'll give you a definite answer as soon as possible," said a pleased Maggie.

"It's my pleasure. I wish there was more that I could offer you, but this is all I could do for now," said Martin.

"It's more than I could have expected, Martin. Thank you, again," said a grateful Maggie.

"Paul, I have something for you," said Martin, reaching under his desk and pulling out Paul's briefcase.

"I was wondering what happened to it. Thank you, Martin," replied Paul, taking it from Martin. It was the same one and had been cleaned up, all traces of blood removed. He had grown attached to the briefcase, even more so since it had saved his life.

"We cleaned it up and made sure all the functions are still working. That's all I have for now. If the two of you will excuse me, I have a few other matters that need attending to," said Martin, rising out of his chair.

Maggie and Paul rose out of their chairs, Paul clutching his briefcase.

"Thank you, Martin," Paul and Maggie said in unison.

"If you need anything, feel free to ask. Oh, one more thing you should know. I've sent the information we gathered on Karl to the local authorities. Hopefully, justice will prevail," said Martin.

"Thank you, Martin," said Maggie, as she and Paul left Martin's office.

Paul and Maggie walked down the hallway holding hands, both lost in thought, contemplating the offers that Martin had put forth and all that had been said. Paul reflected on how much public affection he had been openly displaying towards Maggie.

To some, it would appear unprofessional and he could understand that, but they didn't know the whole story or the totality of it. She was here with him now and he would do whatever he could to make the most of those moments. If the dreams were to be believed, and he knew they were, then these moments could be fleeting at best, leaving either him or Maggie with just memories of their love.

Martin watched Paul and Maggie leave. It had been a good meeting, he thought, allowing him to unload some issues that had been weighing on him. He didn't know which option Maggie would choose, but he was secretly leaning towards the restaurant one. He couldn't remember the last time he had been in a restaurant.

He had devoted so much of his life to the company after Susan's death, that it had left no room for anything else, including dating. It was funny, that he would be thinking about dating now. Seeing the love between Paul and Maggie must have awakened something inside him. Oh well, maybe someday. Right now he had a company to run and some difficult waters to navigate. He sighed and got back to work.

Chapter 33

The Master

Lilith, still in human form, awoke from a deep sleep. She hadn't really been asleep, as humans knew it, but more a withdrawing from the world around her, into a state of energy regeneration. The man, Paul Cross, had drawn heavily on her energy and without the help of Asmodeus, she would have succumbed. Her King and lover had saved her, risking his own existence. She trusted him completely and had been in love with him ever since her creation so long ago.

Lilith stretched out her sensuous form, relishing in the luxurious bed. She noticed

Asmodeus standing at the balcony looking out, still in human form. He turned and walked over to the bed, gazing upon the timeless beauty stretched out before him. He held his composure, though, needing to get some business out of the way first. There would be time for lovemaking afterwards.

"Hello, my love, you're looking refreshed and back to normal," said Asmodeus, trying to keep his mind on business.

"I feel fine, my King. Ready for whatever you have in mind," said Lilith, her lips forming a sensuous smile.

Asmodeus hoped that was the case, from both a business standpoint and a personal one.

"My love, I need you to return to the human dimension and complete your task," he said, with some reluctance. She was still the best choice for the task he had originally sent her to do. Trent had to go back in time and locate the Ark of the Covenant.

Lilith blinked her eyes in surprise, not wanting to believe he was sending her back into danger.

"My King, it's dangerous for me to go back. They have the capability to both see and defeat me," said Lilith, with a look of concern.

"That's true, but it is only one man that can do both. The woman, Maggie, might be able to see you, but can't harm you. If you possess Trent's body, you'll be less likely to be seen. Also, if you see either one approaching, flee to a safe area and return after the danger has passed," said Asmodeus, trying to alleviate her concern.

"I'll do it, my King," said a reluctant Lilith.

"There's one more thing, my love. I'll be sending Belial with you. He will be there only to assist you if there's a problem," said Asmodeus, trying to alleviate her concerns.

"Thank you, my King," said Lilith, relieved that she wouldn't be going alone.

Asmodeus looked at Lilith and felt the lust building within him. Suddenly, her eyes widened with surprise. Asmodeus was about to ask her what was wrong, when an unknown voice called to him from behind.

"Asmodeus!" the voice thundered.

Asmodeus turned to the source of the voice and saw what had surprised Lilith. A tall, glowing, red creature with cloven hooves and large horns on either side of its head stood before him.

"Who are you? No one interrupts me here! I am the King here and will make you pay dearly for this!" roared a somewhat shaken Asmodeus.

"I am Lucifer, your true Master!" thundered Lucifer. He had decided to use the image of what humans thought Lucifer would look like. It seemed the perfect choice and very appropriate for the world of Hell. Turning these demons into believers, however, was proving to be much more difficult.

"You must be joking. Look outside and you'll see demons that are taller, uglier and more powerful than you," said Asmodeus with a sneer.

"Such insolence won't be tolerated! Go to the balcony and witness my power!" commanded Lucifer.

Asmodeus decided to humor the interloper and went to the balcony. He blinked, not believing what he was seeing. Looking out, he saw three lesser demons rising high into the air, then disappearing with a clap of thunder and a brilliant flash of light. The demons were gone without a trace.

Asmodeus turned to Lucifer, rage growing inside him. He dropped his human form and reverted to his scaled demon form. He launched himself towards Lucifer, his long, scaled talons reaching out to tear and rip Lucifer to shreds. Asmodeus slammed into a wall of intense energy, trapping him and slowly drawing his energy. He couldn't move or pull away. His energy running low, he became fearful and frightened. In all his existence, he had never run into a being as powerful as this. Suddenly, a cry came from behind him.

"Stop it! You're killing him!" screamed Lilith.

Lucifer relaxed his hold on Asmodeus, allowing him to regain his composure.

"Lucky for you that we are on the same side and that I need you. Otherwise, I would have crushed you like a bug," said a confident Lucifer.

Asmodeus knew raw power when he saw it, so he acquiesced.

"What have you done with my demons?" asked a subdued Asmodeus.

Lucifer held out a closed, glowing red, hand and opened it, long talons extending from his fingers. Resting in the palm of his hand were three small, reddish orbs.

"They are here, but I have taken most of their energy. They will regain it with time, especially here in Hell," replied Lucifer, as he released the orbs into the air. The orbs floated out the balcony and down to the ground, beginning the process of regaining their energy.

"What is it that you want?" asked Asmodeus.

"I want what you want, the destruction of the angels and the subjugation of the humans. In my case, I need to go one step further and destroy the Earth Collective," explained Lucifer.

"Earth Collective?" asked a puzzled Asmodeus.

"Despite how advanced and powerful you and the angels think yourselves to be, there are beings of vastly greater powers and knowledge. There are seven such beings on the planet called Earth who watch over it. Along with five more on the moon, they form what is known as the Earth Collective. I am similar to them, except that I am much more powerful and second only to the Creator Himself. That is one more reason why you should be kneeling and calling me Master," said Lucifer, his patience wearing thin.

Asmodeus quickly processed what Lucifer had said and knew there was only one thing to do. Having the support of the second most powerful being in the universe could only help in his plans.

"Master," said Asmodeus, as he took on human form once more and knelt before Lucifer.

Lilith, who had watched everything, rose from the bed and knelt beside Asmodeus.

"Master," she said.

Lucifer was pleased. He had held back on telling Asmodeus that he was a prisoner on the moon, not wanting to erode this very tenuous relationship with the demons.

"Continue with your plans, Asmodeus. The Ark must be retrieved and brought to Hell. I'll leave you with two thoughts to consider, one is that I've been secretly watching and helping you since the

Anunnaki rebellion, the second being that it was I, who secretly made your life easier when you first arrived in Hell. Your odds on survival were slim, even with your advanced technology and you had yet to build the Ascension Chamber," said Lucifer.

With that, Lucifer disappeared in a blinding flash of light, leaving a gaping Asmodeus and Lilith to process what had happened.

Asmodeus was the first to speak, turning to Lilith.

"My love, you must go back. We need to find the Ark and Trent is important to finding it," said Asmodeus, feeling an urgent need to please Lucifer.

"I'm ready, my King. Do we have time for another matter?" asked Lilith, her lips curling in a sensuous, inviting smile.

"My love, there is always time for that," replied Asmodeus, changing back to human form and pulling Lilith over to the bed.

Belial waited patiently outside the chambers of his King. He had been summoned here to meet with Asmodeus on an important assignment and was curious as to what it could be. The chamber door opened and Asmodeus stepped out, in human form, wearing a black robe with gold embroidery.

"Thank you for coming, Belial. You're my most trusted general and friend and I need you to do something for me," said Asmodeus, thoughts of Lilith still filling his mind.

"Yes, my King! How can I serve you?" asked Belial.

"Lilith is returning to the human dimension and I need you to keep an eye on her and keep her from danger. The humans have technology that is harmful and maybe fatal to us. Guard her with your life," commanded Asmodeus.

"Yes, my King. With my life," said Belial. How bad could these humans really be? he thought to himself.

"Thank you, my friend. You are free to go," said Asmodeus, who went back into his chamber, closing the door behind him.

Belial walked away with a burning memory that had seemed to grow into an insatiable impulse. The human dimension now held the two humans who were once Valinor and Shaynor. He had always desired the beautiful Shaynor, long before the rebellion, but that scum Valinor had come along and stolen her heart. He now had a chance to fulfill that desire and satiate his pent up lust for her. This was going to be pleasurable beyond all measure, he thought to himself, as a wicked grin spread across his hideous face.

Later, Asmodeus opened a gateway into the human dimension, with Lilith and Belial standing before it in human form, waiting on some last words from Asmodeus.

"Be safe, my love. Remember to hide from the two humans, Maggie and Paul," said Asmodeus to Lilith.

"I will, my King," said Lilith, her sensuous lips curling in a smile.

"Belial, take care of her and stay away from those two humans," said Asmodeus.

"Yes, my King," replied Belial.

Lilith took one last look at Asmodeus and stepped through the gateway, followed by Belial.

Asmodeus watched the two of them step through the gateway with some misgivings. The two were headed into a dangerous environment and would need to tread lightly. Belial concerned him a little more than Lilith. Belial could be impulsive and act before thinking, so Asmodeus could only hope that he didn't do anything stupid. He closed the gateway and went back to the throne room, to consider his next move.

Lilith and Belial stepped out of the gateway and into a cool summer night on the grounds of DarkBridge Technology. Lilith, in human form, felt a cool breeze stirring her gossamer gown and her long dark hair.

"The facility is underground, just below us, by some 500 feet. I know an isolated area that we can enter and not be seen," Lilith said, as a gateway opened before them. Belial changed his form to human, using the one he once had at the time of the rebellion.

"The humans have various sensors, so we must remain undetected as much as possible," warned Lilith.

"Thank you, my Queen. I'll do my best," replied Belial, still not convinced about the danger these puny creatures presented.

They stepped through the gateway and into a secluded corridor, near the residential area. Closing the gateway, Lilith and Belial proceeded to Trent's apartment, pausing outside. Lilith didn't sense any activity inside, so she opened another gateway into the apartment. Lilith and Belial quickly stepped through, into the hallway of the apartment.

The apartment was dark and silent. Lilith led Belial to the bedroom, where Pamela and Trent lay sound asleep. Belial approached Pamela, sensing a protective EM field around her which made it impossible for him to possess her. She was very pretty, triggering Belial's more perverted, lustful side. He would have to make it a point to visit her when Lilith wasn't around.

"My Queen, there isn't much for me to do here. May I look around and see this technology that worries our King so much?" asked Belial.

"You may go. Things appear to be quiet for now," replied Lilith.

Belial bowed and left through his own gateway, which opened up into the hallway outside the apartment. Lilith watched Belial leave, uncomfortable with having him roam free throughout the facility. She silently hoped that he wouldn't do anything stupid.

Shaynor, the name and the woman had been on Belial's mind and he desperately wanted to see her. He remembered a long forgotten memory of being on the colony ship and following Shaynor to her quarters. Still clad in her diamene armor, she had gone inside, closing the door behind her. Belial walked up to the intercom on her door and said that he had an important message to give her from Valinor. Shaynor had opened the door, unaware of the danger. Belial, his lust for her overpowering his sense of control, pushed his way in and closed the door behind him.

He pushed her up against a wall and began tearing at her body armor, succeeding in ripping some of it off. His lust grew to an insatiable thirst to have her. Shaynor kicked him strongly in the groin, doubling him over with intense pain. She reached for the door, opened it and kicked him out of her quarters, telling him that if he tried anything like that again, she would kill him. He believed it, but it didn't stop him from thinking about the perverted, lustful things he would someday do to her.

Belial turned his thoughts back to the present, determined to find her. She had humiliated and refused him back then. Those memories had been like a festering wound, never healing, even after all this time. Now he was in a position to exact vengeance on her. He smiled a wicked, evil grin and cast his mind out, searching for someone who wasn't generating an EM field in this residential area.

He assumed she would be here, near that scum Valinor or whatever name he went by now. He found a couple of humans besides Trent who weren't generating an EM field. There was one that appeared to be living in larger quarters and it wasn't far from his current location. He immediately went there, pausing outside the apartment to rethink his plan.

Even if it wasn't her, there might be someone he could terrorize and expend his perverted, lustful desires on. How similar the situation was to the colony ship, he mused. This time, he didn't need her to open the door and more importantly, he was immensely more powerful. He chuckled with malicious glee and opened a gateway into the apartment.

Chapter 34

The Attack

Maggie had gone to bed early, the conversation with Martin weighing on her mind. She needed some time alone to think, so Paul graciously had given it to her. He had gone back to his apartment, after spending pretty much the whole day with her, even sharing lunch and dinner with her. It hurt her to have him leave and she could see it on his face as well.

He really did love her and she loved him, too, very deeply. They had shared a long passionate kiss before he left and it was a kiss that held a promise of a life together. She had reluctantly let him go, now finding herself in bed alone and thinking about her future.

Maggie soon drifted off to sleep, hoping for pleasant dreams, but Vermont Guardian had other plans. In all the potential futures it had looked at, Belial had found his way to her apartment. So Vermont Guardian opened Maggie's mind to a memory of the past in which she knew her attacker and had successfully fought back. The hope was that it would help alleviate some of the ensuing terror.

The dream began on the colony ship, in orbit around Earth. She was walking back to her quarters after returning from the planet with Valinor. He would soon be joining her, but was performing some post flight checks on the mining ship they had taken down to the planet. She reached her quarters, pausing while biometric scanners verified that it was her.

The door to her quarters slid open and shut as she entered. No sooner had she stepped in, when the door chime sounded, alerting her to a visitor. Not suspecting anything amiss, she went over to the door, pressing a button that allowed the door to slide open. The door slid open and Belial rushed in. He placed one hand on her mouth, pushing her against the wall and with the other hand he pressed a button to close the door.

"Shaynor, you have no idea how long I've been waiting to do this," said Belial in a low menacing voice.

Shaynor kept calm, as Belial took his hand off her mouth and began tearing off her diamene body armor. Belial muttered breathlessly at how difficult it was to get off. What he seemed to forget, was that Shaynor wasn't just some run-of-the-mill female scientist he could have his way with. She was also the daughter of a very powerful military commander.

Ever since she had taken her first steps as a child on her home planet, her father had begun the process of training her in all aspects of self defense and use of various weaponry. A tough taskmaster, he believed in being ready to defend yourself at any moment and had made sure that his daughter learned her lessons well.

Shaynor smiled at Belial, who suddenly realized that he had made a mistake in how he was standing. His legs were spread out, allowing Shaynor to bring her still armored knee up into his groin. Belial went down in a heap, his hands holding his groin, gasping with the intense pain.

"You'll pay for this, Shaynor. Maybe not tomorrow, but someday," he managed to say between gasps.

"Don't ever try that again, or I'll kill you next time," said Shaynor coldly. She pressed a button to open the door and kicked Belial out as soon as it opened. The dream faded, leaving Maggie with a sense of satisfaction as her mind drifted along.

Belial stepped through the gateway and into the hallway of the apartment, still in human form. If Shaynor was here, he would make sure that she recognized him. He proceeded down the darkened hallway and into the bedroom where he sensed someone sleeping. Stepping over to the bed, he saw a beautiful woman there, who looked amazingly like Shaynor. Unfazed by the darkness, he touched her forehead and recoiled. It was her! He exclaimed to himself, a wicked evil grin spreading across his face. He climbed onto the bed, straddling her sleeping body and bent down close to her ear.

"Hello, Shaynor. Did you miss me? Like I said a long time ago, I'll make you pay someday," he said into her ear with an evil whisper.

Maggie stirred from her sleep, drowsy, her eyes slowly adjusting to the darkness. She felt a pressure on her body and terror began to fill her, as she could just make out a dark shape on top of her. Something was whispering in her ear and a vile stench was making its way into her nose. She felt hot, putrid breath on the side of her face and struggled against the force that was holding her down.

Belial let out a wicked, evil laugh, as Maggie struggled against him and he began pulling the bedcovers away from her body. The sight of her beautiful body before him awakened his evil, lustful desires but, to his dismay, it had also momentarily broken his concentration on stifling her vocal cords.

Maggie found her voice and was able to blurt out, "Eva!"

Belial immediately concentrated, suppressing any further speech and began tearing away her flimsy nightgown.

Paul had gone back to his apartment after spending the day with Maggie. He knew she had a big decision to make and needed time to think so he had reluctantly left her alone to do just that. Feeling tired, he had flopped down on the bed, not bothering to undress, still wearing his DarkWeave suit. He fell asleep almost immediately, his mind filling with vague shapes that came into focus.

He was on the hangar deck of the colony ship once again. Having just finished a post-flight check on the mining ship, he was headed to Shaynor's quarters. Turning the corner in the corridor, he was almost at her quarters when he saw someone bent over just outside her door. Walking closer, he saw it was Belial and obviously in some pain. Valinor had an idea of what had happened. Despite his growing anger, he still needed to know for sure.

"Belial! What has happened? Are you okay?" said Valinor, feigning concern.

Belial turned towards the sound of the voice, his face red with anger.

"It's none of your business, Valinor. You and your girlfriend will pay for this someday," he said, using the wall to push himself up.

The dream was suddenly cut short by a chiming sound and a voice telling him to wake up. Paul woke up groggy, the chiming sound filling the room and Eva calling his name.

"Paul, there's something wrong with Maggie. She screamed my name and then went silent. I'm hearing some movement and muffled noises from the bedroom," said Eva with grave concern.

Paul jumped out of bed. Opening his briefcase, he took out his DarkWeave gloves and slid them on, the right one slipping easily over his ring and put his hood on. He wasn't entirely sure of the threat, so he shoved a couple of GAGE devices in his pockets and pulled out a pair of goggles, just in case.

"Eva, I need a gateway into Maggie's bedroom, now!" said Paul with intense urgency in his voice, pulling the hood over his head and then the goggles.

Eva, using her emergency protocol, accessed the briefcase and opened a gateway for him. Paul, his anxiety growing with every passing second, waited for the gateway to stabilize. The instant the shimmering dark blue gateway stabilized,

Paul dove through it into darkness, the gateway promptly closing behind him.

Belial was relishing his terrorizing of Shaynor, but it was time to take it up a notch. "What's wrong, Shaynor? Why haven't you put up more of a fight? Have you forgotten your training? You've become a weak and pathetic human," said an evil, taunting Belial.

Maggie struggled, but against such an inhuman force, she was helpless.

Belial let out a wicked, evil laugh, as his hands turned into huge, hairy paws with long, sharp, talons extending out. He was going to shred Shaynor and enjoy every deliciously, bloody moment of it. Maggie squirmed with terror, trying to break free, but to no avail.

Belial, salivating over the impending carnage, lifted his right, hairy paw. Long talons extended, he brought them down into Shaynor's chest. Or thought he did.

Paul sized up the situation immediately, seeing the part human, part demon form on top of a struggling Maggie. The demon had raised a huge, hairy paw and was about to strike Maggie with its talons. Paul swiftly stepped over to the bed, grabbing the descending paw with one hand and driving his other hand deeply into the back of the demon.

Belial roared with intense pain and coldness. He watched in disbelief as the paw that was about to shred Maggie dissolved into a wispy, black tendril of energy. His concentration broken, Maggie managed to wiggle free and rolled off the bed onto the floor. Sobbing, she crawled into a corner of the room and huddled there with her hand over her mouth, watching wide-eyed as the hooded figure wrestled with the creature.

Paul pressed his advantage, driving a free hand into the head of the demon. Belial screamed with pain and agony. His energy was dwindling rapidly and the attacker was drawing more and more of it from him. Unlike Vagoth, he didn't have the energy of a thunderstorm to draw on.

"Who are you?" screamed Belial into Paul's mind. The pain in Belial's head was so great that he lost control over his physical form and reverted to a formless, smoky black cloud.

Paul could sense the demon weakening and remembered a name from the brief dream he just had.

"Surely, you remember me, Belial, the one you shot in the back so long ago," said Paul, as he continued to drain Belial's energy away.

Belial was momentarily confused, but realization dawned on him and defiant rage exploded into a final attempt to break free.

"Valinor!" screamed Belial into Paul's mind.

"Bingo!" Paul acknowledged in a low voice dripping with sarcasm.

"You will die as you did so long ago. I'll shred you into so many pieces, they'll be burying parts of you for the next 100 years," shrieked a confident Belial.

Paul winced at the power of Belial's words in his mind, but continued the plan to keep getting Belial angry, knowing that the angrier he was, the more energy he lost.

"You always were an idiot, Belial," said Paul, as he immersed himself into the writhing dark mass that Belial had become.

Belial roared with unbridled rage, forming hundreds of talons to rake Paul's body. Talons upon talons fell upon Paul, but every one fell away in a wisp of smoke as they touched the DarkWeave suit.

Belial was getting worried. He could feel his energy draining rapidly, so he fought harder. He formed a huge ax to cleave Paul in two, but the ax dissolved into nothing as it contacted the suit.

Paul remained calm, as Belial struggled and fought mightily against the energy drain. Paul could feel his ring beginning to warm as vast energies were channeled into the QASM unit inside his sanctuary.

Belial continued losing energy rapidly and real fear began to take over his thoughts.

"Valinor, why don't we work something out? I'll give you anything you want, if you let me go. Remember, you and I were once Anunnaki," offered Belial in a last minute sympathy bid to go free.

"Not a chance. Vengeance is ours, isn't that what your Master says? Well it's mine now!" Paul growled, noting that Belial's form had shrunk to that of a large dog.

Belial cried out with anguished pain and frustration, his attacks becoming more feeble and ineffectual.

Maggie watched in terror as the two figures battled. Somehow, even in the darkened room, she could see both the creature and the figure fighting. The hooded figure had saved her from a horrific death and seemed to be gaining the upper hand over his opponent. Maggie thought about her dream. What would Shaynor do in a situation like this? Probably beat the crap out of the creature. The problem was, Maggie didn't feel like Shaynor right now.

Vermont Guardian watched the events unfolding in the facility above it. Looking at all the possible futures, most showed a successful outcome for Paul, but only with some help. It worried about Maggie, however, and her current fragile state. The demon, Belial, had instilled a deep sense of terror in her with his diabolical attack.

Paul had managed to drain a huge part of Belial's energy away but, somehow, the demon was maintaining his strength. Vermont Guardian suspected Lucifer was behind it, meaning that Paul was going to need some help. Maggie was the best option right now, but she needed to find her inner strength and overcome her fear. Vermont Guardian thought for a moment and gave her a little mental push, with something special to go with it.

Paul was finding Belial to be one tough demon and he seemed to somehow be stabilizing at the size of a small cat. Paul could feel the energy still draining from Belial, but it was down to a trickle now. They were at a stalemate. This was where a second ring would have come in handy. Unfortunately, he didn't bring an extra one. He was quickly running out of options, when suddenly, he detected movement out of the corner of his eye and saw Maggie get up and walk over to where he was still struggling with Belial.

Maggie had to do something. The hooded figure was beginning to tire and wouldn't be able to hold onto the creature much longer. She kept coming back to the dreams of Shaynor and how she had dealt with Belial. She had to find a way to tap into Shaynor's no-nonsense attitude and remembered an old adage that if you say something often enough, you tend to believe it.

She started telling herself that she was Shaynor and like a mantra, she kept repeating it over and over again until it permeated her thoughts and blocked out all negativity. Fear rapidly lost its grip on her, as energy suffused her body, giving her the strength to stand up. At that moment, she somehow knew what she had to do in order to help the hooded figure. Wasting no time, Maggie began walking towards the battle with a look of grim determination on her face.

Chapter 35

Inner Strength

Maggie reached the hooded figure and tenacious demon. Instinctively, she reached out with her bare left hand and plunged it into the demon. Belial howled with pain and his anger grew, as he saw that his victim was attacking him. She should be cowering in fear, he thought to himself, as he tried tearing into the flesh of her hand. His efforts proved futile, with all the sharp talons dissolving into wispy tendrils of smoke against her skin. Impossible! he screamed mentally.

Paul could only watch Maggie in stunned fascination, while struggling to maintain his hold on Belial. What came next made his jaw drop. Maggie placed her free right hand on his shoulder, contacting the DarkWeave suit. A blinding flash of light followed and Maggie felt Belial's energy flow into the DarkWeave suit.

To Maggie, it had been like a million ants crawling from one hand to the other. The flash had rendered Paul's goggles useless, so he took them off and noticed that he could still see Belial, or what was left of him, the demon having been reduced to a reddish glowing orb the size of a quarter. Paul immediately grabbed the orb and closed his fist around it.

Reaching into his pocket, he pulled out a GAGE device and placed it on the bedroom floor. He turned the device on, watching the device levitate and begin to hum. A small two foot circular gateway soon formed. The gateway stabilized and Paul placed the orb near it. The orb floated into the gateway, disappearing into eternity. Paul quickly shut the device off, the gateway closed and the device settled to the floor. Threat resolved, he picked up the device and put it back into his pocket. Belial wouldn't be troubling anyone for a very, very long time, thought Paul, a satisfied smile on his face.

Maggie had been temporarily blinded by the flash, but her vision was beginning to clear. She saw the hooded figure take the tiny orb that had once been Belial and place it near a blue shimmering circle. The orb floated into the circle and disappeared. Then she saw the hooded figure do something that shut off the blue shimmering circle. At that moment, the lights came on, but the hooded figure had his back towards Maggie so she couldn't see who it was.

"Well done, Paul and Maggie! I hope you're both okay," said an obviously happy Eva.

It took a minute to register with Maggie that the hooded figure was Paul.

"Paul?" said Maggie.

Paul turned around, pulling off his hood and looked at Maggie. Her nightgown was in tatters and when he glanced at the clothes he was wearing over the DarkWeave suit, they were also in tatters. Together, they made quite a sight, like something out of a post-apocalyptic movie.

"You saved my life," cried Maggie, rushing into Paul's arms.

"That's my job, rescuing damsels in distress. I could also say the same about you. You saved my life," said a smiling Paul, as he held her in his arms.

Maggie hugged Paul tightly, feeling safe and secure in his arms.

"Maggie, you might want to grab a robe. We're not alone," cautioned Paul.

Maggie saw her robe draped over a nearby chair and reluctantly released her hold on Paul and put it on. She returned to Paul's side and followed his gaze. Paul placed a protective arm around Maggie, pulling her closer to him. Standing in a corner of the bedroom was a figure bathed in a golden glow. The figure looked somehow familiar to her, as if she had known him in the past.

"Hello, Gabriel, old friend," said Paul, recognizing his Anunnaki friend from the dreams.

Gabriel tended to forget the time disparities between heaven and the human dimension. To him, he had only spent a short period of time in heaven and here was Paul walking and fighting demons like nothing had happened. The last time he had seen Paul was in the hospital recovering from a critical bullet wound. Then there was Maggie.

Gabriel had sensed large amounts of power being wielded and had followed it here to its source. He had arrived just in time to see Maggie transfer a huge amount of energy from the demon, Belial, to Paul's suit. It was even more astonishing, that it had been done without the use of any technology he was aware of. He was also perplexed that the two were obviously able to see him, despite his efforts to remain invisible. Hoping to gain some answers, he acted as if there was nothing wrong.

"Hello, Paul. Hello, Maggie. I'm glad the two of you are safe," said Gabriel. A frown formed on his face as he got closer. He sensed an unmistakable aura surrounding the two of them. It was an energy that he and his fellow angels knew to reside only with the Guardians. The angels had known about them for eons, but had never had any direct contact, just some indications that they existed. As unlikely as it seemed, Paul and Maggie appeared to have a connection to at least one of them.

"Thank you for saving my life, Gabriel," said Paul, breaking the silence.

"It was the least I could do for an old friend and fellow Anunnaki. Saving you and bringing the two you together, appear to be part of some grander plan. I, and many others, also seem to be part of that plan. Tell me, how is it that you are here and not still in the hospital?" asked a puzzled

Gabriel, trying to shift the subject away from something he wasn't ready to discuss yet.

"It was a miracle! One day he was lying in a hospital bed with a bullet wound and the next day he was completely healed, with no sign of injury, except for a faint scar," explained Maggie.

"Yes, it was a miracle and one that I don't have an explanation for," added Paul, somewhat sheepishly.

"Well, they do happen and it looks like someone or something is looking out for you. I have some other matters to attend to, but I'll be seeing the both of you again very soon. It is good to see the both of you again," said Gabriel, his mind filled with more questions now than he had answers for. He would, once again, have to confer with Uriel and Michael on these recent revelations.

"It's good to see you, too, Gabriel," replied Paul.

Gabriel waved and with that he disappeared, leaving Paul and Maggie alone to recover from their ordeal.

"Paul, Martin and Major Esterbrook are about to arrive," informed Eva.

"Thank you, Eva," replied Paul, as he gathered his thoughts on what had transpired.

Soon after, they heard the door chime sound and Paul hurried to answer it.

Martin had been woken up by Eva, who explained that Maggie had been attacked by a demon in her room, but was okay. She went on to explain, that an emergency gateway had been opened for Paul to step through and his quick action, along with Maggie's help, had dispatched the demon. Even though the situation seemed under control, Martin took the safety and security of his employees and guests very seriously.

"Eva, contact Major Esterbrook and have him meet me at Maggie's apartment," ordered Martin, waiting for the reply.

"All set, Martin. The Major will meet you at the apartment," replied Eva.

"Thank you, Eva," said Martin, as he put some clothes on and made his way over there.

Major Esterbrook was waiting at the door of Maggie's apartment when Martin arrived.

"Thank you for coming, Scott. Eva reports that everything is okay, but I still want a security officer present," said Martin, as he pressed the door chime button.

"Glad to be here, sir. Eva said something about an incursion and I take that very seriously, especially if it involves our guest," replied the Major, as they both waited for someone to answer the chime.

"Sounds like the cavalry has arrived," said Paul, smiling at Maggie.

"Could you answer the door, Paul? I'm not quite ready to receive guests," said a haggard, disheveled Maggie.

"I'll see what I can do. Martin might want to talk to you, but I'll try to dissuade him," replied Paul.

Maggie reached up and kissed him. Paul returned the kiss, before going to the door and opening it. Immediately, he was aware of how he must look. His shirt and pants were shredded, like he'd fought a tiger. He could see the look of surprise on Martin's and Major Esterbrook's faces.

"Hello, Paul. Is everything okay? Is Maggie okay?" asked a concerned Martin

"Hello, Martin. Hello, Scott. Maggie is okay, just physically and mentally exhausted. She's resting comfortably now. Eva was able to get me here just in time to help save her and vanquish the demon. You should have seen Maggie! Somehow, without a suit, she was able to draw the remaining energy from the demon and transfer it to my suit. I'm still awed by what she did. Sorry about my appearance, it was pretty intense there for a while," said Paul, hoping that he had succeeded in allaying Martin's concerns.

Major Esterbrook stood there, appraising Paul. It certainly looked like he had been through Hell and survived. He liked and trusted Paul, so he felt satisfied with what he said. The important thing was that Maggie was okay.

"As long as the two of you are safe, that's good enough for me. I think you'd better stay with Maggie and make sure that she's alright," said Martin, relaxing a bit now that he had talked with Paul.

"I'll take care of her," replied Paul, suddenly feeling rather tired.

"I'll expect a full report in the morning. You both did well tonight and should be proud of what you accomplished. You're a credit to this organization, Paul and I'm proud to have you here," said a sincere Martin.

"Ditto for me," said Major Esterbrook.

"Thank you. It means a lot to hear you both say that. I should get back to Maggie. Good night, Martin. Good night, Scott," said Paul, exhaustion setting in.

"Good night, Paul and give our best to Maggie. Have her stop by and see Dr. Curtis tomorrow morning, just to be on the safe side," replied Martin.

"Good night, Paul. Get some rest. You look like you need it," said Major Esterbrook, as he and Martin left.

Paul closed the door and went back to the bedroom, where he saw Maggie sound asleep in bed. He sat on a nearby chair in his tattered clothes, not expecting any new attack, but wanting to be ready, just in case. For a while, he just watched Maggie, sleeping peacefully despite her ordeal until, unable to keep his eyes open, he dozed off. His mind started to dream, blurry, hazy images once again resolving into distinct, clear images. It was another dream about Valinor, but this dream was different. Valinor and Shaynor had a secret.

He was inside a large cavern located on what would someday be called Antarctica. He and Shaynor had tunneled through two miles of ice using robotic tunneling equipment and then another thousand feet through solid rock, in order to excavate the cavern. After the cavern was excavated, a huge, diamene armored door was installed at the entrance and melt water drainage tunnels were drilled outside the cavern.

Under the auspices of Commander Beleron of the colony ship in orbit, this cavern was to become a military outpost, charged with protecting their settlement outposts as well as their mining and research operations on the planet. From this location, any of those places could be reached within minutes. Shaynor was standing next to him, admiring the five advanced Kyril combat spacecraft parked on the cavern floor.

Off to the side was the mining ship used to excavate the outpost and two hundred assault robots stood against a far wall, awaiting deployment to the colonies. A large dimensional gateway generator was also against a far wall, which was used to help deliver supplies and building materials to the cavern. The gateway was also large enough to send a Kyril spacecraft through, making it an effective means of tactical deployment. Also against the far wall, was a weapons storage area containing kinetic and laser energy weapons, implosion devices, fusion bombs and ten high yield, thermonuclear devices, presumably to be used as a last resort.

Few people on the colony ship knew about the outpost, just Commander Beleron and two others, besides Valinor and Shaynor. This had been deemed necessary due to the current situation back on the Anunnaki home world of Inunak and the technology stored at the outpost. The Anunnaki were at war with the Skarzi Empire and had been for decades. Neither side backing down or giving ground in that interminable conflict.

A reptilian, war-like race, the Skarzi viewed the Anunnaki with revulsion and hatred. Every habitable world discovered by Anunnaki or Skarzi, immediately became a target for the other and Earth became one of those prized possessions. That the Skarzi would someday make it to Earth was inevitable and they would need to be ready. Shaynor turned to Valinor, smiling and he smiled back, pulling her close to him and kissing her deeply.

Shaynor responded with equal fervor, eventually wriggling free, so that they could get back to the task of making the cavern into something more livable. Some time later, their work finished for the day, they boarded the mining ship and flew out, the armored cavern door opening and closing behind them automatically. Traveling up the ice tunnel, they broke out into a clear blue sky and headed back to the colony ship for some rest.

The dream ended and Paul roused himself into wakefulness. The dream, if true, had just made him privy to something that could change the course of events on Earth. The coordinates of the cavern were still fresh in his mind, so he made sure they were committed to memory. As a backup, he decided to do one other thing.

"Eva, confidential storage," said Paul. Eva had the capability to securely store confidential information, preventing it from falling into the wrong hands.

"Yes, Paul. I'm ready. Proceed at any time," replied Eva.

Paul repeated the coordinates he had memorized, without directional indicators.

"Information stored. Anything else, Paul?" asked Eva.

"That's it. Thank you, Eva," said Paul, feeling better now that the information had been backed up in a place accessible only to him. He trusted Eva. Even if the coordinates fell into the wrong hands, they would appear only as a string of numbers.

"You're welcome, Paul. Now get some rest. Maggie seems to have the right idea," said Eva, in a motherly tone.

Paul didn't have to be told twice. He rose from the chair and lay down upon the bed next to Maggie, rolling onto his side and snuggling up to her with his arm draped protectively over her waist. It would be up to him, as to what he did with the information. Hopefully, he would choose wisely. He glanced at Maggie, still sound asleep and realized how important she was becoming to the events taking place. Sleep quickly claimed him, but this time, he was free of such dreams, allowing him to get some much needed rest.

Chapter 36

Dark Justice

Karl stepped through the revolving door into the lobby of the Stanton Aerospace offices in downtown Manhattan. It had been a long couple of days since his visit with Olivia and he still had no idea where Maggie was. No one just disappears like that, he thought to himself. Preoccupied with what he was going to tell Stanton about his daughter, he didn't notice the police presence until it was too late.

Detective Michael Stevens of the New York Police Department had received an APB on a suspect wanted in the murder of a young woman in Connecticut. The suspect was employed by Stanton Aerospace and was possibly in the New York City area. Considered armed and dangerous, Detective Stevens had made sure to bring plenty of back-up, should the suspect be at the company offices. Committing the suspect's picture to memory, he had also sent it to all the officers who would meet him in the lobby of Stanton Aerospace.

Dressed in plain clothes and arriving at the offices, Stevens had positioned the police officers around the lobby, just out of view, so as not to arouse suspicion in the suspect. It was late morning and he had been there for an hour already, waiting for the suspect to show up. His patience was rewarded by the sight of a man exiting the revolving door into the lobby. The man matched the picture of the suspect, so Stevens walked up him with his hand in his pocket clutching his detective badge.

"Karl Schmidt?" asked Detective Stevens.

Karl had seen the man approaching from the corner of his eye, but a quick glance around showed multiple uniformed officers with weapons drawn. He didn't have a reason right now to go out in a blaze of glory, so he remained calm and innocent looking.

"Yes, I'm Karl Schmidt", he replied.

"I'm Detective Stevens, NYPD. Mr. Schmidt, you're under arrest and will be held for extradition to Connecticut for suspicion of murder," said Detective Stevens, as he flashed his badge.

"What murder? I didn't murder anyone!" said Karl, trying to sound innocent. This was beginning to look bad for him and if Stanton found out, he would never make it to any kind of trial and would probably be dead.

"That's for Connecticut authorities to figure out. You'll be held until they arrive to take you back," replied Detective Stevens.

The armed officers moved in, one placing handcuffs on Karl and two more leading him out to a waiting squad car. Detective

Stevens followed behind, contacting the Connecticut authorities about their suspect. Along the way, an officer read Karl his rights and another officer opened the cruiser door as they approached. With Karl tucked inside, the cruiser sped off to police headquarters.

Stanton watched the events happening in the building lobby on the virtual monitor floating above his desk. Security had notified him of the police presence but, when they apprehended Karl, he began to worry. This could be very bad for him, very bad indeed. If the evidence against Karl was solid, then he might talk and finger Stanton as the one who had ordered the murder of Olivia. Added to that, were the deaths of Brian Durham and Susan Weaver, that Karl could lay on Stanton. He had no choice. Karl had been a valuable and reliable asset to him, but now he was a huge liability.

Stanton let out a deep breath that he had been holding and opened a tactical display window on his monitor. He typed in a few commands, relaying them to a security drone stationed inside a hidden gantry on the roof not far above him. Commands received, the gantry doors opened and the limited AI on the drone engaged its rotor blades and flew off, following the departing cruisers.

Stanton sat forward, engrossed in watching the drone footage, as it followed its target. The police cruisers reached headquarters, stopping out front to drop off the suspect. The drone, hovering a mile away, armed its mounted sniper rifle and waited for further instructions. Stanton watched, as the officers unloaded the handcuffed Karl, who was pulled out and briefly left standing alone.

With the nearest officer a scant few feet away, Stanton tapped the figure of Karl on his display, highlighting him as the target and pressed the engage button. The drone quickly maneuvered into firing position, targeting the center of Karl's chest and fired a single armor piercing bullet.

Karl had climbed into the cruiser, his mind filled with questions and fearful of what could come next. If Stanton found out about this, then he was a dead man regardless of the outcome. Stanton wouldn't wait for extradition to Connecticut, much less wait for a trial. Karl exhaled, resigning himself to the inevitable, knowing that his remaining life was being measured in minutes. Reaching police headquarters, he allowed the officers to pull him from the cruiser without a struggle. Standing tall, he paused and closed his eyes.

He felt the intense pain of a bullet strike his chest, passing through the light body armor he usually wore. The impact sent him spinning to the ground, the wound in his chest bleeding profusely. His vision grew black and he felt his soul leave his body. He drifted up, to a point above his now dead body and surveyed the situation. The police were swarming around his body, their eyes searching the surrounding area for the shooter.

Karl saw the drone off in the distance and knew he had been right about Stanton. Not far from the parked cruisers, he saw a man dressed in an all white business suit looking at him and smiling. Karl didn't like how the man was smiling at him and didn't understand how the man could possibly be seeing him. Karl grew fearful, as he felt the evilness of that gaze and wanted nothing more than to escape it.

He began to drift up, a shimmering tunnel opening up before him, drawing him in. Suddenly, he was jerked away, as if an unseen hand had snatched him and he was pulled into another place. It was a place of fiery pits of lava, an orange sky and intense heat. He shouldn't be able to feel the heat or the burning flames, but he did and he screamed a silent scream.

Stanton had watched the drone engage Karl and fire the single bullet. That Karl was dead was clearly evident and it looked as if the authorities had no idea where the shot came from. That was good, but he would have to be careful in case they investigated further. Recalling the drone, he marveled at the effectiveness of the technology his company had developed.

Unseen to Stanton, was Asmodeus who had watched Karl being taken and his demise at the hands of Stanton. Asmodeus opened a gateway to where Karl lay dead, his prone body showing an expanding pool of blood and the humans wondering what had just happened. A smile formed on the face of Asmodeus, as he saw Karl's spirit or energy pattern rise from his dead body.

He hadn't expected to see Karl so soon but, with the apparent disappearance of Belial, there was an opening in the ranks of demons. Asmodeus smiled with evilness at Karl, who had a fearful look on his face. Asmodeus knew there was zero chance of Karl getting into heaven, so he skipped the formality of Karl's rejection at Heaven's Gate and snatched him away.

Asmodeus smiled at the pain and suffering in store for Karl, as his demon followers tortured him and molded him into the demon he needed to be. Karl might not prove to be as powerful as Belial, but he might prove useful over the long term.

Chapter 37

New Beginning

The ensuing days after the ordeal with the demon, Belial, had left Maggie with a new sense of purpose and determination. Looking back, she had been drifting through life after Brian's death. The restaurant had helped overcome some of that, but she had still been searching for something she couldn't define. Paul, and the people at DarkBridge Technology, had been the missing pieces to the puzzle of her existence.

She included Eva in that, too. Even though she was an AI, Maggie thought of her as a friend. Maggie had sat down with

Paul shortly after the attack and they had discussed the options that Martin had given her. Now they were headed to Martin's office to let him know what she had decided.

Martin waited in his office for Paul and Maggie to arrive. The attack on Maggie had left serious doubts as to whether anyone was truly safe here or anywhere else for that matter. He, along with Hiram and the other department heads, would have to develop some new defense initiative to protect the people here.

Right now, his thoughts were on Maggie and what her decision would be. He was impressed with her resiliency after the attack and noted a change in her demeanor, seeming more confident about her future.

"Martin, Paul and Maggie are here and waiting outside your office," said Eva, startling Martin out his musings.

"Thank you, Eva. Send them in," replied Martin, as he stood and arranged a couple of chairs in front of his desk.

Paul and Maggie entered his office and Martin noted that they both seemed rather happy and content.

"Hello, Martin," said Paul.

'Thank you for seeing us, Martin," said Maggie.

"Hello, Paul. Hello, Maggie. Please sit down," said Martin, gesturing towards the two empty chairs.

Paul and Maggie sat down, smiling at one another.

"How are you both feeling?" asked Martin, expressing continued concern.

"I'm feeling much better and Paul is feeling okay, as well," replied Maggie, looking over at Paul and catching a nod from him.

"Maggie, I have to apologize to you about what happened. You're our guest here and we have an obligation to protect you from harm. I'm sorry about what happened," said a sincere Martin.

"Thank you, Martin. I appreciate that," replied Maggie.

"So what have you decided, Maggie?" asked Martin.

Paul watched Maggie with a deep sense of pride and affection. He knew what she was about to say and hoped Martin would go along with it.

"I've given it a lot of thought and would like to do both. I'd like to help Paul and build a restaurant here. I want to be a contributor and be of some help to this facility," said an earnest Maggie.

"That's interesting. I would have thought you would choose one or the other, not both. It'll be difficult, but I think that between the four of us, we can make it work. Isn't that right, Eva?" asked Martin.

"Count me in and welcome aboard, Maggie," replied an obviously pleased Eva.

Paul had wondered what Martin meant by the "four of us" and now he knew. Eva would be very important to making this work.

"Thank you, Martin from the bottom of my heart. I feel like I've been given a chance at a new life," said Maggie with heartfelt sincerity.

"Thank you, Martin," said Paul as he and Maggie rose to leave.

Martin got up from behind his desk, walked over to Maggie and gave her a hug. Not exactly professional, but these were exceptional times.

Maggie hugged Martin back, tears welling up in her eyes. She released Martin, stepping back to stand next to Paul.

Paul smiled at Martin, who smiled back, both men possibly thinking of the nice, juicy steaks they would soon be having at Maggie's new restaurant.

"Now, go you two. I'm sure you have things to do and some plans to make. Welcome aboard, Maggie," said Martin, as he watched the two leave and returned to his chair.

"What do you think, Eva?" asked Martin.

"I agree, it'll be difficult for her to do both, but she is strong and determined. I'll do what I can to make it easier," said Eva.

"Thank you, Eva. You're an important part of the team here and I appreciate everything you do," replied a sincere Martin.

"You're welcome and thank you, Martin. It's my pleasure to serve and help in any way I can," replied Eva.

Martin leaned back in his chair and put his feet up on his desk. Significant challenges lay ahead and he would need every advantage he could find. No one knew what the future held, least of all him, but with preparation and perseverance they might just survive.

Lucifer, still imprisoned on the moon, saw the loss of Belial as being rather trivial. More important, was the obvious lapse in judgment by Asmodeus in sending such an impulsive creature in the first place. Such poor decision making in something so important to Lucifer was troubling. This had the potential to derail his plan to retrieve the Ark of the Covenant, which could give him the edge he needed over the Earth Collective.

He had fed Belial some extra energy so as to make it more difficult for the human named Paul to defeat him and, at the same time, test the limits of the human technology. Their technology appeared to be very effective against the demons. The human named Maggie had surprised him, along with the help she had received from Vermont Guardian. To take such an interest in two humans and actually aid them, puzzled and irked Lucifer.

He hoped that Lilith was more circumspect and less impulsive. She would have to be careful, since the humans would be more watchful now. With so much riding on her success, he would be compelled to intercede on her behalf as best he could, should she find herself in trouble. Biding his time, watching and waiting, the bluish energy shackles flared bright red, as he again tested the attentiveness of his captors.

Belial drifted down into the shimmering dimensional gateway, a feeble orb of energy. He was still in a state of shock over what had happened and furious that Shaynor had beaten him again. Someday, he would get even with her and make her pay dearly for all the pain and suffering she had caused him. The gateway drew him in and he passed into a dimensional bubble, with no apparent energy sources.

It was his new home, an eternal prison with no escape. The realization made him even angrier, and he howled with silent rage, as the gateway winked out. Whether by chance, design, or karma, the GAGE device used by Paul to send Belial here, had somehow retained its previous setting from Maggie's restaurant. Belial wasn't alone.

A vast, featureless dimension, devoid of any significant energy sources had greeted the tiny reddish orb that was Vagoth. He had been defeated and sent to this eternal prison by the human, Paul Cross. Vagoth had been extremely angry at the time, not so much with the human, but with Asmodeus and Lilith.

They had left him alone to deal with the human and had failed to help him. There wasn't much he could do now, so his anger had changed to despair. Alone, he drifted aimlessly through the void, drawing on any energy sources that leaked into this dimension. He had resigned himself to an eternity alone, when things suddenly changed.

In the distance, a blue, shimmering circle appeared, and a reddish orb drifted out. The shimmering circle winked out, leaving the reddish orb drifting alone. Vagoth was intrigued, so he sped towards the orb and was shocked at who he found.

Belial noticed the fast approaching reddish orb, but was too weak to do much about it, so he waited. His wait turned to surprise when he noticed who it was.

Vagoth was shocked to find Belial, in a much weaker state than he was. From what Vagoth could see, Belial had gone through a battle similar to what he had gone through.

"Belial," said a cautious Vagoth.

"Vagoth, you scum. Why are you here?" inquired Belial in a superior tone.

"Like you, I was defeated in battle," replied Vagoth, not liking Belial's attitude.

"It wasn't a fair fight! I was ambushed and outnumbered. What's your excuse? You were always weak and pathetic," said a haughty Belial, too embarrassed to admit that a woman had gotten the better of him again.

Vagoth wasn't hearing anymore of it. Since being here, he had grown somewhat stronger than Belial appeared to be right now.

"You might be right, but here, I am the master and you are scum," declared Vagoth, changing his form into that of a huge foot. He kicked Belial, sending the feeble orb tumbling into the void.

Belial howled with pain and indignation. Vagoth sped after Belial and upon reaching him, kicked him again. Once more Belial howled with pain and indignation, tumbling through the void, thinking that Hell was Heaven compared to this. Vagoth was ecstatic.

Eternity might not be so bad now. He caught up to Belial, lined up for another kick and let loose.

The Author:

I'm employed as a manager at a small electronics manufacturing company outside Boston, Massachusetts and have been in the electronics industry for some 44 years now. During that time, I've witnessed great changes in the industry and the rapid growth of technology. Most notably, would be the numerous computer companies of the 70's and 80's that are now just footnotes to history. Of those companies, Data General Corporation was where I began my career.

All of us have had some seemingly small event take place that sets us on a different path to travel than we would have taken without it. In my case, it was a friend who left the company I work for, in order to seek new opportunities. This small event sparked a creative urge within me, triggering me to produce a short video of a fictitious company called DarkBridge Technology, which led to the creation of this novel. The video can be found at: www.darkbridgetech.com.

I've always been a huge fan of science fiction and the masters of the genre. Clarke, Asimov, Heinlein, Bradbury and many others, fascinated me with both the worlds and characters they created. More recently, Neal Asher and John Ringo have made their own contribution to that fascination and I walk in the shadows of such giants.

In my spare time, I can be found tending my garden, which I find most relaxing in that it takes my mind off the usual everyday worries. I admit to not being a master gardener, but the satisfaction of seeing such a small seed burst and grow into a lush and beautiful plant, becomes an apt metaphor on life in general.